All

I Ever

Wanted

F. Y. Dawn

Dawn2Dawn Publishing

8810C Jamacha Blvd #136

Spring Valley, CA 91977

ISBN-13: 978-0-615-96574-1 (sc)

ISBN-13: 978-0-615-96575-8 (e)

Published by Dawn2Dawn Publishing 08/2015

1

April strutted into Illusions night club. The smoke machine blew billows of fog that added an element of mystery. The glow of a red light illuminated the dark hallway. Some might've found the ambiance a little over the top, but not April. She strolled across the floor as if the hall was her catwalk, jean-clad hips swaying with each step. She stepped into the main dance room and the sway of her backside beckoned eyes toward her, encouraging them to check out the rest of her curves. The dish of the day was the plunging neckline of her blouse, showing enough of her treats to make a man salivate. She knew how to make an entrance. Eyes all across the room burned through her. She tossed a smile to those who caught her eye without slowing her steps.

April ignored the lackluster attitude of her companion for the evening and continued scanning the men in the club. Not really in the mood to club, Candice trailed behind, her face twisted with discontentment. April wished she hadn't talked her into coming. They were more like sisters than friends—especially since April's sister, Sheena, was married to Candice's brother, Paul—and could match each other's *let's get this party started* attitude tit for tat. A good looking man with the finances to wine and dine them was their weakness. April hoped that one commonality would lead them to having a good time.

Rough, sexy men lined the walls. Thuggish men turned some women off, but not April. She loved the power they exuded, the way they walked, talked, and most of all, they were least likely to become attached. They'd stick around just long enough to make her holler, and that's the way she preferred it. At one time, she wanted love and all the things that came with it; however, at eighteen years old she gave her virginity to a man she thought loved her. Truthfully, he was simply understudying the role of soul mate until he got the goods. She preferred keeping things simple: sex, fun, and no emotional attachment. From the specimens filling the space, there were plenty of choices to have a little fun with. Sheena had been admonishing her to slow down, get back into church, and meet a nice young man. That type of man didn't do it for her. She was aggressive and strong-willed. She needed a man whose power exceeded her own, who could congratulate her success and, most importantly, dominate her in the bedroom.

She had finished grad school a few weeks prior, started a new job, and finally felt like the woman she declared she was. She was walking on cloud nine and nothing could knock her down.

Sheena had warned her about being so arrogant, but just about everything Sheena said went in one ear and out the other. April understood Sheena acted out of love, but she was an adult and no longer needed her sister's or parents' guidance.

Moving out of her parents' house and in with her sister a few years prior gave April a sense of freedom she'd never had. She had responded the same way any sheltered child would: partied, partied, and partied some more. Her relationship with God—although it hadn't been much to begin with—was neglected. She'd attended church a few times when she first moved in with her sister, but weekend partying left her too drained to attend service on Sunday. Once she made the decision to stop going altogether, she was free from the guilt and conviction that once held her back.

The bass of the hardcore hip hop music pumped so loudly that the walls vibrated. The thick beat served as a mating call for the females in the room who lacked class. They swarmed the dance floor, performing their mating ritual for anyone who'd watch, but not April and Candice. All that dropping it like it's hot, twerking, and booty clapping the other ladies were doing wasn't their style. They didn't seek to attract men turned on by that. Perhaps the type of men they sought couldn't be found in a club. But, the establishments where classy women were appreciated didn't possess men with the type of power April and Candice craved.

April relished in the beat seductively swaying to the music, effortlessly manipulating libidos. Her small waist and curvy hips accentuated her plump butt. Its hypnotic spell caused grown men to lose themselves. With Candice at her side, they were every man's fantasy come true. Their creamy caramel skin and height were their only similarities. It was Candice's curly mane, draped across her shoulders and slanted eyes that made her stand out. The first question guys asked was, *Is it a weave?* She'd let them run their fingers through it, and they'd be hooked.

April, on the other hand, was a brick house. Her hour-glass perfect shape always stole the show. She worked hard to keep her body toned. Her rigorous workouts kept the appropriate places lean and her voluptuous places high and tight. Her long, silky black hair was dyed blonde at the tips. She wore it brushed back and traipsing loosely along her shoulder blades. Not an inch of her face was covered. That's the way she preferred it. Her slender face, high cheek bones, and pouty lips made her look like a model.

April danced with Candice to loosen her up. Her attempts were met with an eye roll and a halfhearted sway. Candice just wasn't in the mood to party. April abandoned her boring dance partner in search of some real fun. She scanned the crowd, honing in on by far the ugliest face in the room. His body could leave a girl breathless; his face could make her seek salvation. His nose seemed to spread the width of his face. Round, haunted eyes could probably see into the future they were so big. She didn't have a problem with dark-skinned men—she'd had her share of fantasies about Idris Elba—but dark didn't work for that man. On top of all that, he needed some ChapStick. A dark brother with dry, ashy lips was a no-no.

Time to have a little fun...

She made her way toward him. An alluring smile flashed across her face, beckoning him to come closer. He looked around to see if she was actually talking to him. Suppressing an eye roll, she crooked her finger at him, taking more effort to lure him than normal. He still didn't get it. She slowly trekked the short distance between them, playfully grabbed his collar, and guided him to what would be the most mortifying moment of his life. April worked her body to the beat of the music, sliding and grinding her butt against his crotch. His hard body against her was perfect, and when he spoke, his panty-dropping deep voice crept across her skin. His sex appeal was shocking, but his face was the blemish—on otherwise extraordinary packaging—she couldn't deal with.

Too bad, I might've given him some.

He was so drawn into her spell that he couldn't focus enough to dance. He stood in the middle of the dance floor with his mouth hanging open, eyes scanning her from head to toe. He slowly began to sway in the standard male two-step. The song was almost over, but he was just getting started. The music changed to a slower tune and April tried to step away to get rid of him. He locked his arm around her waist and slammed her back against his chest. His aggressive touch was a welcomed surprise that took her breath away.

"It's not time for you to go yet," he whispered against her ear.

That voice! April swooned for a second, but quickly gathered herself. *One more dance, then he's got to go.*

He held her so tight she could barely move. A little aggressiveness was a turn on, but he was getting out of control. She squirmed for a little freedom and apparently he mistook it for her enjoyment. His hand slid across her abdomen and then up to her breast.

Oh hell no! She thought. It was time to put an end to the charade. April jerked out of his arms. The sudden movement caught him off guard and he released her. She turned toward him and could see the sexual energy surging down below.

"Excuse me." April stepped back and walked toward the group of men she had found him with. It was time to put her little ruse to an end. His friends watched their every move, more than likely still trying to figure out why she'd chosen him over them. Her steps slowed, giving him enough time to catch up. Just as she'd anticipated, he grabbed her arm.

"You just gonna run off without giving me your number?"

April spun around and cackled, "Let's not go there. Be satisfied with a dance and let it go." She walked off, leaving him slack-jawed and his boys laughing ferociously.

He mumbled something under his breath and backed away, no doubt trying to save face in front of his friends. She looked back to give him a parting glance and the look on his face—though it was brief—made her skin crawl.

"Can I buy you a drink?"

April shook off the eeriness and turned around. Her face lit up at the sight standing before her. "You most certainly can." She stretched her hand out for him to grab it. He took the cue and lightly grasped her fingers, leading her toward the bar.

Thoroughly liquored up, she followed her new conquest to the dance floor. His hands slid around her waist, pulling her erotically close. She went pliant in his arms, waiting for him to take the lead and sway them to the music. Instead, he pressed her firmly against him and groaned in her ear.

I know he ain't... Her thoughts were halted by him pressing into her. Sure enough, she felt it again, his hardened shaft against her stomach. She tried to ignore it, but he pressed it into her again and again, practically dry humping her right there on the dance floor.

The brother was fine and the watch sparkling around his wrist piqued her curiosity about the contents of his bank account. She wouldn't let a little drunken stupidity keep her from discovering his hidden treasures. She guided his hands to her waist, slung her arm across his shoulder, and tried to rock them into some semblance of a rhythm, but the brother insisted on humping like a dog in heat. He must've been one in his former life, because the fool leaned forward and licked her like a Scooby snack. April stopped dancing and tossed her hand up in his face.

It is time to go.

She walked away without even glancing in his direction. As soon as she stepped away, someone else asked her to dance. She denied him as well as the next three after him. Mr. Doggy Dog had thoroughly pissed her off. She had to regroup.

Candice approached her. April knew what she was going to say before she even opened her mouth.

"I'm ready to go."

"Come on, Candy. We just got here."

"April, I'm tired of these guys who can barely formulate a sentence thinking my breasts are my eyes."

"Relax, we are not here to find our soul mates." April rolled her eyes at that term. A mate made just for her was not something she believed in, "Or, the next Langston Hughes. You look hot. Men are going to stare. Use it to your advantage. Let them buy you a drink and try to have a little fun."

Candice rolled her eyes. She loved April like a sister, but hated this selfish side. Candice often overlooked it, but that night it wasn't so easy. She hated to think they were growing apart, but April didn't seem to be outgrowing the party life; Candice was through with it.

"Candice?" Before April could even finish her thought, Candice walked away. "Come on, Candy. Don't be like that." She called after her several times, but between the inaudible club and Candice's power walking, she never heard a word.

She would deal with Candice later, but the drinks she had consumed were creeping up on her. She desperately needed to find the restroom. She tipped across the room, trying to avoid large clusters of people, swatting away groping hands, and ignoring cat calls until she made it to the hall. As usual, the line to the ladies room was long. At the opposite end of the hall was the men's room with no one in line. She poked her head in, gave it a quick sniff test, and then went inside.

She stepped out of the restroom—grateful for having finished her business without interruptions—and walked smack dab into a wall of muscular flesh. His scent of soap and spice burned through the stench of weed and funk that lingered in the air. She gripped his arms for balance and the muscle flexing against her palm caught her attention. She held on a little longer than necessary.

"You know," he stepped closer to her and she instinctively stepped back, "I should start charging you ladies a cover charge for using the men's room in my establishments."

Her back slammed against the wall as her eyes shot up to his. "You own this club?"

He nodded, trapping her body against the wall with his. "I have three, and every night I find some lady using the men's room. I usually kick them out." He lowered his head to hers and their lips almost touched.

April normally would've kneed him in the balls, but body, looks, and money kept her feet planted firmly on the ground.

"What should I do to you?"

His breath brushed across her lips, shot up her nose, and singed every last hair of her eyebrows. She bit back a gag and held her breath.

All that money and you can't buy a mint?

"I should kick you out like all the rest," his tongue shot out, wetting his dry lips. "But a pretty thing like you deserves to be treated right."

April held her breath until her lungs burned for oxygen. She pushed against his chest, hoping he'd back off, but the fool just laughed. Gusts of his breath puffed into her face with each chuckle. She hated to do it, but didn't see any other way. She let out the breath she'd been holding, sucked in a lung full of his stench, and kneed him in the balls. A great package ruined by a mouthful of rotten garbage. She was disgusted and pissed off. It was definitely time to go.

I should've listened to Candice.

April stumbled toward the exit, pulling out her phone to text Candice. Anger, high heels, and a slight buzz weren't a good combination for walking. The hairs on her back rose and a chill shot down her spine. She turned back to see who was watching her. Seeing no one, she assumed it was yuck mouth trying to get her attention.

Her phone buzzed, and the message, *I already left* flashed across the screen. She bit back a curse word while marching out the door.

2

April's ticked-off tipsy tumble toward the car almost ended with her eating asphalt. She managed, however, to steady herself and took it easy the rest of the way. She turned on the heater to ward off the February chill and tried to clear the haze from her mind enough to drive home. Most of the ride was a blur. When she pulled up to the curb in front of her sister Sheena's house, she mumbled, "Thank you, Lord." Her church attendance was shoddy, but she knew when to count her blessings. She tried to steady herself while inching along the sidewalk. Her stomach rocked with each step, threatening to revisit every meal she'd eaten that day.

"One step in front of the other." She giggled at the memory of that very song from an old Christmas movie that was way before her time, but aired every year. She paused to get her giggling under control and heard footsteps behind her. She turned around and was met directly with a fist to her eye.

Pain exploded through her face like she'd been hit with a grenade. She stumbled backwards and her hands flailed in search of something to hold onto. Finding nothing, she hit the ground. The force racked her body, sending her head flopping back. It cracked against the concrete, making her teeth clank together. Pain shot along her jaw and her mind wafted in and out of consciousness. Before she could fully regain clarity, he was on top of her growling obscenities into her face. His fingernails dug into her skin as he ripped her pants down her thighs leaving a trail of blood behind. With little remaining energy, she tried to fight back, but he punched her repeatedly in the ribs and face until the fight left her. The weight of his massive body held her down and he dug his left arm into her chest for good measure. He pried her legs apart with his thigh. The clank and rattle of his belt buckle was a definite sign of her fate. She clenched to resist him and felt her flesh tearing as he violently plowed in and out of her. His weight against her chest hindered her intake of oxygen. Her pleas for mercy slowly became inaudible.

"Please…no," she managed despite the agonizing pain. The cold concrete burned her bare backside as his unyielding pounding rubbed her against it. His grunting signified the end was near and she praised God that her torment was almost over. He spent himself inside her. The hope of freedom was short-lived. He lifted his weight off of her and balled his fist into her hair, yanking her head back. He used his fist as a battering ram against her face and pounded until it opened up. Her nose ruptured, her lip split, and her eye oozed blood all over her face. She was unrecognizable. He ended his attack with a kick to her stomach so powerful, it scooted her across the ground.

The soft tapping of his footsteps and April gasping for breath were the only sounds of the night. His car engine trailed off into the night, leaving April struggling to find her next breath.

Blood collected in April's throat choking off what little oxygen she had. With all her strength, she rolled to her side and let the blood dribble out of her mouth. Common sense told her to get up and hide in case he decided to come back, but her attempts to stand were pointless. Her weak legs and pounding head forced her to stay put. Her eyes had swollen shut, blood covered her face, and the clothes which once accentuated her body's beauty were now tattered rags. Her battered mouth muffled her cries for help into whispers.

A distant bark piqued her ears and the voice that followed was the sweetest thing she'd heard in all her life. "Paul?" Anxiety escalated when she realized he would never hear her hoarse voice. Each attempt ended with the same result, a barely audible whisper floating across the air.

The distinct sound of padded feet and claws tapping against the concrete headed toward her and she tried another approach. "Roscoe... Roscoe!" She put her heart into each scream. The bark of her brother-in-law's dog picked up as did the pace of his paws as he ran toward her. She sobbed with more vigor than she thought she could muster. Roscoe stopped a couple feet away from April, sniffing the air before he approached. He inched a little closer until he was able to smell her hair. He recognized her scent and his bark became frantic. Paul yelled for him to calm down and get back into the house, but April gripped his leg. If she couldn't get Paul to walk over there, she'd be lying out on the sidewalk—life draining from her—until the neighborhood woke up. Paul yelled some more. Roscoe whined, jerked, and fought to get free, but April held on for dear life. Her weakened body was no match for Roscoe's strength. He twisted and broke free. He was all the way back to Paul before she could muster up a plea for him to come back.

Paul watched in confusion as Roscoe leaped around barking like he'd lost his mind. He had no idea what had gotten into his dog, but figured indulging his curiosity for a moment would get him back in the house sooner.

"Roscoe, I don't know what is so important that you have me outside in the dark with my pajamas on." Paul's footsteps slowed when he looked up and saw where Roscoe was headed. Being a lawyer, he'd heard some pretty gruesome stories, but had never seen any of it. He ran back into the house and called the police.

Paul returned with a blanket and covered her. "Ma'am, everything will be okay. I called the police. Just hang in there."

Ma'am? April attempted to make her identity known, but Paul shushed her.

Emergency response vehicles approached with flashing lights and blaring sirens, waking up the neighbors. Paul stood to greet them and they immediately started tending to April. Paul relayed what he knew to the cops and as he finished up April was being loaded into the ambulance. Before leaving, one of the technicians pulled the officer to the side. Paul turned to head into the house. He was concerned about the young lady, but there was nothing he could do. She was in God's hands. He would pray for her healing and that they catch whoever attacked her.

"Excuse me, sir, but this woman says she knows you." The officer jogged up behind Paul and grabbed him by the elbow.

. Curiously, he walked toward the ambulance with the police following closely behind. "Oh, my God!" Paul's heart dropped when he looked at April's face. "This is my sister-in-law. She lives with us." Paul reached out to touch her and the police grabbed him.

"Sorry, you can't touch her until she has seen a doctor."

The look on the officer's face let Paul know right off the bat where his mind had gone. "You think I did this to her?"

"Well, it is a little suspicious that you didn't recognize her. Maybe you guys had a little argument. You lost control and are now feeling a little remorse..."

Paul stepped into the officer's face making no effort to hide his annoyance. "She was on her stomach and I didn't want to roll her over. That's why I didn't recognize her. Besides, I saw her car parked here and just assumed she was already in the house. It didn't dawn on me that..."

April's hoarse voice cut him off before he riled up. "Get Sheena." Her words were barely coherent, but her reaching for Paul's hand halted the cop's accusations.

April sank into the stretcher, gritting her teeth at every bounce of the ambulance. Each dip and turn intensified the pain throbbing through her body. Her eyes were so swollen that trying to force them open hurt just as bad as the beating that had gotten them that way. She kept her ears trained on Sheena's voice. She turned her head to hear Sheena more clearly. That simple movement sent pain radiating up her neck and swelling into her head. She sucked in a breath trying to cope with the pulsing. It was too much. She reached for Sheena, fighting to stay conscious, but her body went limp. She was out.

"April!" Sheena hovered over her shaking her shoulders, ignoring the EMT's request to calm down. She hysterically screamed April's name over and over again. The EMT tried to console her by telling her they still had a pulse and that it was common for patients to pass out from pain, but it was pointless. It wasn't until they left the ambulance and April grunted at the movement that Sheena calmed down.

April regained consciousness, but wished she hadn't. Excruciating pain wracked her body as she teetered on the brink of lucidity. She was motionless as they picked at her body collecting evidence, running tests, and taking x-rays. Vaginal tears, a broken nose, a couple of broken ribs that punctured a lung, and God forbid any diseases that monster had deposited in her.

Officers hovered about hoping to get a statement, but her oxygen stats were low and the swelling around her mouth made talking nearly impossible.

"Oh, April." She heard Sheena's despair at her bedside and wanted to comfort her, tell her to stop crying, and tell her how she'd gotten what she deserved. Crying for her was a waste of tears and time. Every kick, every punch, and the sheer brutal force of her attack were all deserved. For all the men she'd humiliated and treated like the scum on the bottom of her shoe, she had this coming.

"Oh God, how could you let this happen to my sister?"

April reached to comfort her, but it took more strength to lift her arm than what she actually had. She listened to her sister's grief. Her eyes were so swollen that no one even noticed she was awake. She tried to speak, but her mouth had almost doubled in size since they put her in the ambulance. She only managed an incoherent mumble. The barely audible sound was no match for her sister's sobs. Paul tried to console Sheena, but there was no consoling her. He called on God to do what he couldn't.

April listened intently to his prayer, trying to find comfort in the words but couldn't. Apparently Sheena could. Her wails tapered off to a soft whimper and then disappeared altogether. April wondered how he could ask God to help her knowing the kind of life she'd been living. *God won't help me.*

She was glad when the nurse stepped into the doorway. She didn't have to listen to her brother-in-law pleading for a lost cause.

"Sorry, I don't mean to interrupt," the nurse softly spoke. "All of the admittance paperwork has been finalized and I am here to take Ms. Walker to her room. She will be in Room 429. Sorry to say, but visiting hours are over on that floor. They'll give you a few minutes, but no more than thirty."

They filed out of the room and Paul immediately made a phone call. He saw the look of distress on Sheena's face and didn't like it. His company afforded him business connections that could make a hospital stay seem like a dream vacation. Within the hour, the hospital administrator was on-site. April was switched to a private room. A doctor and nurse were called in and Paul paid them double-time to tend to April's every need. Her visitors were free to come and go as they pleased, without limitation.

When the administrator showed up and started calling the shots, Sheena knew exactly what had happened. She looked at Paul, blew him a kiss, and mouthed the words *thank you.*

3

Pastor Richard Hawkins stood at the podium looking out over the congregation. Over six hundred pairs of eyes looked back at him full of expectation, as if their existence depended on his next words. He'd given all he had in hopes that the people would receive strength. He had exhausted his energy, and when he felt he had nothing left to give, their souls begged for more. Silence settled over the sanctuary. He stood there with sweat trickling down his face. Everyone waited—the musicians to accompany his squalling delivery, the deacons to shout 'Amen', but there was nothing. He was officially depleted.

He grabbed a towel and dried the sweat from his face. He sipped his water, hoping to descend from his adrenaline-induced high. His heart thumped like he had just completed a cardio workout instead of what he was actually doing, preaching the word of God. Half the congregation was on their feet in expectation. They cried out "Amen" and "Hallelujah," hanging onto his every word. They wanted more, but hadn't he already given enough? He looked down at his notes. Of course, there was more he could say, but he couldn't bring himself to utter another word.

He gripped the sides of the podium. His head hung so low between his shoulders it almost rested on his notepad. Discouragement had crept up on him at the most inopportune time. He inhaled deeply, begging his mind for just five more minutes of clarity, so he could finish the sermon.

"There's a season of blessings with your name on it." He closed his Bible and downed the rest of his water, trying to ignore the confused faces. He had been in the climax of a message that seemed to be exactly what they needed to hear. The abrupt change in pace had thrown them off. "No matter what you're going through, no matter what the devil says, that season will come. It's not the time to tuck tail and run. Stand strong and see the salvation of the Lord." He stepped down from the pulpit and exited the sanctuary without an explanation.

The on-duty deacons scrambled to their posts and followed him out. Sweat continued to pour from his face and every pore on his body. The battle between his flesh and the Holy Spirit buckled him at the knees. The deacons caught him before he hit the floor and assisted him to his office. He felt the Lord urging him to go back and finish delivering the message. He was exhausted—spiritually, physically, and mentally. *Wait, Your Season will Come,* was the message for the morning, which was probably more for him than anyone else. He was tired of the Lord telling him to wait. Hadn't he waited long enough?

He wanted to preach something else, but he vowed to never get before the church and deliver a sermon that wasn't from the Lord. Seeing how he had stepped into the office of pastor to fill his father's shoes, it was a vow he didn't take lightly.

Before his father passed, Richard had never seen himself as a pastor. His mind flashed to the day his father passed. Richard definitely wasn't pastor material, but that night, the man he was came crashing to a halt.

The champagne was perfectly chilled, a tray of chocolate sauce and strawberries were placed on the center of the bed, and a beautiful woman waited for him on the other side of the door. Some men preferred to feed their women chocolate-covered strawberries, but he couldn't get with the hard chocolate. He chose to dip the strawberries himself. Chocolate dribbling from his fingers onto her bare skin added to the fun.

He smiled at the beauty standing on his threshold and stepped aside for her to enter. His eyes followed her curves as she swayed into the room. He took a moment to enjoy the view and then slipped a do-not-disturb sign onto the handle. Renting a hotel for a night of adult fun might have seemed like a waste of money, but it kept things private and as far away from his church life as possible. People—mainly his father—didn't understand he was a grown man with needs. The only thing his father cared about was him being a pastor's son and how his actions affected the church. Well, what good ole dad didn't know wouldn't hurt him. And God...well, He was merciful and faithful to forgive. Richard was barely twenty-six, and with the ladies throwing themselves at him the way they did, how could anyone expect him to behave differently?

He coaxed her into one of the chairs in the sitting room and kneeled before her, traipsing his fingers down the curve of her calf. She shivered and he smiled. It was definitely going to be a good night. He unbuckled her shoes. They looked expensive, but he couldn't care less. He tossed one shoe aside and turned toward her other leg.

His buzzing cell phone caught his ear, but he ignored it. The buzzing started back up and he regretted not shutting it off. He excused himself and grabbed his phone. It was his mother. There was no way he was answering that call. The sound of her voice would dampen his evening. He sent the call to voicemail and was getting ready to turn the phone off when he realized he had more missed calls and text messages from her. He couldn't explain it, but dread swelled up in him so thick, it clogged his throat. He felt like he was suffocating. On autopilot, he dialed his mother back. The anguish in her voice let him know something horrible had happened. The words rushed out of her mouth in a jumbled wail of sorrow and grief.

"He's dead."

"What do you mean he's dead?" were the last words he spoke before his life changed forever.

Richard shook the memory away. He couldn't allow his dad's vision to be passed on to anyone else. So, when the board requested a meeting with him and his mother, he made his intentions clear. Without a second thought, he picked up where his father had left off. Though he was only twenty-six at the time, the congregation willingly followed his lead.

His toughest battle was getting his mother to let him run the church without interfering. Lillian had dedicated her life to the church right along with her husband. She had a hard time taking a back seat to her son. She was used to calling meetings, allocating funds for programs, and making decisions that should've been his to make. The final straw was when she called a meeting with the deacon's board to discuss problems she had with their performance. Richard respectfully put her in her place and told her to back off. She still tried him, but once Lillian saw the same passion for souls and love of the people in him that his father had, she gracefully relented. Each Sunday, she sat with pride as she watched her baby minister.

Five successful years as a pastor had come with a price; he was lonely. He yearned for someone to share his life with. He had witnessed many couples in the church marry and start families. He was excited for them, but envious as well. Patience wasn't his strongest trait, so occasionally he got off track and sought his own mate instead of waiting on the Lord. Foolishly, he had tried dating a woman in his congregation. He had noticed her during the church's car wash and dinner sale. Her beauty was undeniable, but what Richard noticed most was while all the other sisters were in the air conditioned church selling dinners, talking, and having a good time, she was outside with the brothers sweating and washing cars. She'd sweated out her hair and had no makeup on. She was gorgeous but looked worn out. He kindly told her to go inside and rest. Her simple response piqued his interest even more: "The more people washing cars, the faster we can go. The faster we go, the more money we can raise," she had said. He followed her lead and washed cars right alongside her. They had a good time laughing and joking with each other. A few days later, Richard asked her out to dinner.

They dated for a couple of months. He enjoyed spending time with her, but there was no romantic spark. They talked about their goals, disappointments, and seemed to build a good friendship. When he broke things off, she lost all good sense, ran his name into the mud, and ran members from his church. She claimed he misrepresented his intentions and that he had vowed to commit to her. Her heart was set on being the first lady of the church, and she couldn't handle her dream being crushed.

The rumor mill made it into a scandal and the executive board was furious. Meetings were held to discuss whether he was the right pastor for the church. They deemed his actions inappropriate for a pastor. If it hadn't been for the persuasiveness of his mother and the influence she still had on the church, he would've been ousted. He was forgiven, but they warned him future indiscretions wouldn't be taken lightly. Since that day, he pledged to never date a woman in his congregation again, but the desire for a mate was constantly in his dreams and prayers.

Some nights, an alluring woman visited his dreams. She was always elegantly dressed with an air of class that made her seem like royalty. Her smile drew him in. In the dream, she was always working. Other workers bowed as she walked by and protested when she picked up a tool to help. She would simply smile, instantly calming their angst and assuring them she would be fine. She was so enthralled by what she was doing, she never saw him getting closer. Every time he got close enough to speak, she would disappear and then reappear further away, working just as hard. Restlessly, he tossed and turned as he pursued her identity, but after each recurring dream he would wake with the same confusion and dissatisfaction. Her face seemed vaguely familiar. He felt like he'd seen her before, but couldn't figure out where. When he asked the Lord who she was, Habakkuk 2:3 rang out in his mind. *For the vision is yet for an appointed time; But at the end it will speak, and it will not lie. Though it tarries, wait for it; because it will surely come, it will not tarry.*

He'd sacrificed so much of himself, spent long days and nights at hospitals and nursing homes, received phone calls in the middle of the night, and had driven all over the city, tracking down members who had gone astray. He had pulled people out of crack houses and dropped them off at rehab, stood toe to toe with abusive spouses, and even confronted gang members who were trying to recruit the youth at his church. All was done in the name of the Lord; he didn't regret any of it. He just wanted something for himself. Was that too much to ask?

Sitting in his church office, Richard tried to erase all of the negativity from his mind. He leaned his head back, closed his eyes, and tried to meditate on the good things in his life. The more he tried to relax, the more his thoughts raced. Even while awake, he could see the woman's face and desperately wanted to feel the warmth of her skin as he rubbed his hand across her cheek. He wanted to run his fingers through her long silky hair as she rested in his arms. Just like any other man, he had his own urges and desires that needed to be laid at the altar, but his desire for that woman was different. Sexual gratification was the least on his list. It was her companionship and the peace he felt emanating from her that he craved.

There were plenty of women vying for the position of first lady at the church. There was a joke around the church about a first ladies club, where they touted all women who had claimed to be his soul mate. He shook his head at the ridiculousness of it all. There was only one woman for him. No matter how crazy it sounded, he knew exactly what she looked like. None of them were it.

Now that he had resolved in his heart that he wasn't going to settle for anything less than the best, bitterness was setting in. He had suffered over the fact he'd already sacrificed and endured so much for the ministry—never asking for much in return—and the one thing he wanted more than anything, the Lord refused to give him. *Lord, how long do I have to wait?* echoed through his mind as he locked up his office and nodded at Jaleel, head deacon and good friend, who faithfully waited outside his office every Sunday until Richard left.

Jaleel locked the last door to the church and escorted Richard to his car. "You all right? You seem a little down."

"Got a lot on my mind right now." Richard shook his head in frustration as he slumped into the driver's seat.

"Well, I was praying for you this week. I know this situation with Cole and your mother is crazy, but God will help you sort it out."

"Thanks, man." He stepped out of the car and gave his boy a hug. "Now, get home to your family." He had to end that conversation. Cole and his mother were an ordeal all within itself. He'd done his part and extended the olive branch. Now it was their turn to do something with it.

The drive home seemed to take longer than usual. Richard had purposely moved far away from the church to have some semblance of privacy. Growing up, he'd heard his father complain many times about people watching his every move. He refused to live like that, opting to live clear across town, so that he and whomever he married could enjoy each other without prying eyes. In that moment, his choice didn't seem so wise. He turned on the radio to drown out his mental ramblings and forced himself to sing along. He couldn't sing a lick and eventually grew tired of hearing his own voice.

He sighed deeply as his mind focused on the empty house that awaited him. His moderately furnished home could use a woman's touch. The voice of children would definitely liven up the place. There was no personality in the house, no pictures on the wall, plants, or decorative figurines, just white walls, a black leather sofa, and a love seat facing the fireplace. In the kitchen were just the bare necessities, a dining table and kitchen appliances. The only room with a bit of flair was the bathroom which had a decorative trash can, matching toothbrush holder, and soap dispenser. He took one last deep breath and made a U-turn. Even his mother's company sounded appealing.

He walked into her house and hid his shock behind a smile. Her living room was filled with visitors. He greeted them, but was confused as to why his mother would cook a big Sunday dinner and invite all those people except for him. She walked into the living room carrying two cups of lemonade and started fussing at him before she could pass them on to their intended recipients. "What took you so long to get here? We've been waiting on you, so we could eat."

"I'm sorry, but I think you forgot to invite me. I just came by to see what you were up to."

"What? I told Deacon Williams to tell you I cooked and wanted you to come by." Lillian bit her lip to keep from saying what she wanted to say in front of all her guests. "Well, let's not dwell on that. Praise God for sending you this way. Now we can eat."

Richard kissed his mother on the forehead as he walked past to join the others at the table. Lillian was elegantly flawless, hair styled to perfection, suit pristinely pressed and tailored to fit, and her skin was smooth and blemish free. The only hint of her true age was the bit of crow's feet gathering at her eyes.

Since the day he'd questioned her about Cole, her smile had lost a little of its sparkle. When he tried to get more information out of her, she would quickly change the subject. He wanted her to confess and release the burdens she had been carrying, but she held on to them like precious jewels. Richard guessed that her son being her pastor was just as hard as having to pastor your mother, so he didn't push.

The dinner and fellowship turned out to be exactly what he needed. Everyone was full of compliments. They praised his steadfastness, the growth they saw in him, his ability to teach, and his love for the people. They even expressed their gratefulness for all the sacrifices he'd made for the ministry. God had taken a simple dinner to inform him that his work wasn't going unnoticed.

4

April laid in the hospital bed with her back to the window and her face toward the door, a habit she'd picked up her first night. Two weeks later, the habit was still as prevalent. She didn't want anyone to sneak up on her again. It wasn't good for her broken ribs. Fortunately, they weren't on the side she needed to rest on.

She suffered through the pain and refused to use her morphine pump. The doctors said if her attacker had kicked her any higher, he would've hit her chest and possibly stopped her heart. Some nights she wished he had. Living with the guilt of the person she had become and the torment of her nightmares was almost just as hard as coping with the pain.

Her last nightmare had shaken her so bad that she woke trembling and her cheeks saturated with tears. The image of her attacker was so vivid and the pain so excruciating, it felt like she was back on that cold concrete, skin scraping against the cement, and body being violated in the worst way possible. She had been awake ever since, fighting sleep for over twenty-four hours. Her body pulsed in agony, but pain meds meant sleep. She couldn't risk it.

She couldn't see much from the position of her room. She guessed the private rooms were designed to keep the patient away from the hustle and bustle of the hospital. All of her other senses were on full alert. She could distinguish between the clack of a high heel against the linoleum, the clunk of a male shoe with a bit of a heel, and the thud of a sneaker. Her sense of smell was even heightened. From staff lunches, to overindulgence of perfume, to soiled bedpans, she smelled it all.

She had to be on full alert and aware of her surroundings at all times, but her eyelids were heavy. Her eyes fluttered as her brain struggled for clarity. Her blinks became longer. Her body demanded sleep and she had exhausted her power to stay awake. Her head sank into the pillow and tension left her body as she finally gave into fatigue.

୨◦ୡ

What seemed like just minutes later, April felt a soft touch on her arm. Her eyes fluttered open and the man standing before her almost scared her to death. She screamed and jumped to her knees on the mattress, flailing her arms in his direction. Her heart pounded out of control and her head spun from such a sudden change in position, but that didn't deter her. "Get away from me!" she shouted over and again as she slapped and clawed his face.

31

The nursing staff rushed in to see what all the commotion was about. They walked in on April dishing out one final slap that sent her unsuspecting victim tumbling back away from the bed.

"Dustin, what are you doing in here?" one of the nurses called out as she helped him to his feet.

"Langley is running late and asked me to cover for her."

"Yeah, well you don't cover in here." The doctor stepped in, furious that despite all the briefings they'd had about that particular patient, a male staff had still gone into the room.

April, still kneeling on the bed—her chest heaving from the physical exertion and adrenaline pumping through her veins—watched the aftermath of her panic.

I'm losing it.

"Ms. Walker, we need you to calm down. Let us give you something to help you sleep." Dr. Mills slowly approached the bed.

"No!"

"We're going to have to call your sister. You can't stay on this floor if you're going to attack our staff. I need you to understand that there is no physical reason for you to still be here. We are going to have to transfer you to mental health."

"I'm not crazy."

"I know. You've experienced something traumatic. Sometimes a little counseling can help you work through your fear and anger."

Dr. Mills walked out of the room followed by the other nurses who had rushed in. April slumped down onto the bed. *I'm not crazy.* She tried to convince herself, but the more she thought about her actions, the harder it was to believe. She turned on the television, attempting to find something to rid her mind of its chaos.

"Hey, kiddo."

The deep, masculine voice startled April out of her TV-induced trance and she hopped up on her knees, ready to defend herself again. "Paul!" She instantly relaxed and sank back into bed. She hadn't realized how much time had passed. "Where is Sheena?"

"She's out talking to the nurses." He cautiously made his way toward the bed. He was the only man she allowed in the room, but the way she jumped up when she heard his voice and what she'd done to the male nurse put him on alert. "You care to tell me what happened?"

"Please don't let them send me to the crazy ward."

"It's going to be hard to convince them not to. That nurse is pretty shaken up and you marked his face pretty good. You're lucky he's not pressing charges."

"I know," she blinked away the tears. "But, I think I had fallen asleep and started having a nightmare, and then he touched me. He scared me."

"I know." He kissed the crown of her head. He loved her like his own flesh and blood sister. Seeing her like that was killing him. "The doctor said you still haven't been sleeping well. What's up with that?"

"The nightmares…I can't."

"Come home and let us take care of you."

April turned her head and gave her attention back to the television. She couldn't go home. She was attacked right in front of their house. How could she live there without seeing his face, smelling his scent, and reliving the torment day after day?

"Hey, hun." Sheena made her way into the room and sat on the edge of the bed. April tried to ignore her, but she wasn't having it. Sheena cupped April's cheek in her palm and turned her face. "This has got to stop. I can't imagine what you're going through, but this fear is destroying you. I'd take the wild, carefree April over this weak one any day. I've always admired the fire in you. Don't let the devil snuff it out."

April slung her arms around Sheena's neck. It was that same fire that had gotten her attacked. Humiliating a man in front of his friends just for kicks and giggles, she should've known it would end badly. She would never be that person again.

Sheena hugged her tighter, fighting back her emotions. She was determined to be the strength her sister needed. She had cried for her enough. It was time for tough love. "I've convinced the doctors to let you stay, but I'm giving you until the end of the week. It's either home or the psych ward. I won't allow Paul to pay for anything else. Insurance will only pay for the doctor's psych recommendation, which he adamantly thinks you need. On the other hand, I think all you need is Jesus."

April held her breath trying to contain her feelings and shrugged her shoulders. Maybe she did need Jesus, but after all she'd done, He didn't want her, so why even bother?

"Have you prayed?"

April shook her head.

"Then, don't you think it's time?" Sheena laced their fingers and bowed her head, hoping April would take the opportunity to cry out to God.

She didn't. Silent tears rolled down her cheeks. She pressed her lips together to contain her wails. Her body shook from the buildup of emotions threatening to erupt.

Sheena wanted to wrap her tightly in her arms, soothe her sobs, and pray for her, but she couldn't. She had prayed all she could. It was April's turn. If she wanted the restorative power of the Lord to touch her life, she had to ask for it herself. It was the hardest thing she had to do, but Sheena passed April some tissue and stepped to the side until she got it together, and then reminded her, "You have until the end of the week."

April watched Paul and Sheena walk out the room and couldn't help but feel angry. Why couldn't they let her stay where she felt the safest?

5

Richard rounded the corner of his street. The early morning sun hadn't fully risen, but it provided the perfect temperature for his run. He had added an extra four blocks onto his run, hoping to rid his mind of the chaos. In through his nose and out through his mouth, his breaths were steady. With each breath, he hoped to exhale frustration and inhale peace. His sweat-soaked white tee clung to his chest like a layer of skin. The muscle exertion and adrenaline pumping was exactly what he needed.

His steps slowed as he approached his house and saw his mother's car parked out front. Just as quick as the exercise had cooled his angst, seeing his mother made it rise again. He'd been ignoring her calls for two days. He should've figured she would show up. One of the extra blocks he added to his run had her name on it. One belonged to his brother and the other two to the Lord. Sad to say, he was losing his patience with all of them.

Lillian saw him approaching and hopped out of the car before he could run into the house. Richard slowed his steps and stopped right in front of her. It would've been better for her if he had kept trotting into the house, but she wanted to keep pushing him, so he would give her what she came for.

"When I don't answer the phone, it doesn't mean you just show up," he barked out between labored breaths as he removed his headphones. He had never taken such a forceful tone with his mother, but he was not in the mood.

"So, you're just going to keep ignoring me?"

"Mom, I'm a grown man. Every now and then I need some time to myself. I have other things going on in my life that are not centered on you."

"I'm sorry. It's just..." she paused. She walked a little closer to him, afraid someone might overhear. "This whole situation with Cole is driving me crazy."

Richard shook his head and walked away.

"Can you at least give me his number?"

Richard kept right on walking.

"You know, life wouldn't be so bad if you stop being so picky and get married."

That made him stop. It wasn't the first time she'd tried that method. It was a classic mother move. She wanted to talk about Cole, so she brought up a subject he outright refused to discuss, hoping he'd gravitate back to talking about his long-lost brother. Usually, he humored her, but he wasn't in the mood.

Richard forced a calm he certainly wasn't feeling. He didn't want to lash out at her again, but she was asking for it. "Isn't that what got you into trouble—settling?" He slowly turned toward her, and as he suspected, shock was all over her face. "You settled for someone you never really loved and your actions destroyed lives."

She gasped and Richard could see the hurt in her eyes, but that didn't stop him. She had peeled the scab off his wound without concern for his feelings.

"That's not true. I loved Cole's father."

"Really? You have a funny way of showing it. I'm not marrying for convenience. It will be for love. She will be the only one that excites me."

She charged toward him and Richard braced for the slap he knew was coming. She had never slapped him before, but he earned that one. He crossed a line and disrespected her with his insinuations. She stood in front of him and instead of her hand slapping him across the face, the pain in her eyes did. "Is that what you think of me? That I moved on to the next man because he made me feel things my husband couldn't? I loved Cole's father. Do I wish we had waited until we were a little older to marry? Yes I do, but I loved him. Marriage and all the burdens of caring for a family changed him. He was a verbally abusive drunk, but I loved him. And yes, I made a mistake. When I met your father, I was broken. Slowly and patiently, he put me back together. I fell in love with him and loved him more than I ever thought possible. I won't apologize for it. We had talked about taking Cole and moving away. I hesitated and my husband found out I was cheating. He disappeared with my baby and I was devastated."

"Please spare me all the details. I've heard them before. I'm not the one you need to be explaining it to."

"I tried telling him that day at the hospital, but he's so angry."

"He has every right to be, but you have to keep trying. You owe him that much."

"What about you? Do you forgive me?"

Tears streamed down her face and that was Richard's undoing. He wrapped his arms around his mother and held her tight. It couldn't have been easy, but he couldn't help but think there had to be a better way. She had no control over what her husband did, but she did have control over what came out of her mouth. The lies and deception were uncalled for.

"I was a wife and a mother. I should've pushed your father away, but I couldn't. When you fall in love, maybe you'll understand it more."

"You're right, which is why I won't settle. Don't you want that same kind of love for me?" He stepped back and hunched down to her eye level.

She nodded and he was satisfied.

"Now," he said, releasing her and wiping the tears from her cheeks, "I'll help you with Cole, but you have to realize that he is my brother. That means something to me. I won't do anything to jeopardize it. He and I were good friends until he suspected you were his mother. It's going to take time to soften him up. Go home and I'll call you." He walked away from his mother feeling like he needed to run a few more laps around the block.

Richard walked into his house determined not to allow the quiet loneliness to creep up on him. He walked past his prayer room and felt the Lord pulling him inside. Turning back, he placed his hand on the knob.

Not today...

He internally spoke the same sentiment he felt the Lord had been throwing at him. He walked right past the door and into his room to take a shower.

He stepped into the shower, allowing the cool water to beat down on his head. It rinsed away thoughts of his mother and how she'd robbed him of an opportunity to know his brother. He took a few deep breaths while his mind honed in on the root of all his frustration. Her face floated to the front of his mind, causing his heart to beat a little harder. Maybe he should go see a shrink, because he had to be losing his mind. How could he be obsessed over someone he didn't know? He didn't even know if she existed. She could've just been a figment of his imagination; he needed help. Some pastors were dead set against their members seeing psychiatrists, preferring they seek spiritual counsel, but not him. He'd be the first in line if need be. The more the dreams intensified and the nights dragged on without knowing her identity, the closer he was to making that phone call.

What happens if I never find her, was his final thought as he finished up his shower. He stepped into his room, and before he could begin putting his clothes on, he felt the pull of his prayer room. Praying was a daily ritual for him, but it had been two days since he set foot in that room. Whatever he called himself doing—mad at the Lord, on strike, or neglecting his duties—wasn't working. He had less peace than before, which he didn't even think was possible. He was falling apart and there was no relief in sight.

"What am I doing?" Richard plopped down on his bed shaking his head. He wiped his hand across his face and huffed out a breath in frustration. Before he could talk himself out of it and before anger could rise up, he slid to his knees and bowed to the Lord. The simple act of reverence, of humbling himself and acknowledging God's sovereignty was enough to get God to move mountains on his behalf.

"I'm sorry," he whispered as the shame of his anger toward the Lord set in. He wasn't in prayer long when God reminded him of the duties he'd been neglecting. His pity party was over. It was time to be about the Father's business. He wasn't dead yet. With life came hope. He just had to keep believing that God was working things out for him.

He continued praying and one name dropped in his spirit; that's who he centered his prayer on. Some people saw faces and prayed for them, others prayed from a list. He heard names and usually received direction on what to pray for, but not that time. He already knew what she was in need of. He prayed harder than he had

41

in days. When he was done, his instructions from the Lord were, *Go to the hospital and pray.*

With his issues still weighing in the balance, he dressed and made his way to the hospital to try once again to pray for his friend's sister. Obedience was better than sacrifice.

6

Richard sat in his car outside the hospital, trying to force his mind into pastor mode. His friends needed him. He had gotten the call days ago about Sheena's sister being attacked. This was the same sister that had hidden in her room or snuck out of the house, rudely refusing to meet him every time he came over. When he received the call, he rushed to the hospital to pray with the family anyway. Most people raised in the church knew what was right, but they often refused to live it and didn't want anything to do with church. Even still, he didn't take it personally.

On his first visit, April had been too traumatized to meet with a man she didn't know, so the doctor felt it best he wait until she was ready to see him. He had no idea if she was ready for male visitors, but if the Lord was sending him, He would most definitely work all that out.

Richard was a little uneasy walking through the hospital halls. Many times, he'd been sent to speak a word from God;

however, this would be the first time God told him to go without giving him a word to speak. He stood outside her room and took two deep breaths, racking his brain for something encouraging to say. He searched for a scripture or even one of the popular phrases people used during testimony service, but his mind was blank. Richard stepped into the room waiting on the Lord to give him anything.

"What are you doing? Don't come in here!" April jumped off the bed wincing as a sharp pain shot through her injured ribs. She rocked back and forth on the balls of her feet readying herself for his next move.

"I'm Pastor Richard Hawkins…"

"I know who you are. Please, don't come in here." Her voice trembled and her eyes were as wide as saucers.

Richard didn't have anything spectacular to say, but he knew what he could do. He eased further into the room without making eye contact. He kept watching her out the corner of his eye to gauge her reaction. She was terrified.

"Please go."

Her whispered plea touched him more than he let on. It was for her good, so he continued. God didn't give His children the spirit of fear. He refused to allow that spirit to keep her locked away from the world. He grabbed a chair by the window and slid it to the opposite side of the bed. He casually took a seat and tossed his foot onto his knee.

"Please, go."

Richard didn't budge.

"Get out of here!" She banged her hands on the bed and barked with such force he jumped. He hid a smile, relaxing his face to show he wasn't affected. He was impressed. She was scared and injured, but she had some fight left in her.

Slowly, he lifted his eyes to hers. "You know if I…" Richard stuttered as he tried to regain his composure. His eyes firmly settled on her face for the first time. He compared it to the images in his mind.

It can't be.

There was some swelling and bruising, but he was almost totally sure that she was the woman he'd been dreaming about. Her jet black hair, creamy, light brown complexion, and bright prominent brown eyes that sparkled in the sunlight.

"If you what?"

Her gruff voice snapped him back to reality. "If I wanted to hurt you, I would've done it by now. I'm not leaving, so please sit and talk with me." All the anger and bitterness he had felt toward the Lord vanished with one glimpse of the woman standing before him. Clips of his dreams floated across his mind as his heart hammered against his ribs. She was even more beautiful in person.

She stood in fight stance, chewing her bottom lip, her hands stretched out, gripping the bed sheets. She considered his words, but wasn't buying it.

"He's already robbed you of so much. Don't let him take your sanity."

April let those words sink in. It was easier said than done. Some of the tension left her shoulders and she let go of the sheets. Richard stood and moved toward her. His six-foot-three frame was domineering and she backed away from him.

"I need you to fight this." He touched his hand to her cheek and she trembled.

April couldn't breathe. His proximity sucked the oxygen out of her lungs. She stood there, immobilized and on the verge of passing out. "I'm scared," she managed to say, just above a whisper.

"I know, but I'm here for you."

"He hurt me and it's my fault."

What?

She wailed into his chest and it nearly broke his heart. He wrapped an arm around her waist and guided her onto the bed. Touching her made his heart thump so hard it felt like he was back outside running laps around the block. He looked at her face and saw past the bruises. She was damaged and God had a great work to do before he could pursue her affection, but at least she was there.

She's been here all this time.

Richard shook his head in amazement. God truly worked in mysterious ways. What would've happened if she hadn't refused to meet him all those times? What if she had joined his church months ago like Sheena and the rest of her family had been praying? Would the Lord still have given her to him? He was done trying to figure it out. He was just going to try not to mess it up. His first step should've been to leave before his hands and emotions got him into trouble, but he couldn't very well leave her like that.

"This is not your fault." He grabbed some tissue off the counter and dabbed her face dry. "No woman—regardless of what she's done or said—deserves to be attacked and violated the way you were."

There was something about him that soothed April. The warmth in his eyes, the authority in his voice, the compassion in his touch, she felt safe. She sucked in a deep breath and slowly let it out, gradually calming her sobs.

"Your first step to conquering this is getting out of this hospital and talking to the police. From what I hear, you haven't done that yet."

April turned her head away, fighting back the instant tears that rushed forward at the thought of leaving. That hospital room had become her fortress and she outright refused to leave. Talking to the police was out of the question. She let that suggestion go in one ear and out the other.

Richard caressed her cheek and turned her face back toward him. "God's got you and so do I." He smiled at that last statement. He wanted to let her know just how much he had her, but it wasn't time.

"I know you aren't a member of my church yet, but I want to extend to you the same privilege all members have." April watched in disbelief as he wrote his number down for her.

"All of your members have your personal number? How do you ever rest?"

Richard tilted his head with an unbelieving smirk. This woman was in the hospital battling demons, but was concerned about his rest. The bastard that attacked her may have wounded her, but he didn't break her spirit. Sparks of her fire kept flying up and he couldn't wait to see her at full capacity. "Yes they do. I'm a full-time pastor and I want the members to be able to reach me."

"I understand, but I work full-time during scheduled work hours. After that, I'm unavailable. The church can call you at all hours of the night? You have to change that or they are going to wear you out."

Richard sat back in his chair and smiled at April. Jokingly he saluted her, "Yes ma'am, I'll fix it right away."

"I'm so sorry," April gasped, momentarily clasping her hand over her mouth. "Sheena is always telling me I can't say everything that comes to my mind."

"There's no need to apologize. You're absolutely right." His mother as well as a few other pastors had told him the same thing, but he refused to listen.

"From what I hear you're a really good pastor. I'm going to need you to be around for a long time, so take care of yourself."

"I will, but enough about me. How are you feeling?"

April leaned back to rest her head on the pillow. She sighed as she searched for the words to explain how she had been feeling.

Seeing the grief on her face, Richard moved his chair closer to the bed and grasped her hand. The gesture was soft and endearing. Richard instantly felt the connection. He glanced down at their joined hands and his heart swooned. What if he hadn't prayed that morning? Would the Lord have made him wait longer? There was no more wondering or searching; she was there in the flesh. He lifted his eyes and she turned her head to face him. Tears crested her cheekbones and he caught them with the pad of his thumb.

The strength and warmth of his hand was comforting and helped her relax. He stroked the back of her hand and continued drying her tears, listening attentively as she spoke.

"To be honest with you, Pastor, sometimes it feels like I'm losing my mind. I know who attacked me, but just about every man who walks into this room terrifies me. I can't sleep at night because of the nightmares. What am I supposed to do?"

Richard gripped her hand a little tighter. "Just relax, I'm here for you. You don't have to be afraid anymore." Before he could stop himself, he had kissed the back of her hand. He realized his error and instantly wanted to take it back. She didn't know what he knew and he didn't want to run her off before the Lord revealed it to her. Not wanting to give her time to analyze his actions, he grabbed her other hand and prayed for her.

"Great and mighty God, our peace, our joy, our refuge and strength, a very present help in the time of trouble, be the God we know You to be, display the power we know You to possess." Although he'd just prayed for her, he prayed with an enthusiasm he had yet to experience. Knowing who she would soon be fueled his fervor and he prayed until the power of God arrived in that hospital room

April gripped his hands as tight as her weakened body would allow. He finished praying and she looked into his eyes. The tears she saw confused her. "Why are you being so nice to me? You don't even know me."

"I know you better than you think I do. The Lord has shown me some things regarding you. I wish I could reveal it to you right now, but God has to complete his work in you first. Just know that God has allowed for you to go through this to strengthen you for the work He has for you to do."

"What could he possibly want me to do? I'm a mess..."

"Shhh." He placed his finger over her lips. "Only speak the positive; you are fearfully and wonderfully made. God is going to do a great work in you. He is going to do it quickly. Soon you won't even recognize the person you are today."

"I'm pretty sure there are people who won't let me forget."

"You are absolutely right. People are going to be jealous and hate you because of what God has chosen you to do. Even your family may not understand, but you have to trust God. I have to go, but you can call me whenever you need me." He would've loved nothing more than to continue sitting with her, but he was having a hard time fighting the urge to wrap his arms around her and place his lips on hers. The more she cried, the weaker he became.

Richard felt the weight of his burdens being lifted as he walked out of the room. He no longer felt as though the Lord had forsaken him. Although he still had to wait to be with her, being able to put a name to her face and touch her was appeasing.

The tapping of his shoes against the linoleum floor as he walked made a rhythm with the beat of his heart. He felt like dancing for the Lord. The people he passed in the hall made strange faces toward him, more than likely trying to figure out why he was smiling so hard. He made it to the elevator, but he didn't know how much longer he could contain himself. Praise for God was bubbling over inside of him. He was seconds away from dancing right there in the hospital. His cell phone rang and put a temporary damper on his praise.

"Hello?"

"Is it too soon?" a female voice asked.

"Who is this?" Richard asked.

"It's April. You said I could call whenever I needed you. Is it too soon?"

Immediately, Richard did an about face and headed back to her room. The quiver in her voice beckoned him. "No, of course not, how can I help you?"

"I was hoping maybe you could come back and sit with me until Sheena gets here. I felt more at ease with you these past few minutes than I have all week."

"Well April, you know I'm a very busy man."

"Say no more, I totally understand. I really enjoyed your company and I hope to see you soon." She hung up the phone, feeling foolish for asking and even more foolish when her eyes misted.

"Why are you crying? I told you I'd be there for you when you needed me."

Startled by his voice, April's eyes shot up to the doorway. The shock of him standing there overwhelmed her. Although she tried to fight it, her tears became more than just a mist. The elation she felt was confusing, but she was too enthralled by his presence to analyze it.

Richard pulled his chair close to the bed and grabbed her hand. He leaned forward, giving her his undivided attention. She relaxed in the bed and turned to face him. They talked for almost an hour. They were so engaged in their conversation that neither heard Sheena and Paul enter the room.

"So, tell me April, how is it that you don't go to church?"

Sheena heard the question as she stepped into the room and didn't want to interrupt the moment that could turn her sister's life around. She tiptoed out of the room and signaled for Paul to follow.

"I've met several members of your family and they all serve the Lord. What's your story?" he further prodded at her silence.

She hesitantly spoke, pulling her hand from his. "When I was a kid, I was forced to go to church. It wasn't always enjoyable. Don't get me wrong, I have some fond memories of vacation bible school and youth retreats, but all that is overshadowed with the negative. My sister was a saint in everyone's eyes. They expected me to be the same. It was hard living up to everyone's expectations. I got tired of falling short and being condemned for it, so I stopped trying. There is nothing worse than giving your all and then finding out it's still not good enough. So I took that energy and started giving it to other things: boys, sports, friends, and did I say boys?" They laughed at her emphasis. "Before long, I was involved in so much stuff that I was missing church all the time. Then, college gave me a taste of the party life. And when I moved out here to live with Sheena, I had the freedom to come and go as I pleased. I just got carried away."

She shrugged her shoulders as if to say what's done is done. Turning her head toward the window, she waited for the judgment and the condescension to come spewing out of his mouth, but there was none. What she heard made her head snap back around and she stared at him with shock.

"Good for you. There are so many members of my church that are living the same kind of life as you but come to church every Sunday pretending to be holy. God knows and sees all. They are fooling no one but themselves. I have always believed if you aren't ready to live this life, then you shouldn't. Now don't get me wrong, I pray they get ready before their time runs out, but even the word of God says that we should be hot or cold. That lukewarm, in the middle, straddling the fence mess is ridiculous. No man can serve two masters. You will love one and hate the other, so why bother putting up the front? By living a life contrary to the word of God, you have already chosen which master you love. Coming to church on Sunday trying to praise God harder, louder, and longer than everyone is a waste of time."

"Wow," was all she could say. A smile tugged at the corners of her mouth as she continued to stare at him.

"Sorry, I just don't like when people play games. When they play games with God, it infuriates me."

Her smile faded. She was the queen of game playing and it was her stupid games that had landed her in the hospital. She didn't know why his opinion mattered so much, but she hoped to God he never found out why she was attacked. April fidgeted as she wracked her brain for something else to talk about and almost leaped with joy when Sheena walked into the room.

"Hey hun, it's good to see you allowing visitors." Sheena walked into the room, acting as if she hadn't been outside the door eavesdropping. Paul couldn't stand listening to people's private conversations and tried several times to step around her, but she had pinned him with a look that warned him if he made another move her wrath would make hell look like a vacation. He choked back a laugh at her horrible performance and she shot him the look again.

"Maybe you'll be ready to go home soon." Paul kissed the crown of her head and went to greet Richard. "We really appreciate you stopping by."

"Don't mention it, man." Richard accepted Paul's hug and tried to hide his disappointment over his time with April being interrupted. "So, are we still balling in the morning?"

"Of course. Make sure you get plenty of sleep tonight. I don't want to hear any excuses."

"Don't worry about me and my sleep. Just bring your A-game, because I'm feeling pretty good. Y'all might not be able to keep up." They slapped hands as they exchanged their usual brotherly banter.

"We shall see," Paul chuckled as Richard stepped toward the door to make his exit.

April's heart dropped into her stomach as he said goodbye and headed out the door.

As always, Sheena was being overly observant and had picked up on her mood change. "What's wrong?"

"Nothing," April mumbled, still looking at the doorway hoping he came back. "I just feel bad for refusing to meet him all this time. He's a really nice person." A smile touched the corners of her mouth as she remembered their conversation and how he comforted her. "I think I'm ready to go home." She ignored the shocked expressions and packed her things.

Richard sat behind the wheel of his black Lexus GX. The heat from the sun-soaked leather seats burned through his pants, but he didn't care. He gripped the steering wheel and let out a deep howl that echoed through the vehicle. Triumphantly, he threw his hands into the air as if he'd just won an Olympic gold medal. In a sense, he had. God had brought the mystery woman into his life. He remembered all the times he visited and she refused to be cordial, sneaking out of the house to avoid meeting him. Richard clapped and laughed out loud at how the Lord had worked. Anyone on the outside looking in might've thought he'd lost his mind, but it was fully intact and he was already contemplating his next move.

The effects of meeting April lingered for the rest of the day. He was no longer consumed with loneliness that almost made it hard to breathe. He thanked God for everything that had taken place. For the first time in months, he climbed into bed with gratitude instead of anger toward the Lord.

7

Richard strutted around his house like the man of the hour as he prepared to meet his boys for a game of three-on-three basketball. A good night's rest and finally meeting the woman of his dreams had him feeling good. His other problems faded into the background.

He loved the early morning games. They were the rare instances he stepped outside of his title just to have a good time. The white tee that stretched across his muscular chest, nylon basketball shorts, and Jordan's on his feet hid his ministerial persona well.

Richard stomped into the gym like he owned the place. He had always been very charismatic, but this particular day, his swagger was off the chain. The few women hanging around stopped in their tracks to admire his smooth chocolate skin, thick lips, and soft brown eyes that lit up in the sun and hoped he'd do the same. He saw them, but didn't have the time of day to give them. He only wanted the attention of one woman. He went around fist pumping and shoulder hugging familiar faces and then headed toward his boys.

"What up, fellas?" Richard's jovial attitude was a stark contrast to the sullen faces that greeted him. He barely got a good-morning reply. The only one who looked ready to play was Jaleel. "You guys need to shake that sleepiness. I don't want any excuses on the court."

"I came home from the restaurant ready to climb in to bed with my wife and get a good night's rest." Marlon plopped down on the bench. "But, somebody was up and ready to play. Don't get me wrong, I love being a dad, but I just need one uninterrupted night of sleep."

"That explains him. What about you and Tim?"

Paul smirked, "Let's just say my wife didn't just have a baby, so we spent the night trying to make one."

"I second that." Tim slapped Paul's hand and then turned to Richard "You rolled up in here looking like you might have partaken in the dirty deed yourself. Is there something you need to tell us?"

"You know I don't roll like that, but I did meet someone."

Every eyebrow shot up in shock and they spent the next five minutes trying to pull more details out of him. When he'd had enough of the interrogation, he threw his hands into the air and asked, "Are we balling or not?"

"Have you talked to your brother?" Jaleel asked as he kneeled to tighten up his shoelace.

Richard rolled his eyes. He was still trying to get used to everyone referring to Cole as his brother. "I've gone by the hospital several times. He's looking worse than Meme." Richard turned to Marlon, concerned etched on his face.

"I know what you mean. I went by there yesterday to talk to the doctors about this infection she can't seem to get rid of and Cole looked like a zombie. I reminded him that she was my sister and that I'd be more than happy to sit with her. He looked at me like I was crazy."

"Let's go down there." Without any prodding, they gathered their things and went to the hospital to support their friend.

Richard, Marlon, Paul, Tim, and Jaleel walked into the hospital looking like an ebony dream. Women stopped what they were doing just to stare at the sight. They were so mesmerized no one bothered to tell the men that there was a two-visitor limit. The outward appearance was just the surface of how wonderful these men actually were. Their group was comprised of a lawyer, accountant, chef, computer engineer, and a man of God. That, combined with their tender hearts and overflowing bank accounts, and these women would be rushing to the locker room to change out of their scrubs and into something a little more appealing.

They walked into the room and Cole was stretched out on the hospital bed with the television remote in his hand with Meme sprawled across his chest. Marlon took the chair on the side of the bed closest to Meme. Richard took the one closest to Cole. Tim hopped up on the counter by the sink and Jaleel and Paul leaned up against the wall. Cole watched them all. "My bad, brothers. I didn't realize it was basketball Saturday."

"Would you have come if you did?" Richard made sure his skepticism showed.

Cole chuckled. "Hell no."

"I hope to God I'm not this sappy when I fall in love." An image of April popped into his mind and Richard knew he had just spoken his fate.

"You came pimping into the gym this morning smiling from ear to ear just because you met someone. That's a good indication you will be exactly like Cole. Maybe sappiness runs in the family," Marlon said, laughing as the others joined in.

"Who did you meet?" Cole's question cut through the laughter and everyone listened for the answer.

Richard looked around at everyone eyeing him and let out an exasperated breath. "Y'all are about the nosiest bunch of men I know."

They didn't bother to deny it and sat silently waiting for his answer.

"Look, we aren't at that point yet. We haven't even gone out, but so far I like what I'm seeing." He let the conversation die with that. "Besides, it looks like playa-playa is going to beat me to the altar."

"I hear that. I thought hell would freeze over before this fool settled down. I spent many long nights praying for him to get some sense." Marlon shook his head as he thought about Cole's relationship with Meme.

Richard couldn't help but laugh at the look on Cole's face.

"All that talk about us being whipped and one look at Meme and she knocked you to your knees." Marlon had sensed an attraction between them, but they fought it for so long he thought maybe he was imagining things. "Look at you, nose is so wide open I can see your thoughts. They have Meme written all over them. I hope when she gets out of this hospital she decides to marry you, because I'd hate to knock my boy out for stalking my sister."

Laughter roared through the room. A few of the nurses poked their heads in to see what was going on, but were too awestruck by the masculine splendor to say anything. The rumble of Cole's laughter vibrated his chest and woke Meme.

Her head popped up.

"Sorry, baby. I didn't mean to wake you." He caressed the side of her face, guiding her head back to his chest.

"Pastor Hawkins." She finally noticed him sitting beside the bed. "Your brother." Her head popped back up. She had been so out of it, she'd yet to express how amazing them being brothers was. She looked at Cole and then at Richard. "Oh my God, you guys look alike."

"Yes, they do," everyone else chimed in at once.

Meme's head snapped around as she noticed the other people in the room. The quick movement made her woozy and she gently rested her head on Cole's chest to keep the room from spinning.

"You all right, baby girl?" Marlon leaned forward and rubbed her back.

"Yes," she smiled weakly. Everyone could see she was lying.

"Well, let's pray," Richard beckoned for the other men to circle the bed. "And then I want you to convince my brother to trust the Lord is working it out, so he can go home and rest."

"We can pray, but I won't rest until she's home with me," Cole firmly asserted.

Richard watched Cole pull Meme a little tighter and brush his lips across hers. He knew it wasn't up for discussion. Since Cole was determined to be her strength, he might as well learn to be her strength in prayer. "You pray for her," Richard suggested. Cole cocked a brow at him, but he didn't care. "Pray for her," he repeated, placing his hand on Cole's shoulder. The others followed suit, placing a hand on his arm, head, or wherever they could reach. Cole sat motionless, listening to the words flowing from his brother's mouth. He wasn't an atheist, but he wasn't a child of God either. Up until recently, he'd rejected even the thought of a higher power. Something he couldn't explain overwhelmed him and gushed out over him in a powerful heat that surprisingly didn't singe. He shut his eyes to hold back the moisture that was collecting, but it did no good. His body trembled and he held onto Meme. He tried to fight off whatever was happening to him.

Richard felt his resistance and wasn't going to sit idly by and let this move of God pass by. "Open your mouth and ask God to heal her. If you love her, then ask the only one that can heal her for help."

Cole took a deep breath and that emotional riptide broke free. "Make her better, please." He had said a few quick prayers throughout her hospital stay, but more so to make sure all his bases were covered. This particular cry out to God was because he believed. The power he felt surrounding him was proof of God's existence. It was unreal. His trembling transferred to Meme. He looked down to see if she was okay and she was crying, too. "God, I love her too much to lose her." He didn't have big words, scriptures, or Christian anecdotes. All he had was hope. "Please God, I need you."

Tim shut the door. He remembered how the Lord had saved him in an unlikely situation and knew God was getting ready to do a great work. They didn't want any interruptions.

Cole's trembling persisted. He clamped down his teeth trying to fight off the sensation coursing through him. Richard opened his mouth to tell Cole to stop struggling against the Lord and start praising him, but Cole chanted over and again, "God help her, please help her." The breakthrough and salvation Richard was hoping to be rained down on his brother rushed through Meme instead.

She clung to Cole's chest as an energy and strength she hadn't felt in weeks surged through her veins. She'd gone through so much, but had survived to tell the story. In that moment, God washed away all her lies, betrayal, and everything keeping her from surrendering to Him. She had walked away from the Lord years before. In that instant God reclaimed her. Her heavenly language broke free and she spoke to the Lord.

Richard smiled down at her feeling hopeful. He wanted his brother to get over his issues with the church and give his life to Christ. Maybe he still had more things to work through, but a sanctified woman could sanctify her man. The way Cole loved Meme, there was no way she'd live for the Lord without him. His brother was coming to the Lord whether he liked it or not.

8

April stood staring out her bedroom window. The spot where she was attacked was dead center in her view. She tried to focus on the beauty of the sunset with its violet hewn sky specked with streaks of amber trailing the sun, but it did nothing for her except haunt her mind.

Her eyes strayed over to the spot where nearly two months ago her pleas for mercy were unanswered, where her flesh was singed from rubbing against the concrete, and where her face was pounded, body battered, and her dignity raped. Her throat clogged with despair, which she tried to hold back. She didn't want to cry or be afraid anymore. No matter what she did, she couldn't shake her fear. She had imprisoned herself in her room, refused all visitors, and hadn't eaten more than one meal a day since leaving the hospital.

Sheena had been pushing her to go to church, but she refused. How could she sit in a church full of strangers when she could barely tolerate being around her family?

"Lord, help me." April rested her head against the cold glass window and let the tears she'd been holding back trickle down her cheeks.

Her cell phone buzzed on the nightstand.

It's probably another family member checking up on me.

Their calls and texts had been frequent, so she took her time checking it. The screen flashed with a text from Pastor Hawkins, and her heart rate picked up a bit. She cleaned her face and nose with the sleeve of her sweatshirt, fluffed her hair like he could actually see her through the phone, and then shook her head at why she'd actually care.

I prayed for you today.

I really need it, thank you.

You need to talk?

No, don't want to bug you.

It's no bother.

You're busy and I have to learn to deal with it...how's your day so far?

April waited for a response, but it never came. Her phone rang instead.

"Hello?"

"Hey."

That one word washed over April, sending a tingle that radiated from her ear to her neck and throughout her chest. It was so powerful and scared her so bad, she almost hung up the phone.

"Do me a favor."

"Anything for you."

Richard knew that was a common phrase when someone asked for a favor, but he couldn't help how those words—coming from her—affected him.

"Wrap your arms around yourself and squeeze tight."

She smiled at the silliness of his request, but something in his voice made her do it anyway.

"If I were there, this is how I'd hug you," he continued, choosing his words wisely, so he wouldn't scare her away. "I'd hold you, pray for you, and remind you that you are more than a conqueror until you believe it yourself."

"But I…"

"Shhh. You are a conqueror. Focus on that."

She sniffled and he was on the verge of running out to his car to go to her.

"Now get up and take a shower. Put on a cute outfit, like you're going shopping with your girlfriends."

"I can't."

"You can and you will." Silence ticked through the line. Richard thought he had offended her, but her whispered concession urged him on. "You don't have to leave the house, but you will leave that room. Are you still hugging yourself?"

"Yes, sir." She felt thoroughly chastised. How else could she respond to him?

"Squeeze a little harder. I give you my strength until yours is restored, my courage to help you stand against giants, and my—" He started to say heart, but thank God he caught himself. She had captured his heart in his dreams without even knowing her. He was falling hard. "...And my prayers to fortify you for the journey ahead."

"Thank you." April closed her eyes and basked in the warmth engulfing her. She ended the call thinking he had to be the best pastor in the world. If he gave all his members that kind of one-on-one attention, he would undoubtedly burn out before turning forty. April ignored the feelings that popped up at the thought of him giving other women in the church attention and hopped in the shower.

A little over an hour later, she stood at her bedroom door with her hand on the knob. *I give you my strength until yours is restored.* Richard's words soared through her mind. She locked them in her heart and opened the door. The house was quiet. She took a couple of deep breaths and kept moving.

The kitchen was empty, but the aroma of the foil-covered pans cooling on the stove was too tempting to resist. She grabbed a plate out of the cabinet and helped herself. The sight of roasted chicken and vegetables made her stomach growl. She was hungrier than she realized.

"April!"

She was so caught up in making her plate, she didn't hear Sheena sneak up behind her. Her heart slammed against her ribs at the sudden voice. The plate in her hand fell to the floor, cracking into pieces, and what little food she'd managed to get on the plate splashed up onto her pants. She spun around, on the verge of taking off running, but held it together.

"I'm sorry. I'm just a little hungry." She ran a shaky hand through her hair and reached for the paper towels on the counter.

"It's okay. You go back up to bed. I'll bring you something to eat."

"No, I need to get out of that room."

"Why? You've been through a lot. Everyone understands you need time to recuperate."

"He told me to."

"Who?"

For some reason, April didn't feel comfortable letting her sister know she had spoken to the pastor. So, she ignored her question and proceeded to clean up her mess.

Sheena recognized that attitude and didn't know whether to be glad her sister was returning to her normal pain-in-the-butt self or to push her to divulge who had forced her out of her room. She didn't have the strength to argue, so she let it go and made them both plates.

Before they could sit down to eat, Paul walked in with the twins. "Aunt April!" Paul Jr. and Page swarmed around her. She hadn't seen them since before the attack. It looked like they missed her as much as she missed them.

She duck-waddled to the table with them attached to her waist and plopped down into the seat. She pulled Page on to her lap and cuddled little Paul real close.

"Aunt April, where were you?"

"What happened to your face?" The ever-observant Page scanned her face and traced the last bruise with her finger.

"A very bad man hurt me and I was in the hospital."

"You should tell my dad. He'll have him arrested," Paul Jr. added. He idolized his dad and thought he was superman. The way he handled business and had means to rectifying any situation made him a super hero to everyone, April included.

"Don't worry, Auntie. I'll keep you safe." Page's little hand cupping April's cheek was one of the most endearing moments of her life.

"We'll all keep you safe. Now you two give your aunt a break and go wash up for dinner." The kids ran off to the washroom and Paul kissed April on the crown of her head. "I'm glad you decided to come out of hiding."

"Are you?" April tossed a questioning glance to Sheena.

"I just want you better. Whatever it takes, I'm happy with it."

April enjoyed dinner with her entertaining niece and nephew. She hadn't laughed that hard in days, but their exaggerated stories, whining over who'd had more juice, and burping at the table in spite of their parent's chastisement pulled it out of her.

She hadn't realized how hungry she was until she looked down at her plate and every last crumb was gone. She leaned back in her chair and patted her full stomach. "You can cook your butt off."

"Thanks…"

"Not as good as me though."

Sheena threw her head back laughing. "You know I'm always down for a cook-off; care to put your money where your mouth is?"

"Yeah, right. Who's going to judge? Paul?" April looked at Paul and shook her head. "I don't think so."

"What? You think I can't judge fairly?" he asked.

"Sure you can, but I think if you ever wanted a home-cooked meal from your wife again, you'd be persuaded to vote in her favor."

"You do have a point," Paul laughed and popped a piece of bread in his mouth.

"Okay, my dear little sister." Sheena sat up and scooted her plate to the side, actually getting excited about the idea. "How about you do your best dishes and I'll do mine. We don't tell him who cooked what. The dish he likes best is the winner."

"Nope." Paul got up and started clearing dishes from the table. "Pick someone else." He kissed his wife on the cheek and escorted the kids out of the kitchen.

They watched him walk away and leaned toward each other laughing. "It is good to see you smile." Sheena sobered and embraced April.

"I didn't think I'd be able to again." April leaned into the embrace and rested her head on Sheena's shoulder. "So about this competition, I don't think I have the energy to cook for a bunch of people."

"Okay, what about Pastor Hawkins?"

71

April's head popped up and she pulled away to look Sheena in the face.

"What? You seemed pretty comfortable around him the other day."

"Okay, you're on but two weeks from now." April got up from the table trying to hide her excitement over seeing Pastor Hawkins again.

9

ichard was still soaring from meeting April. They hadn't spent time together, but knowing who she was and that the Lord had finally brought her to him was all he needed to put joy back into his life. The last thing he wanted to do was interfere with the Lord's work or even scare her off. So, he would keep his distance until he felt the Lord leading him to do otherwise.

Richard sat in the pulpit, scanning the congregation. He was halfway listening to his secretary read the church announcements. He blew a kiss to his mother and gave a head nod to his boys. His attention was drawn to the door opening at the back of the church as April walked in. The dress she wore had no right being in church and Richard loved every inch of it. Her curves were hidden by the hospital gown the last time he saw her, but that dress molded to the curvature of her body like a second skin. The bounce in her walk made her hair float in the air. The definition in her calves and her flat abs…

My God! he thought. Richard had to drag his eyes away before someone caught him staring. *Thank you, Jesus!* He had to bite his lip to keep from groaning. He was worried that when he decided to get married the docile demeanor of church women wouldn't be enough to get his blood pumping. He wanted to give God a fist bump and say, *Good looking out for a brother.* Without a doubt, April had gotten his blood pumping and he said a quick prayer to get his mind back in the right space before he had to preach.

It was her first Sunday and her presence affected him in a way he hadn't expected. First off, he was proud of her for venturing outside the house. Secondly, she was already his woman, plain and simple. Possessiveness overwhelmed him and he felt like pounding his chest and swinging from the ceiling fans like Tarzan as he carried April out the church. *My woman.*

That particular Sunday, Richard switched his style of preaching. Instead of the high energy exhortation, he was more calm and personable. He stepped down off the pulpit and walked around the altar as he spoke. "I had a dream about the church. In this dream, I saw a few faces and God told me to pray for you today. There may be more of you out there who find yourself dealing with this same issue and when the time is right you can come to the altar. But in this dream there was a boxing ring. The same kind you see on TV. Inside the ring was a few of the saints."

Pastor Hawkins paused to scan the faces in the congregation. "I know you're thinking that this is another 'People of God Stop

Fighting' message, and you're right. The only difference is, when I looked closely, each person was fighting an image of themselves. The struggle and the fight that a person has within them can be greater and more damaging than any physical altercation." He began to walk the aisles, asking certain people to meet him at the altar. "There are some of you who love the Lord and desperately want to live right, so you beat yourself up about mistakes you've made. You are tearing yourself apart over something the Lord has long since forgiven and forgotten."

Returning to the altar, Pastor Hawkins smiled. He knew the word God had for them. He looked each of them in the eye as he spoke. "The Lord instructed me to tell you that the fight is over. Just that simple, the fight is over. There is therefore now no condemnation to those who are in Christ Jesus. Why are you condemning yourself for the person you used to be? God has moved on and so should you."

He prayed for those at the altar. April was at the end of the line. He wanted to pull her to his chest and wrap his arms around her while he prayed but knew that wouldn't be perceived well. He placed his hand on her forehead and her warm soft skin almost made him lose focus. She needed his prayer, a touch from the Lord, and the reassurance that she was forgiven. He wouldn't allow his selfish desires to get in the way of that. He prayed for her, giving everything he had left. He rebuked, declared, commanded and encouraged. April buckled to her knees under the intensity and Richard went with her. The deacons tried to support him, but he didn't let them get in the way. He warred in the spirit until he heard the undeniable sound of the Lord working. He signaled the musicians to stop playing and placed the microphone to April's mouth. The sound of her heavenly language filled the sanctuary.

Richard stood and, right on cue, the female ministers were in his place. He looked over to Sheena and she just about lost it praising God. Paul wrapped his arm around her waist trying to contain her, but she was having none of it. Richard dried his face with a towel and made his way back to the pulpit, barely able to contain his own praise. He watched them working on the floor all the while praise swelled within him. They helped April to her feet. Without thought of what she looked like or what people might think, she praised the Lord. With her hands raised in submission, she leaped for joy. Once, twice, and on her third leap Richard lost it. He was out of the pulpit and running around the church before anyone could comprehend what was going on.

He considered himself a more reserved pastor when it came to dancing in the aisles. He'd always been that way, but didn't judge those who did dance. That day, he stepped out of his norm to give God the praise He was due. Praise spread around the sanctuary like fire. Before long, just about the entire congregation had joined in. Richard finished glorifying God and then went to his office. Service was over. What else could God do?

April hung around after service to see him. Normally, the deacons didn't allow anyone in his office on Sundays, but made an exception for visitors. He really didn't feel up to visiting, but knew how important it was to make visitors feel welcomed. When the deacons told him someone wanted to talk with him, he accepted the visit. He was pleasantly surprised when she walked in.

"April, it's good to see you." He came from behind his desk and greeted her with a handshake. "How are you feeling?"

"For the most part, I feel amazing. Not just physically, but spiritually as well. All that clubbing, drinking, and partying I used to do, and all the pain I've experienced lately seems to be washing away."

"Praise God! Keep up the hard work."

"I will. I'm not going to hold you too long, but I wanted to tell you two things real quick. I had a dream about you."

Richards's ear perked up. The Lord said He was going to work quickly, but that was quicker than what Richard imagined.

"You were building a wall out of bricks, but your wall had holes in it, like a few bricks were missing. I had the missing bricks and was standing next to you filling in your holes. I have no idea what that means, except for maybe I should work with you."

Words nervously came out of her mouth. "Anyways, it made me think of what you said to me when I was in the hospital. You said that God is preparing me for a special job. Thinking about my being in the hospital made me remember that I never thanked you properly for being there for me that day. I don't know if it's customary, but I would like to take you out to lunch just to say thank you. Would today be fine?"

She nervously glanced around his office as she waited for his response. It was moderately furnished. She thought a man of his stature would have more. Her eyes zoned in on a cake plate sitting on his desk and she tried to inconspicuously focus her eyes to read the note taped to, but all she could make out was *there is more where this came from.* Her mind ran wild with assumptions. Every possible meaning made her blood boil. At that moment, she couldn't explain it nor did she understand it, but she wanted to find the woman who had cooked for him and slap some sense into her.

"Well, I try not to go out alone with sisters. It's how rumors get started." He desperately wanted to say yes, but had learned a long time ago not to let his good be evil spoken of.

"I understand." April turned to leave his office, but came back for one last attempt at giving him a proper thank you. "Paul and Sheena are cooking dinner today. Would you like to join us?"

Richard thought for a moment. He was ecstatic about her dream, even though she was clueless about the true meaning of it. The progress she was making excited him and he was anxious to be with her. He didn't want to jump the gun and have his eagerness to spend time with her delay God's plan. Waiting was something he had done plenty of and didn't want a slip of the tongue, misplaced touch, or a misunderstood glance to cause more waiting. Then, there was that dress she had on which was making their conversation even harder. Weighing the ins and outs, he decided that there would be plenty of people around the dinner table to keep him on his best behavior. He could join her for dinner.

April was elated that Richard accepted her dinner invitation. She really enjoyed his company and felt like she could be herself around him. Usually, she was made up from head to toe before she let a man see her, but he had already seen her at her worst. She felt no need to put up a front. Nervously, April piddled around the house as she waited for Richard. Every time the phone rang, she feared it was him calling to say he couldn't make it. All the food had been arranged on the table and they were gathering to give thanks when the doorbell rang.

"Praise him, bruh. Is everything all right?" Paul answered the door, shocked to see him there.

"Is April here?"

"Yeah, follow me."

No one noticed how April's face lit up when Richard walked into the room. "Thank you for coming. I really appreciate you."

"Don't mention it. Thank you for inviting me. It looks like I made it just in time."

"Yes, you're just in time," Sheena cut her eyes toward April to let her know she wasn't happy. She was all for having guests and was always welcoming to visitors, but a little notice would've been nice, especially with Richard. Yes, they were good friends, but he was still the pastor and she liked to reverence him as such.

As he took his seat at the table, Richard looked at the family seated around him. One day soon, they'd all be his family. That thought put a smile on his face. He really liked the Matthews and all the extended family they had brought to the church. They were genuine men and women who loved God. Richard's eyes landed on April and he caught her staring at him. She quickly shifted her eyes away, but it was too late. He laughed to himself as he watched her fidget to keep her eyes averted. She straightened out her silverware, placed her napkin in her lap, took a sip of water, and then settled in on her bowl of gumbo.

"Did you get my email about coming to dinner next week?" Sheena's voice interrupted his thoughts.

"I have to meet with Sister Johnson that day. She's spearheading the citywide revival committee. I'm checking to see if I can move the meeting to another date."

"You know, giving her responsibilities in the church just feeds into her fantasy of being the next first lady."

April nearly choked on the food in her mouth. She tussled, fumbling for her glass of water and spilled it all over the table. Sheena patted her back and gave her another glass.

Richard held his breath until she settled down and then looked her directly in the eye. "As long as I know what's up, that's all that matters. I'd prefer one of you to take the lead on organizing everything, but your plates are already so full with the children's and prison ministry. Sister Johnson will get the job done. I know how to deal with all that other foolishness."

"Well, you don't have to rearrange your schedule for us. Just let me know what Saturday you're free."

"I appreciate that, but you know y'all are my people and I'll drop everything to be there for you."

April couldn't help but think he was talking about her. She stared at him, hoping he'd look in her direction. When his eyes flashed to hers, her heart climbed into her throat, nearly suffocating her.

Richard wanted to kick himself. He tried to keep from looking at her, because he didn't want her to see the truth in his eyes. He would drop everything and everyone if she needed him. She couldn't know that yet. He averted his eyes and dug into his bowl.

"Hey Rich, you mentioned the prison ministry and it reminded me that I forgot to tell you about Jason. Some woman has taken to writing him." Paul washed his food down with a gulp of soda and patted his mouth with a napkin. "He won't tell me her name. He said he doesn't want me running a background check on her."

"What's so wrong with a woman writing him?" Candice froze mid-bite, waiting for him to answer.

"Calm down, little Sojourner Truth. Save the feminism for someone else. All I'm saying is, you have to question a woman's character when she randomly picks an inmate to befriend. Jason is getting out in a few months and I don't want him to get caught up with another bad element."

"She might not be that bad."

The room fell silent and every eye was on Candice.

"You okay, Candy?" April made eye contact trying to understand where that hostility was coming from. Candice rolled her eyes and dug back into her bowl.

Two bowls later, Richard was stuffed and sat at the table feeling like he was going to explode. He looked at Sheena and mumbled, "Man, that was good," breaking the uncomfortable silence that had settled over the table.

April watched Richard from across the table. His presence fascinated her. She wondered how a man who exuded such power and authority could be so sweet and kind. Those words were never in her vocabulary when considering a man. Her first thoughts were always money, cars, and wardrobe. When she looked at Richard, she didn't appraise his monetary worth. She saw his heart. The compassion it held intrigued her. The way he had held her hand, spoke to her, and listened to her fears was exactly what she needed. He looked her in the eye and seemed to absorb every word she spoke. His approach was tender, but he possessed a power that commanded her respect.

Sitting quietly as everyone cleared the table and cleaned the kitchen, Richard marveled at their family unity. At all the dinners they had when he was growing up, his mom was always left to do the dishes and clean by herself. He would occasionally help out, but he was much more interested in playing with the kids that had come over. He couldn't remember a time where his father helped with the dishes. Watching Tim, Jaleel, and Paul clean with their wives while he sat around made him feel like a chauvinist. He gradually made his way toward April to assist her with sweeping the floor. When he grabbed the broom, she resisted and snatched it back. She insisted he didn't have to help, but he wouldn't relent. She swept while he held the dustpan and when they were done, April smiled and said, "I guess we make a pretty good team."

Richard smiled back, "I guess we do."

With everyone working together, the kitchen was clean in no time. They coupled up, holding hands, and walked toward the living room. Richard was enjoying himself and wanted to stay, but he didn't want to overstay his welcome. Even though they were friends, he set boundaries to keep from losing their friendship. "Well, I guess I'm going to head on home. I enjoyed myself, the food was delicious, and I hope to see everyone soon."

April shook his hand and said goodbye, trying to conceal her disappointment. Her breath caught in her throat as he clasped her hand between his. For the first time, she acknowledged feeling more than respect for him. She wasn't ready for him to leave, but didn't want to further upset Sheena by asking him to stay. As she watched him shake hands and say goodbye to everyone else, she pleaded with the Lord to make him stay.

When he finished his goodbyes, April volunteered to walk him out. "I'm really glad you came over." She held her head down, trying to hide the discontentment on her face. They stood face to face. April refused to make eye contact.

Richard took her by the hand, delicately kissing the back of it, he whispered, "Walk me to my car."

Hand in hand, they walked toward his car. April's heart beat out of control and she breathed deeply trying to calm her nerves. Approaching the driver's side of the car, April blurted out, "Please don't leave. Can you stay with me a little longer?" She wished her outburst had come with a little less desperation. "What I mean is...I was really enjoying your company. Everyone is going to watch a movie and it would be nice if you could stay."

"I think it's best if I leave now."

April's head dropped in defeat and Richard stroked her cheek as he lifted her chin.

"Don't be upset—"

April interrupted his sentence with a kiss on his lips.

Richard froze. The gesture caught him off guard. He couldn't decide whether to pull her in closer and return the kiss or push her away, so he just stood there. April swept his mouth with her tongue, nibbled his lips, ended with a soft peck, and ran away before he could react. He called out to her, but she didn't reply.

With her back leaning against the inside of the front door, April breathed deeply as panic started to set in. She tapped her hand against her forehead, scolding herself for doing something so crazy. Then, the doorbell rang. April halted her mental rebuke and paused in fear. She peeked out of the peephole and the look on his face made her pulse thump even harder. He looked upset. The last thing she wanted to do was upset him.

"April! Why are you just standing there not answering the door?"

April nearly jumped out of her skin when Sheena yelled her name. "I already know who it is. It's Pastor Hawkins."

"Then don't just stand there; let him in."

"I can't."

"Why can't you?" Sheena was fed up with April being so inconsiderate, inviting someone to dinner without checking to see if it was okay. Now leaving a guest on the porch was plain rude.

"I did something stupid."

Sheena's eyes widened with fear. "What did you do?"

There was no answer just that ridiculous fidgeting April had been doing a lot of lately.

"I don't know what is going on with you, but I love my church, so you better fix this." Sheena pushed past April and opened the door.

Richard was shocked to see Sheena at the door, but managed to keep his cool. "Can I speak to April alone for a minute?"

"Sure, come on in." Sheena stepped aside and allowed Richard to enter, and gave her sister the evil eye as she walked away.

They stood in silence for a moment, each waiting for the other to speak first. April dropped her head again, this time in shame. "I'm sorry. I don't know what got in to me. Please forgive me."

"April, look at me."

"I'm so embarrassed. I don't know if I'll ever be able to look at you. You are my pastor and I crossed the line. I promise it'll never happen again."

Richard pulled her into his arms. "Please don't tell me that you'll never kiss me again. I don't think I could live without your kiss."

April stepped back to look in his eyes, "So, I wasn't off base about what I feel developing between us?"

"No, but I'm not just some guy off the street. I have a certain standard to uphold and certain obligations that supersede my own personal desires."

"So, in other words forget about what I feel."

"No, what I'm saying is I'm a pastor, and if I'm in a relationship, there are activities that unmarried Christian couples can enjoy that I have to abstain from."

April smiled as she placed her arms around his waist. "Are we in a relationship?"

Richard took a deep breath as he placed his forehead against hers. He was conflicted. Was he jumping the gun or was the Lord finally giving him the okay to be with her? In his mind, he prayed for wisdom and the words to say that wouldn't ruin his chance at happiness. Words flowed from his mouth to her ears, but God was speaking to both of them. "Before we were created in our mothers' wombs, before the foundation of the earth, our souls were formed to love each other. The journey to each other just took longer than expected." The journey to each other might've taken long, but once

God brought her to him, things moved quickly. Barely two months had passed since he'd laid eyes on her in the hospital and already he was holding her in his arms.

April's head sank into his chest as she relaxed in his arms. The vibration of his voice traveled through her body sending chills up her spine. "I've never been with a man like you."

"You've never been with a real man before. Don't worry. I won't hurt you the way you've been hurt in the past. But be warned, being with me is going to be tough. There are women who are members of the church only because they are hoping to be my wife. When they get wind of me being in a relationship, things might get nasty. I'm sorry to say you are going to catch all the gossip, snide comments, and dirty looks. So, if you choose to keep things quiet for a while, I'll respect that. Your family may not even understand. I know you share everything with them, but their response to us being together may not be what you expect."

"I think my family will be more concerned about you than me. Sheena looked at me like I was crazy when I told her I'd done something stupid and didn't want to let you in." They laughed.

"Okay, let's just keep things quiet for right now. You think about what you want and let me know." Richard kissed her forehead, "But I have to go."

April moaned and pouted like a five year old. "Do you have to?"

Tightening his embrace Richard whispered, "It's for the best. You can call me and we can talk for as long as you like."

April took him up on his advice. She called him before his car left the block. He connected his blue tooth and they talked the entire drive. Richard wanted to blurt out, *You're my wife. I dreamed about you months before meeting you.* She'd probably freak, block his calls, and tell the church he was crazy. He held his peace and decided to let things progress naturally.

Minutes turned to hours as they both lay in their beds talking. Richard had to remind April several times to stop calling him Pastor Hawkins. She would apologize, but sure enough she'd say it again. By the end of the night, she had no problem calling him Richard.

The next morning, Richard woke up with his cell phone stuck to the side of his face. Smiling, he remembered April begging him not to hang up. His eyelids were heavy and he could barely form a complete sentence, but he wanted to keep talking to her as much as she wanted to talk to him. Checking the phone display, Richard chuckled; the call was still connected. He said hello a few times and was getting ready to hang up when April's groggy reply resounded through the phone.

"Good morning." He could hear the smile in her voice and it touched him deeply. "You fell asleep on me last night." When she realized he had fallen asleep, she was going to hang up. She decided, rather, to listen to the soft purr of his breathing. Before she knew it, she had drifted off to sleep as well.

"I'm sorry." Richard settled back onto the bed. "But, falling asleep to your voice helped me have the best sleep I've had in a long time."

"You want to meet for breakfast somewhere?"

"I would love to, but going out together wouldn't be wise right now."

This relationship was definitely going to be different than any she ever had. Privacy and discretion sounded more like hiding and secrecy. Although she understood the need for it that didn't mean she had to like it. "So, when can I see you again?" she asked, trying to take the little girl whine out of her voice. Not only was Richard a lot older than her, but he was an important man who didn't have time for foolishness. It was time to put her big girl panties on and grow up. The games she played with men in her past wouldn't be tolerated, nor would she dare subject him to the same foolery and selfishness as she had with her exes.

Richard contemplated her question. He definitely had to come up with some ground rules. He didn't want any of the church members, including her family, to find out about their relationship until he could address it properly. He couldn't do that until she was ready to be with him openly. Until then, he would do what was necessary to protect their privacy.

10

April sat at her vanity mirror removing her make-up. It was the end of another day of playing dress up just to wander aimlessly around the house. She wiped her cheeks clean and sure enough, the last lingering bruise popped up. Her eyes zeroed in on it. It was merely a small dot, but it served as a reminder of that horrible night. She could still see his face hovering over her, smell his breath, and hear the sick sounds he grunted. She stared at her reflection, and for a moment, became lost in the memory of her attack. How could someone do something so violent to another person?

Tears filled her eyes and she quickly blinked them away. She was tired of letting the memories control her and take her to a place of grief and despair. She'd dug herself out of that place many times in the weeks following her attack. A large teardrop slid from the corner of her eye and she shut them to ward off the onslaught threatening to follow suit. Despite her efforts the tears still came.

She climbed into bed and allowed herself one last cry. She promised it would be her last. The emotional roller coaster had to stop. It felt like joy and sorrow were playing tug-o-war with her mind. She silenced her sobs with a pillow. She didn't want someone walking by to hear her. She grabbed her cell phone to call Richard—his voice alone could calm her—but thought better of it. He needed to rest. She took a few deep breaths to get her wailing under control and let the tears silently flow.

Her bedroom door creaked open and she held her breath, hoping whoever it was thought she was sleep and left her alone.

"Auntie, are you sleeping?"

April hurriedly dried her face. Her niece was relentless and would come in and have a full conversation whether she answered her or not. "No sweetie, I'm up. Come on in." She slid her head out of the covers, hoping Page didn't pick up on her puffy watery eyes and start asking questions.

"Look what Roscoe did to Maddie." She thrust a slobber-soaked baby doll into April's face and she almost gagged. "He bit her. Daddy said it's my fault. I didn't put my toys away."

She had always had a soft spot for Page. It wasn't that she loved her more than Paul Jr., but he was a boy through and through. Toy trucks, sports, rough housing—if it was boy related, Paul loved it. He was the ultimate tough little boy. Page, on the other hand, was an emotional, loving, nail-polish wearing, baby-doll-toting girl. April loved it.

She sat up and gathered Page into her arms, welcoming the distraction from her troubled thoughts. "Where is your mommy? What did she say?"

"She's not here."

"Okay." She paused to come up with the right words to say. She was by no means parent material, but her sister on the other hand was the perfect mother. "Well, where did you leave Maddie?"

"I was playing with her before school and left her in the living room."

"And where are you supposed to leave her?"

Her head dropped and she fidgeted with the doll, totally ignoring the question.

April touched a finger to her chin and lifted her head. "Where are you supposed to leave the toys?"

"In my toy box."

"If you left her in your toy box, would Roscoe have gotten her?"

Her little head dropped again and her voice was so soft April had to strain to hear her. "No."

April was silent, giving Page a moment to think about it. "How about we give her a bath and get her all cleaned up?"

They went to the bathroom to prepare a bath for the baby doll. April turned her back on Page to check the water temperature to ensure she wouldn't burn her hands. She turned back around and Page had removed her clothes and hopped into the bath tub.

"What are you doing?"

"I have to take a bath with her, so she won't be scared."

April smiled thinking she'd definitely been played by her niece who loved to play in the water. She poured bubbles in the water and helped Page slosh the water around until a nice frothy layer built up. She stacked bubbles high on her head and gave her a bubble beard. Page giggled and splashed water all over the place, the soiled baby doll all but forgotten. It was moments like these with her niece when thoughts of motherhood slipped across her mind. She usually shut them down, but not this time. Images of Richard mingled with her thoughts of childbearing and for the first time she welcomed the possibility.

"Are you still mad at me?"

April was so caught up in her thoughts she hadn't noticed Paul stepping into the bathroom. She jumped and knocked the container of bubbles into the tub.

He moved into the bathroom and April stood, so he could sit on the edge of the tub. He gripped her chin and lifted her face so he could examine it. His eyes connected with hers and she knew he saw what her niece didn't.

"I'm fine." She answered his unspoken question and moved out of his way. She watched him soap up a rag and begin washing his daughter. She couldn't help but smile at how sweet they looked.

"Are you still mad at me?" Paul asked the question again, but pouty lips should've been his indication that Page was in fact mad at him.

"Daddy loves you, but you have to pick up your things, so Roscoe doesn't get them. He isn't smart like you. He sees things on the floor and thinks he can eat them. So, he needs us to look out for him. Can you do that for me? Be a big girl and watch out for Roscoe, so he doesn't hurt himself." He rinsed the suds off of her and bundled her in a towel.

"Yes, Daddy." She wrapped her little arms around his neck, blew a raspberry on his cheek, and waved goodbye to April as he carried her out of the bathroom.

April cleaned Page's mess and for a moment allowed her mind to ponder the possibilities. A loving relationship with a man that was everything she wanted and more. A home with a baby and a happiness she'd never allowed herself to consider. Could she have that? Did Richard want that? Surely he must, since he was a man of God. Casual relationships had to be pointless. Her heart leapt at that thought. A future with Richard didn't sound bad at all.

11

April stepped into the church foyer and her eyes locked with Richard's. He smiled but quickly turned his attention back toward the elderly woman holding his hand. It was one of the rare Sundays when he stood at the exit shaking hands with members as they left. He stood in the doorway with the air of a king. He was regal in his stance: broad shoulders, strong jaw, clean shaven, and a body to die for. She took a moment to truly take him in. If beautiful could be used to describe a man, he was definitely it. He captivated her to the point where she hadn't realized she was blocking the exit. People squeezed by saying excuse me, but she noticed no one but Richard.

The bass of his voice and low rumble of his laughter reached her ear—even above the clamor of the lobby—and lassoed around her, pulling her toward him. He ended his conversation with one person and she glided into their spot.

"Hi." Her wispy voice floated to his ear. She didn't care one bit that she sounded like an awestruck teenager.

"Hey." His lop-sided smile lit up the darkness that had been trying to consume her. He extended his hand in greeting and her heart leapt at the opportunity to touch him again. Why did he affect her so much? How could he command respect with just his presence? And what made her so willing to bow to him?

"I enjoyed—" She lifted her hand to his only to have it brushed out of the way by Sister Johnson.

She slipped in between them, entirely too close to Richard, and April literally had to bite her tongue to keep from cursing Sister Johnson out in God's house.

"Praise the Lord, Pastor. I just wanted to say you preached your face off this morning." She plucked a piece of lint off his shoulder and smoothed her hand across it.

Richard stiffened and gave her a look that would have made a more civilized person drop to their knees and repent. Sister Johnson had long passed civilized and stood there grinning like a kid at Christmas.

Richard cut his eyes to April, hoping she had the decorum to not make a scene, because Sister Johnson certainly didn't. April took a deep breath and walked away. Richard excused himself and darted to his office.

He passed smiling faces and gave halfhearted greetings. Surely they saw the urgency in his stride and would understand his curt response. He brushed past the on-duty deacon, unlocked his office door, and slammed the door shut. He couldn't grab his cell phone fast enough. Without thinking of the consequences or what his actions might look like, he texted April.

Meet me at my place.

He gave her the address, changed out of his sweaty clothes, and left the church faster than he ever had since becoming a pastor. He had waited too long for the Lord to bring the woman of his dreams into reality to have the likes of Sister Johnson come along and ruin it. He had to keep reminding himself to obey the speed limit. Anxiety over April not responding to his text shot from his heart, down his leg, out through his foot, and pressed down on the gas pedal. He made it home in record time, hoping to see a car parked in front of his house, but there was nothing.

April made it all the way home before she read Richard's text. When she did, she didn't know how to respond. Sister Johnson's intentions toward him were pretty clear, and she didn't know how to deal with it. Did she even want to be with a man who was the objection of every single woman in the congregation's affection?

Probably some of the married ones, too.

Rumor had it that most pastors slept around. She really didn't want to deal with it. Her mind flashed to the look on Richard's face when Sister Johnson touched him. That one image alone was enough to get her to start her car and plug his address into her GPS. Sister Johnson's touch had pissed him off.

They lived on opposite ends of the city and she used the long drive to mull over what she was doing. Dating a pastor? For crying out loud, how crazy could she be? She'd decided a long time ago the Christian lifestyle wasn't for her. The Lord certainly knew how to make her see the error of her ways, but did that mean she had to get married and do the white-picket-fence thing? Then, she didn't just go after any man, she'd shot straight for the top. Anyone with him would be scrutinized to the nth degree and expected to be found as pure as gold. Besides that, there were plenty of women like Sister Johnson in the church—or the world for that matter—who wanted Richard. Would she be able to bow out so gracefully when the next Sister Johnson approached him?

Her mind was made up. She wasn't going to be a pastor's mistress, dirty little secret, or oblivious girlfriend. She rang his doorbell, poised to end things before she got in too deep.

"Hey." She forced a smile when he answered. "Richard, I'm not going to be able to do this."

He reached for her hand, interlacing his fingers with hers. His heart pounded against his ribs. He wasn't about to let her break up with him. He tugged her toward him, cradling her in his arms. "Yes you can." He brushed his lip across her cheek and she nearly collapsed.

She thought herself to be a strong woman, but the heat of his embrace and the commanding tone of his voice had weakened her. Her resolve to end things—so resolute before he opened the door—crumbled.

"We can do this. Just remember that all these seductive gestures from desperate women mean nothing to me. I only care about you."

"I don't share."

"You'll never have to."

"Why me? Sister Johnson is beautiful and probably closer to your age."

"How can you ask that question? Can't you feel this chemistry between us?"

She dropped her head, staring at the dark space between her face and his chest and closed the gap.

He felt her nod yes against his chest and exhaled the tension that had been building. "Look at me."

At his command, she looked into his piercing brown eyes and was further dragged under his spell.

"This doesn't happen again. I'm yours. Don't let anyone, anything, or any situation convince you differently."

She tried to lower her head again, but he crooked his finger under her chin and made her look at him. His eyes roamed every inch of her face, smooth creamy skin, brown eyes, high cheek bones, and that mouth.

God, she's beautiful. He couldn't have chosen better if he'd picked her himself. His lips, hovering above hers, slowly made their descent. The voice in the back of his mind warned *careful, careful...* So, he stopped.

April felt him retreat and wanted to scream. That night she had forced a kiss on him made her lips tingle every time she thought of it. It was wonderful and she wanted to see how much more potent it could be if he joined in.

"Stay for dinner." His easy smile left no room for objection. He wouldn't have accepted it anyway. He offered her his elbow and she looped her arm around it. He escorted her into the living room and took the opportunity to kiss her cheek before helping her get comfortable. "I ordered Chinese. It should be here in a few minutes."

He excused himself to get her a drink and April was finally able to breathe normally. She loved powerful men, but Richard was more than she had bargained for.

Waiting for him to return, she looked around his living room. She had never been in a house that had absolutely no décor. It was a lot like his office. When things progressed between them, she would definitely have to change that. April shook her head at her thoughts. What had gotten into her? She chuckled at herself. She couldn't believe she was actually thinking about more than the here and now with a man. She wished she could talk to Candice about it, but Richard said *everyone or no one.* So, she would just have to figure out everything on her own.

"Thank you." She accepted the glass of lemonade as he sat beside her. She saw him sipping his drink and watching her out the corner of his eye. Mustering up some of the woman she once was, she brazenly turned toward him with one eyebrow raised in question.

Richard laughed to himself and mimicked her actions, raising a brow of his own.

She reached out to touch him and he caught her hand by the wrist. Her eyes shot to his and she couldn't hide the emotion that rushed there.

Am I not allowed to touch you? Her eyes seemed to implore.

He brought her palm to his lips. The warmth of his breath fanned across it. That alone sent heat racing up her arm and flooding her body. His lips made contact and scorched her as if she'd been struck by lightning.

She snatched her hand back and faced forward. *What the hell? Chemistry...yeah, I definitely feel it.* She coughed, clearing her throat of nerves and arousal. "If you can put your lips on me, then I can touch you."

"Is that so?" Richard downed the rest of his drink and leaned back against the sofa. He watched her nod while barely looking at him and had to hold back a chuckle. He loved how he affected her and how she wasn't afraid to show her reaction. When he had realized that the woman God revealed to him in a dream and Sheena's wild, promiscuous sister was one in the same, he was a little worried. It had been years since he'd been with a woman. He knew she'd had a plethora of male suitors. What did he have to offer? But, it looked like God had worked that out as well.

April felt him caressing her with his eyes and desperately needed to switch his focus before she corrupted the man of God.

Wanting to get a man's focus off her body was unfamiliar territory. "I enjoyed your sermon today."

"You did?"

"Especially the part where you said, 'Why are you asking a supernatural God for simple stuff? Pookie down the street can fix a leaky pipe'." She chuckled at how comical he had sounded, but the truth was she probably needed that word more than anyone. She needed the supernatural power of God to overcome the demons that had been chasing her since her attack. "You're really good at what you do. It seems like you put everything you have into your messages. It has to be draining."

"It is." His brief response hung in the air as her eyes scanned his face, seeing the truth in his words.

Without second thought, April slid toward him and placed her hand on his neck. He stiffened and April gave him a look that warned him not to move away. Her warm palm and slender fingers against his skin was the best thing he felt in a long time. When her other hand touched the opposite side of his neck, he closed his eyes to enjoy the moment. Her hands glided from his neck down to his shoulder and back again, gripping and massaging his tense muscles. His head sank into the sofa cushion and the tiniest moan escaped his lips.

He wanted to protest and let her know she didn't have to massage him, but it felt too good. He clamped his mouth shut and let her ease his stress. Maybe he should've stopped her. Soon his breathing was even, mind relaxed, and his eyes shut. He was asleep.

The doorbell rang and April slid her hands from his neck. He didn't budge. She lightly tapped his chest and he still didn't wake up. She smiled at how peaceful he looked and went to answer the door. She paid for the Chinese food and went in search of a linen closet for a blanket to help Richard get more comfortable. She carefully took off his shoes, hoping not to wake him, but failed.

"What are you doing?"

She jumped, startled by his voice, but quickly recovered. "You need to rest. Promise me you'll take better care of yourself."

"I don't need to." He lay back on the couch and allowed her to cover him with the blanket. "I have you now." He lifted the corner of the blanket offering her a space to lay with him.

On autopilot, she inched closer to him. Intimacy was the one part of relationships that made her stay away from them. It was during those moments a man could see the weakest part of her and she refused to let a man exploit her weakness. Maybe if the men in her past had shown her a fraction of the compassion Richard had, she would've been happy to open her heart to them.

Instinctively, she touched her finger tips to his scalp, gently caressing it. He exhaled and closed his eyes. Thirty minutes went by. She didn't know what to do or say, so she kept right on massaging his head. She thought he'd gone to sleep, but his hand slid up her thigh and wrapped around her waist. She cupped his cheek and he kissed the palm of her hand.

For a moment, they sat in silence staring into each other's eyes. She rested her forehead against his, lost in the synchronized rhythm of their hearts. She had never laid that close with a man without him pawing all over her. The warmth of his hand splayed across her back warmed her entire body. She yearned to feel his lips against hers, but didn't want to ruin the moment.

Richard inhaled her scent, allowing himself a moment to connect with her on a deeper level. She trembled against him and he knew it was time to release her.

"Do you know Cole?" He removed his hand and ignored the look of confusion she gave him. He wasn't ready for her to leave. The next best thing was to focus on something else. "Apparently, we are half-brothers."

"Um…Cole, Meme's boyfriend?" He nodded and her mind scrambled to find something to say. "Well, is it possible that your dad cheated on your mom?" She was honored that he chose to talk to her, but was so out of her realm of comfort she had to inwardly coach herself to stay put.

"We have the same mother."

"Lady Lillian?" He nodded and April fumbled over her words. "Oh…well, um…let's not overreact. Have you talked to her?"

"I have and I'm having a hard time forgiving her. Who abandons their own child? She has her excuses, but I'm not buying it."

"I know that we have to forgive." She stroked his head and smiled when the crease between his brows eased. "And not forgiving your mother may seem hypocritical, but sometimes you have to give it time. What does Cole say about all of this?"

"It helps that we were friends before. We acknowledge that we're brothers, but we haven't actually discussed it. We've kind of pushed the issue aside, because he's in the middle of a crisis. He needs me, so everything else can wait."

"What's going on? Is it anything I can help with?"

"It's Meme. One day she's fine and the next day not so much. Cole won't leave her side. He won't eat. He barely sleeps. The guilt he's carrying over what happened is killing him."

"He loves her so much. He'll probably never forgive himself. Bad things happen all the time. I know that better than anyone. Maybe I should go talk to him. Meme is my friend. Maybe I can sit with her while he gets a break."

He pulled her hand down from his head and kissed the back of it. "That would be nice, but he won't let anyone sit with her."

"Well, at least I can pray." She rolled off the couch to her knees. She waited for Richard to join her and connected their hands. Her prayer for Meme was just as fervent as the ones he'd offered up on her behalf over the past few weeks.

Richard should have been praying, too, but he was too amazed to utter a word. A prayer that started as a timid conversation with the Lord turned into a spiritual war cry. She praised God so sincerely that Richard felt God's presence enter the room. She didn't know the details of what was going on with Meme, but was able to spiritually hone in on her need. She declared Meme's safety, her healing, asked God to rid Cole of the guilt, and when she turned toward Richard directing that same power and spiritual authority toward him, he was floored. She cradled his head to her chest and linked her arms around him. His mother was the only other woman in the world that had prayed for him so selflessly. Richard returned April's embrace and gave into the power of God enveloping them. On his behalf, she called down peace, direction, and wisdom. If he had ever doubted whether she was strong enough to lead the church with him, it was put to rest in that moment. She ended the prayer by asking God to help her love Richard the way he deserved to be loved.

He lifted his head to look at her face. Her nose was red and running, cheeks wet with strands of hair stuck to them, and eyes puffy and glossed with unshed tears. She had never looked more beautiful. She grabbed a tissue from her purse to clean her face. He took it from her and dabbed her cheeks dry. He even wiped her nose. She protested, but he didn't care. He continued his inspection of her beauty, falling for her more than he had any woman. Because of his dreams, he had been enamored since the beginning. However, in that moment, he saw her outside of the fantasy and recognized the woman—the treasure—God had truly blessed him with.

"Richard," she playfully punched his chest. "Stop staring."

He ran his fingers through her hair gripping a handful in a makeshift ponytail and twisted it around his wrist. He slightly tugged her head back, raising her chin and exposing her neck. His eyes honed in on her erratic pulse thumping at the base of her throat, gradually moving up the slender column of her neck and back down.

"Richard?" Her tongue darted out, trying to moisten her suddenly parched mouth. As independent and strong willed as she was, she loved the domination of a man. Nothing kinky like whips and chains, but just the power of a man was what she craved.

The innocent gesture captured his attention and her full plush lips became the new focus of his inspection.

"Richard?" His examination had weakened her and his name was a wisp of sound on an exhale.

"What, baby?"

"Kiss me…please kiss me." She had never begged a man for anything, but his eyes had kissed her a thousand times over and she was desperate to feel the real thing.

Oh how he wanted to kiss her. The agonizing need was becoming harder to resist. He trailed his nose up and down her neck, inhaling her scent as he contemplated the consequences of his actions. There was nothing standing in their way and nothing to stop them if things got carried away. Would he be able to kiss her and stop at just a kiss? Yes he could, but what scared him was the fact that he didn't want to. He wanted to take advantage of God's mercy, lose himself inside of April, and repent later. Knowing that, he released her and put some space between them.

April watched him get up and pace the floor. She took a few minutes to get her disappointment under control before she went to comfort him. She blocked his path and slid her arms around his neck. He towered over her and her arms barely met behind him. "It's okay. Just knowing that I affect you like that is enough for now." She stood on her tippy toes and softly pecked his lips. "I know I have to leave." She didn't want to, but didn't want to be his downfall either. "Get some rest."

He escorted her to the door and watched her walk to her car, longing for the day when his home would also become hers.

12

April rested on the couch nibbling saltine crackers. She was plagued with nausea and wished she'd just throw up and be done with it. She didn't know if she was actually sick or just lovesick. It had been five days since she'd seen Richard and she craved his presence. If she had never been attacked, she wouldn't have been vulnerable enough to let her guard down to meet a man like him. She couldn't help but think her tragedy may have been the best thing for her. Maybe if she hadn't been so hard headed, God wouldn't have had to use such drastic measures to get her attention, but the Lord worked in mysterious ways. She was grateful for the changes and progress she had made.

She sat up to brush cracker crumbs off her chest. Out the corner of her eye, she caught a glimpse of someone standing in the doorway. She jumped up, ready to defend herself, knocking over a can of ginger ale and nearly breaking her neck as she stumbled over the coffee table.

Her eyes finally settled on who it was, and she wanted to throw something... "Candy, don't sneak up on me like that." She wondered if she would ever get over the jumpiness or if being easily startled was something she'd have to permanently deal with.

"I didn't mean to scare you. I just wanted to see you."

April sat back down on the couch and took a moment to think. She had to admit she was a little mad at Candice. "Where have you been? You're the only friend I have. I've seen you once since I got out of the hospital and even then you were acting weird."

"I know and there is no excuse, but I can explain if you give me a chance." She took April's silence as permission to continue. She tossed her purse on the coffee table and sat next to April on the couch. "I should've never left you."

Confused, April turned to Candice, but the tears in her eyes explained everything. "Oh Candy, this isn't your fault."

"How can you say that? I should've never left you. You would've stayed with me all night regardless of how you were feeling. But me..." Her voice trailed off as she shook her head at how she'd let her friend down that night. "I had been feeling so..."

"So what?" April grabbed her hand and patted the back of it.

The gesture was comforting and so unexpected from April that, although Candice hadn't gone over there to talk about her problems, she found herself spilling her guts anyway.

"So...unhappy." She looked April in the eye and the tears she'd been fighting to hold back rolled down her cheeks. "I want so much more out of life. I'm tired of clubbing and hooking up."

Me too!

"There has to be more to life than this."

"What do you want your *more* to be?"

Candice paused for a moment, and suddenly it was all clear. "Love! I want love." At April's silence, she jumped on the defensive. April always talked about silly women who fall victim to love. "Don't you want a boyfriend?"

"What makes you think I don't already have someone?" Smirking, April tried to get up and walk away, but Candice grabbed her arm.

Candice scanned April's face and didn't see the face of a woman who had been brutally raped. Her friend was glowing. Candice couldn't help, but smile. "Really?"

"I didn't think God made men like him. He's soft and compassionate but exudes a power that's out of this world. He's the man to champion my own strength and isn't a chauvinistic jerk while trying to do it."

"Aww April, now I'm jealous," Candice laughed and dabbed at the tears in the corner of her eye. "I'm really happy you found someone."

"What's his name?" Sheena jumped into the conversation as she walked into the room. She hadn't heard April talk about being with one guy since she moved to San Diego over four years ago. The one good thing that had come out of April being attacked was that it had definitely calmed her down. Sheena loved her sister and had been more than concerned about her lifestyle. It looked like God was using what the devil meant for bad to bring about a positive change.

April picked up another cracker, busying her mouth, so she didn't have to answer.

Sheena rolled her eyes and sat next to April on the couch. "I'm getting a little worried about you. You seemed to make a little progress and now you've been lying around the house barely eating."

"I'm fine, Sheena. Weren't you the one who said I deserved to rest?"

"I just want you to talk to someone."

"Well, I was talking to Candy until you interrupted."

Sheena had to bite her tongue to remain calm. She had no idea where all April's hostility was coming from or why it seemed to be only directed toward her. "I invited someone over for you to talk with," she mumbled under her breath as she stood and walked across the room. Sheena hastily walked out, trying hard to keep from arguing.

Paul stepped aside, allowing Sheena to exit. Then, in strolled Richard following behind him.

"You called the pastor on me?" April yelled out, trying hard to sound upset.

"I called him over to talk with you." Sheena marched back in, losing a bit of her restraint. "You sleep all day, you haven't been eating like you used to, and you look a little pale. Shoot me for being concerned."

April hoped she was doing a good job at masking her excitement with anger. For once, her meddling sister had done something right. Trying to hide her eagerness, April rolled her eyes at her sister and told Richard to follow her. Once alone inside Paul's home office, they stood on opposite sides of the room staring at each other, both waiting for the other to speak.

Richard's palms were sweaty like he was on his first date. Her hair was tussled as if she had just woken up. She had on sweats and a tank top and was as beautiful as ever.

Every butterfly ever created floated around in April's stomach. She had never seen him dressed so casually. His simple polo shirt, jeans, and Nikes enhanced his good looks, taking her breath away.

"Are you all right?" Richard was the first to break through the silence. "The things Sheena told me have me a little concerned."

She chuckled. "I'm not depressed. I've been sleeping a lot because you keep me up on the phone all night."

"What about health-wise? You do look a little pale." Richard crossed the room toward her and caressed the side of her face. Her face dropped into his hand and he caught her chin with his index finger raising her face to look into her eyes.

"I'm fine, but I miss you. When do I get to be with you?"

"You're with me now."

April placed her arms around his waist, placed her head against his chest, and waited for his embrace. The warmth of his hands slid across her back, causing her to sink further into his chest.

He heard her sniffle and pulled back to look into her eyes. A tear rolled down her cheek. That single tear was his undoing.

"Baby, I know this isn't what you expected, but I promise I'll do better." He kissed the top of her head and pulled her back into his embrace. "Let's go to the movies tomorrow."

"You promise?" she whined, smiling up at him. She was tempted to get on her tippy toes and join their lips

"Of course I do. But, I need you to promise me something." He kissed the top of her head again. "Go see a doctor."

"Richard, I'm fine."

"Just indulge me, please. I can't be here every day to take care of you. Knowing that you saw a doctor would put my mind at ease." He pulled her closer and whispered against her ear. "Baby, please…"

The soft-spoken endearment melted her resolve and she promised to see a doctor. With the sincerity and concern she saw in his eyes, he could've asked her for anything and she would've done it.

"Will you dance with me?" Richard asked.

She giggled, looking at him with confusion as he pulled out his cell phone.

He opened his music app, put it on his favorite station, and Teddy Pendergrass's *Feel the Fire* was playing. He hoped no one was standing outside the door listening, but he was willing to take the risk. He pulled her as close as possible and swayed with her in his arms. For a few minutes, they were lost in the moment. They forgot about their surroundings and the other people waiting for them and focused on each other. His touch was like no other. April couldn't recall a man ever holding her so tenderly.

As the song came to an end, Richard whispered, "It's time for me to go."

"No," April whined, squeezing him tighter.

"We can't stay locked up in here too much longer without them coming to check on us."

Her lip poked out as she pouted.

"Hey." He lifted her head until their eyes met. "If you are ready for everyone to know about us, I'll go out there right now and tell them the truth."

"It's not them that I'm worried about, it's everyone else. Can't we just tell my family? We can be out in the open around them and worry about everyone else some other time."

"I'm sorry, but it's too risky. I don't want to risk someone finding out and starting rumors before I have time to properly announce our relationship. It has to be everyone or no one." He truly sympathized with her. It was going to be vicious once all the single women found out he was off the market. That's why he had left it up to her to decide when they would inform everyone. He would also have to deal with the church board, but once he explained the vision the Lord had given him, they would be on his side. April, on the other hand, would have to deal with vindictive, spiteful, jealous, desperate women who would probably never be on her side.

April's shoulders slumped in defeat as she stepped away from him. She wasn't ready to deal with the church yet. "So, the movies tomorrow, right?"

"Yes, we will talk more about it when I call you tonight."

April turned her back to him and fanned her eyes dry before the tears had a chance to roll down her cheeks.

When they got themselves together, they walked back into the family room. Richard told Sheena that April promised to see a doctor, said his goodbyes, and left.

"April, we need to talk." Sheena grabbed her sister by the hand and dragged her down the hall. Once they were alone, her eyes burned through April. "Please tell me I didn't see what I think I just saw." She combined the besotted look in April's eyes, the comment she'd made earlier about her possible boyfriend, and feared the worst.

"Sheena, what are you talking about? Stop speaking in circles and say what you need to say."

"I saw the way you looked at Pastor Hawkins just now. Please don't tell me you are becoming one of those silly groupies, claiming God said he was her husband. Don't get me wrong, he is a good guy and good looking. I see why you would be attracted to him, but…"

April silenced Sheena's next thought with an open palm in front of her face. "You're overreacting as usual. Speaking of you overreacting, let's talk about why Pastor Hawkins was even here. My sister—whom I've told over and over again that I'm fine—

called him. Your meddling is getting out of control. I'm going to see my doctor and once he says I'm healthy, I expect you to back off."

Throwing her hands up in surrender, Sheena agreed.

13

April had been giddy all day in anticipation of her date with Richard. Other than church and a visit to his house, she had rarely gone out of the house since being attacked. She was a little nervous to face the world, but knowing Richard would be by her side eased her anxiety.

She stepped out of the shower, humming her own tune when her cell phone rang. She looked down at the caller ID and a grin split her face.

"Hi, baby."

"Hey, are you getting ready for our date?" His swoon-worthy deep voice vibrated across the line. Goose bumps pebbled across her exposed skin. April wondered if he would ever cease to have that effect on her.

"You're not calling to cancel are you?"

"Of course not, but I do have a small request."

April held her breath. As long as he wasn't cancelling, she could handle anything else.

"I'm going to leave a ticket for you at the booth. I will be waiting for you in the back row with all the candy and popcorn you could ask for."

"Oh, hell no!" April bit her lip to keep fire from popping out of her mouth. "I'm not a jump off, side chick, pity date, or whatever else you want to call it."

"Baby, it's not like that, and you know it."

"Look, I understand your need for discretion, but if you want to date me, you will pick me up. I'm not going to sneak around like I am ashamed to be seen with you. I will be ready at 9:30. If you're not here, don't bother calling." She hung up and finished getting ready. She tried to stay positive, but something told her he wasn't going to show up.

You're so stupid. Would meeting him there have been so bad?

April nervously continued getting ready. Her hands shook so bad that she dropped bobby pins all over the floor. Any attempt to use the curling iron was like playing with fire.

When Richard hadn't called by 9:30, her heart dropped into her stomach. She sat on the edge of her bed trying to face the fact she'd messed up something that could've been great. Five minutes later, her cell phone rang.

Before she could say hello, Richard's agitated voice cut her off. "I'm outside. Do you expect me to ring the doorbell? But, know that if I ring the doorbell, all of this secrecy is over. I'm telling whoever answers the door that we are dating."

April was bubbling over with excitement. "I'll be out in a minute." She grabbed her purse, put on her sweater, and practically ran downstairs.

"Hey April. Where are you rushing off to?"

She brushed past Sheena in the hall and didn't even bother to respond. She didn't want to deal with all the questions that would follow. She was out the door and hopping into Richard's car before anyone could follow her out.

"Hey." She kissed his cheek and buckled her seatbelt.

He tapped a finger under her chin and lifted her head to look into her eyes. "You have your requirements and I have mine. Don't hang up on me again. It's childish and I won't tolerate it." He pulled the car away from the curb and tried to get in the right frame of mind to enjoy their date.

"Are we having a fight?"

Richard glanced in her direction and turned back to the road without saying a word.

April smiled. "You're sexy as hell when you're angry."

Richard shook his head to ward off the smile spreading across his face. "Stop cussing."

"Hell is not cussing."

"It is, and it's unladylike."

"Yes, Daddy."

"Daddy?" Richard chuckled and shook off his rebuttal. He reached across the center console and entwined his fingers with hers. He brought the back of her hand to his lips and tugged her a little closer. "I have something for you." He fought the urge to kiss her endearing little smile and told her to reach into the glove compartment. She pulled out an envelope with her name on it and when she saw the contents, her jaw dropped in shock.

"Why are you giving me money?"

"Before you get mad, let me fully explain." He put on his most charming smile and hoped it smoothed her over. "I want to buy you some new clothes for church."

"You don't like the way I dress?" She snatched her hand from his and folded her arms across her chest.

"I do, but a little too much. Those jeans and tight dresses on those curves..." He took his eyes off the road and scanned her body. "...Are going to drive me crazy." He grabbed her hand and kissed the back of it again. "I'd love to take you shopping myself, but..."

"Yeah, I know. You can't risk it." April leaned back in her seat and stared out the window. "Thank you," she finally said after minutes of silence.

"You're welcome. You're not upset are you?"

"No, it's just that." She turned to him and dropped her head, studying her fidgeting fingers, hoping he would understand. "I've been to church and your place. I haven't really been out by myself since..."

Richard pulled to the side of the road. He reached across the center console and held her face between his palms. "Trust me when I say, God's got you." He caressed her cheek and made her look into his eyes. "Every day, I pray for your safety. I ask God to cover you and heal you. He knows how special you are to me and how much I need you. He's going to keep you safe."

She snuggled her face against his neck as he wrapped his arms around her.

"I know you're scared. After what you went through, I don't blame you. If you'd feel more comfortable taking Candice or Sheena, I won't object."

"What do I tell them when they ask where I got the money from?" The vibration of her voice and her warm breath against his skin was driving him crazy. It was definitely time to get to a public place.

"You tell them to mind their business."

Now there's a thought. She couldn't remember the last time Sheena had minded her own business. She was probably sitting at the kitchen table as they spoke plotting an interrogation.

"I'll wait to the side while you buy our tickets." He pulled into the parking stall. She unbuckled her seat belt and grabbed the door handle.

"I bought the tickets before I picked you up." He kissed her cheek and reached across to remove her hand from the door. "When you're with me, you wait. I'll get the door."

He escorted her into the theater and led her to their seats. She wanted to hold his hand but didn't want to press her luck.

"What do you want from the concession stand?"

"Popcorn and Raisinets."

"Who under fifty eats Raisinets?" He laughed and she punched him in the arm. He made sure she was settled before going to buy snacks. They sat in the corner of the back row. The light lowered and he lifted the middle armrest to be as close to her as possible. With his arm wrapped around her, she had no choice but to rest her head on his chest. She looked up at him, questioning whether the closeness was okay. He responded with a tender kiss to her forehead.

The movie previews were long as ever, but they didn't seem to notice. She fed him kernels of popcorn, kissing his chin as he chewed. He returned the favor and she sucked his finger into her mouth, running her tongue down the length.

"Behave," he moaned and spanked her thigh.

"Sorry, I couldn't resist."

He could feel her smile against his chest and he spanked her again. He was grateful God hadn't chosen some weak-willed, mousy woman with no passion. He needed a woman with fire. April had that and some. She continued feeding him and he was tempted to give her a little taste of her own medicine. However, he had a feeling she'd straddle his lap right there in the theater.

April barely paid attention to the movie, being in his arms snuggled up in the dark felt heavenly. The rise and fall of his chest as he breathed, the caress of his hand up and down her arm, his heartbeat against her cheek—how could a woman be expected to concentrate? She looked up at him and his eyes met hers. It felt incredible to be with a man who wanted more than just her body.

She dropped her head back to his chest, trying to calm her racing pulse. She was in unfamiliar territory and she hoped she didn't screw it up.

The walk back to the car was quiet. He politely opened her door. She touched her hand to his cheek. His eyes connected with hers as she confessed, "I really like you," and hopped into the car before he could respond.

14

The next day, April woke up bright and early. Richard was right. God was looking out for her. It was time for her to stop hiding and get back into the world. There was something she really needed to do. She rolled out of bed and slid to her knees. Every day since she'd been home from the hospital, she had taken time to communicate with the Lord.

She showered and dressed as modest as her wardrobe would allow. Richard's statement about her attire made her more conscious of what she put on and the image it portrayed. Shopping was on her to-do list that day, but first, she wanted to check on her friend.

She stepped off the elevator and was greeted by the chiming of heart monitors. Although they were essential to saving lives, the sound was creepy, and they instantly took her back to her own hospital stay. She had passed out in the ambulance and awakened to a bright light shining in her face. She thought she had died and was standing before God.

Oh no! I'm not ready. I'm supposed to have more time. She'd been raised in the church and warned that if she didn't get her life together, she'd have to stand before God in judgment. She wasn't ready. There was still so much she wanted to do and so much she needed to repent for. How many Sunday school lessons had she heard about the five wise virgins who were prepared for the bridegroom's return and the five who weren't? Yet, she wasn't prepared.

Then, her ears opened up and the sounds of despair filled them. Heart monitors beeping, babies crying, and doctors giving instructions—there was still time. Right then, she repented. Her jaw was too swollen and painful to talk, but in her mind, she confessed all her sins.

In the nights that followed, she laid in that hospital bed too afraid to sleep because of the nightmares that haunted her. So, she lay awake listening to the chirping heart monitors of patients nearby, such a simple sound to indicate life.

April paused outside the room, taking a deep breath to clear her mind of those horrible memories. "Good morning." She stepped into the room and smiled at Cole. They'd only met once before, but knowing his relation to Richard, she couldn't help but notice their facial similarities.

Recognition flashed on his face and he stood to greet her, offering her a seat. His stature was just as overwhelming as Richard's, but his closeness had no effect on her.

"How's she doing?" She looked over at Meme who was sleeping and looking so helpless. She would win the award for worst friend in the world for not visiting sooner. She had been too selfish and used the excuse that they weren't that close as a reason why she hadn't visited. She was ashamed. Since being attacked, that emotion seemed to be popping up more and more.

"She's a lot better. How are you doing?"

One look at his face and she knew he had heard about her attack. "Same as Meme, doing a lot better." She was so tired of discussing the details. She hoped he didn't ask any questions. When he went on to talk about Meme, she let out the breath she'd been holding and relaxed into her seat.

Richard stepped into the room and she saw him before Cole did. Her heart skipped three beats and her mouth ran dry. His presence sucked the oxygen out of the room. April suddenly felt faint. Her eyes scanned the length of him, from his Ferragamo-clad feet to his black slacks to his argyle sweater. She usually hated those sweaters, but the way this one molded to the cut of his chest gave her a new appreciation for them. Her mouth hung open with her tongue stuck to the roof of it. She took a moment to enjoy his sculpted physique before moving up to his face. The look on his face cut her assessment short. He was clearly amused.

"Good morning, Sister April. How are you doing today?" He bowed his head in her direction, trying his best to keep from laughing at her flustered expression.

"Um..." Her eyes shot over to Cole.

His raised eyebrows and slight smirk let her know he'd seen her checking out the pastor.

"I'm going to go. When Meme wakes up, tell her I stopped by." She fumbled for her purse and was out the door before Richard could come up with an excuse to make her stay.

Cole's laughter echoed through the hospital. "How do you put up with that? Beautiful women throwing themselves at you? It can't make being a pastor easy."

"The same way you're going to handle being off the market."

"That's different. Meme is it for me. There is no one else that does it for me like she does."

Richard reflected on that for a moment. He could definitely understand.

"All right, spill it man. What has you smiling like that?" What had started as a small smirk, Cole watch evolve into a full-on grin.

Richard leaned forward in his chair and rested his arms on his knees. "No one else knows this, so keep your mouth shut." He ignored the look Cole flashed him and kept talking. "That is all me," he pointed toward the door April had just exited. He would later regret saying anything, but it felt good to tell someone.

"Get out of here," Cole chuckled. "There is no way you're hitting that."

"I'm a man of God. I'm not hitting anything. But, trust and believe, that's all me."

"Hold up. Hold up." Cole scooted his chair a little closer. "You mean to tell me you're not sleeping with anyone?"

Richard nodded.

Cole chuckled with doubt.

"When you do it God's way, He blesses you with something like that." He pointed back toward the door and leaned back in the chair.

"Man, get out of here!" He tried to contain his laughter to keep from waking Meme. "There is no way that's you."

Richard shook his head and pulled out his cell phone. "Baby, come back up here." He put his phone away and sat quietly, waiting.

Not even five minutes later, April poked her head around the corner.

"Come in and shut the door."

She hesitated, but did as she was told. She looked at Cole and then back at Richard.

"Now come here."

"Pastor…"

"Don't pastor me. Come here."

She loved his dominance. She looked at Cole one last time and slowly made her way toward Richard. He took her by the hand gracefully guiding her onto his lap.

"Why are you doing this?" Her voice shook with fear and anticipation.

"I just wanted someone to know how much you mean to me."

She leaned forward and pressed her lips to his. He wasn't giving nearly as much as she needed, but it was enough to satisfy her. She was on a slippery slope to love, and each day she slid deeper.

"I thought you were going shopping today."

"I wanted to see Meme first."

"Who's going with you?"

"I'm going by myself. You prayed for me this morning, right?"

"Of course, but still be careful, and have fun."

She smiled and shook her head. "Can I go now? Or, do you want to keep showing off?" She stood and walked toward the door.

He watched the sway of her hips as she walked away.

She turned back and caught him in the act. It was good to see he was just as infatuated as she was. "We will talk about this later." She blew him a kiss, opened the door, and walked out.

Cole could barely wait for her to get down the hall before he started laughing. "There is no way you ain't hittin that."

Richard laughed right along with him. "First, you don't believe that I'm with her. Now, you think I have to be getting some."

They laughed and talked for a good while. It wasn't lost on Richard that they were having their first brother moment.

"It's good to hear you laugh."

"It's good to have a reason to." Cole scrubbed his hand down his face and stared out into space. "She lost my baby, almost lost a kidney, and nearly died in the process. It's been a long few months, but the infection's gone and they said twenty-four hours without a fever and she can go home."

"Which home is that going to be?"

"You don't even have to ask."

"So, I'm assuming you plan to make an honest woman out of her."

"I do."

"Just let me know when and I'll put it on the church calendar."

Cole almost choked on his laugh. "I'm not getting married in a church." He knew he had made God a lot of promises while he was praying for Meme and would have to work that out. He had no problem with God, but the people he chose to work for Him were a different story.

"One day, you are going to tell me why you hate church so much."

"My reason is simple, your mother."

Richard dropped his head and sighed. They were having such a good conversation and he had to go and ruin it. "She's your mother too and I'm not getting in the middle. She's my mother and I love her. You're my boy, and now you're my brother. I love you too. Now, back to this wedding. Don't let your hang-ups keep Meme from having the wedding of her dreams."

Meme moaned and stretched. Cole was at her side before she could fully open her eyes. "Good morning." Her smile greeted his.

"You have a visitor."

131

"Oh God, Cole. I probably look like crap."

"You're just as beautiful as the day I met you."

"You mean the day you seduced me."

"More like the day you couldn't resist me." He helped her sit up and she gasped in shock.

"Why didn't you tell me it was the pastor?" She swatted his arm. "You have me talking inappropriately in front of the man of God."

"It's all good. He's family."

"Aww, you're finally accepting him as your brother."

"He was like a brother before we found out. There's no reason that should end."

"Agreed." They shook hands and pulled each other in for a quick hug and slaps on the back.

"Excuse me." The nurse walked in with a bucket and towels to assist Meme with a wash down.

"I'll take care of it." Cole grabbed the items and placed them on the counter.

"I'm sorry, but doctor's orders, you're no longer allowed to give her a bath. The last time you bathed her, you set off her heart monitor."

"It's okay, he'll behave this time." Meme was so embarrassed she wanted to disappear.

Cole waited until the nurse left and then turned toward Meme, "Don't make promises you know I'm not going to keep."

Meme gasped, "Cole." Her cheeks heated and she turned her head to avoid looking at Pastor Hawkins.

"On that note, I think it's time for me to go." He made his way toward the bed and put his hand on her shoulder. "Don't be embarrassed. It's that type of love and obsession that the world needs more of," he said, smirking at Cole. He offered a quick prayer, promised to stop by once she was released, and went home.

Talking about love and marriage with Cole made him think of his own relationship. There was no doubt in his mind whether or not he wanted to marry April. God had led him to her in such a way he couldn't deny she was the woman for him. With so many women vying for his affection, he had been leery of dating anyone. God knew it would take a lot to convince him she was the right woman. He was grateful God had made every provision for him to accept April. The only question was would she marry him.

15

Richard dragged himself out of bed. His head was pounding. The last he checked, his temperature was 101.2 degrees. The incessant doorbell ringing was impossible to ignore. The buzzing rang through his ear, sending sharp pains shooting through his head and throughout his body. He walked slowly, trying to steady himself and his queasy stomach. Each step rocked his stomach and threatened to send him through another round of dry heaves. He had already revisited every ounce of food he'd consumed the day before.

It took all the strength he had to open the door. He leaned against the frame for support and tried to lift his head to see who was standing in front of him, but the walk had again unsettled his stomach. Beads of sweat formed on his head and his mouth salivated. His poor unsuspecting visitor stood right in his line of fire as his stomach convulsed and erupted with another round of heaving.

April's heart broke when she saw how sick he was. The night before, he had ended their phone conversation early because he didn't feel well. She chalked it up to him not getting enough rest. Seeing how weak he was, she regretted not rushing over. Feet covered with vomit, April grabbed Richard by the waist and supported him as he walked back to bed.

Richard fumbled into bed then wrapped himself with a blanket. He was shivering to the point that the bed was shaking. April grabbed the thermometer off the nightstand to take his temperature. It read 104 degrees. She rushed to the bathroom, turned on a cool shower, tore the covers from his body, and practically dragged him into the shower. She had never seen anyone with a temperature that high and feared for his life.

It had been over a month since they'd started secretly seeing each other. In that short time, they had built a relationship stronger than anything April ever experienced. Although they were limited on the time they spent together and the places they could go, they enjoyed each other's company. He treated her like royalty, and every second they were together, the rest of the world didn't exist. She was able to relax and be herself around him without the pressure of sexual intimacy. She knew the affection and gifts he showered on her were free of ulterior motives. Richard loved how she always spoke her mind without sugar coating her thoughts just because he was the pastor. Her spicy flare added flavor to his life. Even though they didn't see each other often, he didn't feel lonely. Just knowing he had her made him a better man. He could finally serve the Lord without resentment.

The impact of the water from the shower sent Richard into shock and he collapsed, twitching and shivering as he attempted to get away from the water. April was relentless. Everywhere he moved, she aimed the showerhead directly at him. After fully saturating him, she turned the water off and assisted him back into the bedroom. He stood soaking wet in the middle of the bedroom, as April pulled every last blanket off the bed. His pulse throbbed in every inch of his body as his cool outer body tried to balance out his overheated core.

April stripped him naked. He had no energy to protest. Wrapping him in a sheet, she helped him lay on the bed, made him swallow two Tylenol, and then climbed in next to him. She pulled his head to her chest, cradling him in her arms as she sang him to sleep. Her voice was beautifully melodic, one of her hidden gifts not even her sister knew about. She sang and prayed while planting small kisses on his head.

About an hour later, his eyes popped open. His fever had broken and he was more alert and focused. April felt him budge and released her hold on him. She smiled as he looked up at her. "Good morning, are you feeling better?"

There was no response. Richard looked around to assess his condition. "How did you get in here?" His voice was raspy and weak. The pained look on his face revealed just how much it hurt for him to talk.

"You opened the door and let me in. I came to check on you, you answered the door, and threw up on me." She lifted her feet showing the fluids that had now begun to crust over. He shook his head in disbelief and opened his mouth to apologize, but she stopped him. "It's all right. You just worry about getting better. Do you know how high your temperature was?"

"Yeah, 101.2." He rested his head back on her chest, snuggling up against her. He knew he should tell her to get out of his bed and that being so close to her could lead to sin, but it felt so good to have someone take care of him that he overlooked the proper thing to do.

"No honey, it was 104. You had that robe on and were wrapped in all these blankets. Praise God I arrived when I did. I hate to think what would've happened if it had gone any higher. I kind of panicked and put you in the shower with your clothes on."

Richard's eyes widened at her statement, "You took my clothes off?" He pulled his head back to look her in the face.

"Yes, I did. Please don't be mad. I had to get your fever to break. Don't you feel better?"

"I do. I understand you did what you had to, but now you have to go home."

April chuckled. "I'm not going anywhere."

"We shouldn't be together like this. I'm naked and you're in my bed. It's not acceptable."

April rolled her eyes. She was really getting tired of the whole *that's not acceptable* speech. "I'm sorry you feel that way, but I'm not leaving you like this, so get over it."

"April, you have to respect the man that I am."

"Well Richard, you need to decide what you want—my respect or my affection, because right now you can't have both." She looked him straight in the eye, standing her ground, hoping he'd choose her. She watched his eyes roam her face and smiled when he lowered his head, surrendering to her wishes. "If it will make you feel better, I will grab some underclothes for you to put on. I'll even turn my back while you put them on."

Not waiting for his response, she went to his dresser and found his underwear. Her steps halted when she turned around. He was sitting on the edge of the bed with his torso uncovered. In her haste to break his fever, she hadn't noticed the perfection which sat before her. The silver cross he always wore hung around his neck, shining against his perfectly chiseled chest. Her eyes rolled down every ripple of his abs and back up again.

Richard looked up and caught her staring.

They made eye contact and she began apologizing. "I'm sorry, you just caught me off guard." She rushed over and tossed him his under clothes whispering over her shoulder as she turned around. "I didn't think you could be more gorgeous."

Richard looked at her backside perched in his face. *My dreams never revealed all of this.* But, he kept his observations to himself.

April could feel his eyes burning through her and didn't mind one bit. He stood behind her and the proximity of his body sent chills down her spine. The kiss he placed on her bare shoulder gave her goose bumps. She turned to help him back into bed, but the sight of his six-foot-three-inch muscular body wearing a t-shirt that hugged his chest and boxer briefs that barely hid his magnificence made her think twice about staying. "Okay, okay, okay," April frantically announced. "Get back into bed before I lose my mind."

Richard chuckled. "I will, but come here first." He pulled her forward by her hand into his embrace. Lightly kissing her on the crown of her head, he whispered, "Thank you for taking care of me." There was so much he wanted to tell her, but he had to follow the leading of the Lord.

Love was a foreign emotion to April, so she didn't know if she loved him or not. The more time they spent together, the more she wanted to be with him. She hated when their dates were over or when it was time to get off the phone. One thing she was sure of, she was tired of having to hide their relationship. Every time her sister asked why she seemed so happy, April wanted to scream out, *It's Richard!* Instead, she would cop an attitude and ignore her.

"You don't have to thank me for that." She tried to build up the courage to tell him she was ready to go public with their relationship, but she couldn't do it. It was more than being able to tell her sister. It meant telling the whole church. She wasn't ready for the ridicule or judgment. She knew she wasn't good enough for Richard. She didn't need an entire church telling her that. "Now get back into bed before your fever spikes. Do you want to see if your stomach can hold some crackers?"

He laughed as he climbed into bed, "You won't find anything like that here. It is rare that I buy groceries, because I don't cook."

April rolled her eyes. *Typical bachelor.*

"Okay, you lie down and rest. I'll run to the store. Where are your keys, so I can lock up and let myself in when I come back?"

"They're in the kitchen, on the counter by the phone. My wallet is there too. Get my ATM card."

"Richard, I don't need your ATM card."

"Take it anyway. You might decide to get more than crackers. While you're out, make yourself a copy of my key."

The expression on her face was priceless. She stood for a second, processing what he'd said and mischievously smiled when she decided to accept his offer. "Okay, I'll be right back. You stay in bed and rest."

She rushed to the store and purchased everything he could possibly need to settle his stomach, plus a few extra things to cook for him when he started feeling better.

It took two trips to bring in all the groceries. She was glad she had taken his card, because everything she purchased was well out of her price range. She hadn't gone back to work and was slowly consuming the little money she'd saved for getting her own place.

Once everything was put away, she tiptoed into Richard's room to see if his temperature had risen. She touched his forehead, trying not to wake him, he felt all right. April borrowed some basketball shorts and a t-shirt from his drawer to take a quick shower. She still had vomit on her foot and it was sickening. Instant relief washed over her as she stepped into the stream of water. She showered and allowed her mind to wander to the day when she would be a permanent fixture in Richard's home.

Get your mind out of the clouds, April. She shook her head and focused on showering.

She slid the shower door back and stepped out just as Richard busted into the bathroom. Their eyes met for a second before he dropped to his knees and hurled into the toilet. No towel, no shower curtain, and Richard was kneeling on her clothes. She was stuck. Frantically, her eyes searched for something to put on, but found nothing. She rushed into the bedroom and grabbed another t-shirt from his drawer. By the time she put the shirt on and turned to head back into the bathroom, Richard was standing in the doorway. She was too ashamed to make eye contact. With her head hung low, she simply mumbled, "I know, I have to leave. Give me a few minutes to collect my things."

April fought back the tears. Just when their relationship had gone to a new level, she had gone and screwed it up. One tear fell from her eye when Richard—not saying a word—crawled back into bed. She wiped it away before he could notice and went to pick up the wet clothes off the bedroom floor. She placed her soiled clothes along with his wet clothes in the wash and then slipped on the basketball shorts. She grabbed a few bottles of water and a pack of crackers out of the kitchen.

She returned to the room and sat on the edge of the bed, still afraid to look him in the eye. "Your stomach is not ready for food, but start taking small sips of water every twenty minutes or so." She opened a bottle of water and made him take a sip. "I'm going to leave these crackers on the nightstand. Try eating a few in a couple of hours." She grabbed the Tylenol. "You have to take two every four hours to keep your temperature under control. Your next dose will be at five." It was killing her that he still hadn't spoken to her. Feeling the tears gather at the corner of her eyes, she stood to leave.

Just like her life had suddenly been looking positive and took a nose dive, so had their relationship. He had given her a key to his house, which meant so much to her. Then, her need to take a shower knocked them ten steps backward. Glancing at Richard out of the corner of her eye, she could tell he was trying his best not to make eye contact. That was fine with her. She was too embarrassed and afraid of what she might see in his eyes. She gathered her things and, with one last peck to his forehead, she was out the door, leaving her key to his house on the kitchen table.

Richard watched her walking out of his room, hoping it wasn't for good. He wanted to beg her to stay, but with the way his body had responded to seeing her naked, he knew it was best she leave while he still had some control. Nausea and fever aside, he was ready to sample every inch of exposed flesh. *Don't speak, don't touch,* is what his mind chanted over and over. He saw the tears in her eyes and literally had to clench his fists to keep from caressing her. It wasn't until he heard the front door open and close that he realized he was holding his breath. He sucked in a long deep breath and expelled it as he collapsed against his pillows.

Images of her naked beauty danced around in his head and his body ached in places that hadn't felt the inside of a woman in the five years he'd been a pastor. It was going to take the power of God to get him over his sudden lust for April. His carnal side—the side that wanted to toss her on the bed and wreak havoc on her body—begged him to chase after her. His spiritual side, which wasn't ignorant concerning the devil's devices, refused to give in to temptation.

April raced out to her car, the wind from her fast pace drying the tears streaming down her face. "Get it together," she whispered as she slumped behind the steering wheel. It wasn't that big a deal any way. If he was that bothered by a woman's naked body, then he needed to get over it. They were both adults, and it wasn't like she purposely exposed herself to him. "He is entirely too uptight. I can't be with anybody like that."

She pulled away from the curb, trying to convince herself to cut Richard loose. The kind of relationship they had was totally different from the ones in her past. Normally, she would've slept with the guy by now or kicked him to the curb. She could barely get a kiss out of him and it seriously made her doubt his feelings for her. She tried to summon the old April, the one who would stomp on a man's heart and keep it pushing, but she was nowhere to be found.

She could definitely use that cold-hearted demeanor to mask her feelings for Richard. The more she tried to say *screw him,* the more that ache in the pit of her stomach intensified.

April arrived home and made her way to the kitchen, not remembering one inch of the drive from Richard's. Her mind was in a haze. She felt sick. She touched her hand to her stomach, hoping to stave off the nausea. She was trying to process what had just happened, but too many thoughts cluttered her mind at once. She was so caught up in her mental ramblings that she hadn't noticed Sheena sitting at the table.

"Is everything okay?"

Startled, April spun around. One look at Sheena and tears flooded down her face. She filled her lungs with air to gain some control, but the torrent of her emotions was already rampant. That nausea turned into a pain unlike any she'd felt before.

Sheena was on her feet and gathering April into her arms. "Oh honey, I wish you'd talk to me. You don't have to deal with any of this alone." She guided April to the table and grabbed some paper towels to clean her face.

April hid behind those paper towels. She couldn't believe she was crying over a man. The more she thought about Richard, the more the tears streamed down her face. How many times had she ridiculed silly women who let their emotions lead them? There she was lumped into a pile with the rest of the sad, disgraceful women who had let a man break them. For the first time, she totally understood why they continued to let it happen. "He made me feel things I never thought possible."

Sheena cringed, seriously doubting whether she wanted to hear the rest of what April had to say. But, her baby sister needed her, so she'd grin and bear it.

"He never makes me feel like a sex symbol. If anything he makes me feel like royalty. Being around him makes me want to be a better person."

"He sounds wonderful, so why all the tears?" She felt April pulling away and didn't want to let go, but learned a long time ago not to force her to do anything.

April sucked in a breath, trying to sober her mind. "Even great things come to an end." She stood and walked away.

"But the greatest things are worth fighting for."

April's steps slowed, but she didn't turn around. What if she fought and lost? The look on Richard's face as he let her walk out of his house ate at her. He loved Jesus first and foremost. Anything threatening that relationship had to go. Sadly, it was her. She would just have to accept it and move on.

16

"The sad part is, I don't think I'll ever be able to have another relationship after being with a man like him," April sighed into her pillow trying to fight off another bout of tears.

Candice saw the tears and held April a little tighter. They had been tight since meeting nearly four years ago, and in all that time, she'd never seen April cry over a man. The fact that she had let any man penetrate her hardened exterior was shocking. Knowing that man hurt her was enraging.

"Candice, you have no idea how much it hurts to want a man that has too many issues for y'all to be together."

"Okay, enough of this moping around. Let's go to the mall. A little retail therapy will do you some good."

April plopped down on her bed, trying to come up with an excuse to stay home and her cell phone chimed on the nightstand. "Oh God." She checked the display and slammed the phone on the bed.

"What's wrong?"

"Just a reminder for a doctor's appointment that Sheena and Pastor Hawkins made me promise to schedule." Just speaking his name made her heart skip a beat.

"Well, get dressed. I'll go with you."

"I'm not going to that appointment."

"A check-up will do you some good, or at least the fresh air would. It would certainly put my mind at ease. I don't like seeing you like this." At April's hesitation, she said the one thing that would definitely get her up and running to the doctor. "At least get your injuries checked. Did you ever get an HIV test at the hospital?" Sure enough, April got up and made her way to the bathroom without another word.

The ride to the doctor's office was silent and the ride back home was depressingly quiet. Candice alternated between watching April and keeping her eyes on the road. She didn't have to be a genius to figure out there had been bad news at the doctor's office. "You okay?"

April sat up in the seat and turned her body more toward the window. Pain filled her eyes, but her face gave no hint to the turmoil inside. That was the April that Candice knew, closed off, always hiding her emotions.

"April, what did the doctor—"

"Let's go to the mall."

Just like that, the conversation was over. She'd have to wait until April felt like sharing to find out what was going on. From the bag of prescription medication sitting on April's lap, Candice assumed she'd been diagnosed with some disease and was too ashamed to talk about it. Her heart went out to April and she questioned how such a great God could allow something like that to happen to such a good person. April had her issues and flaws like everyone else, but she was truly a good person. Being raped and then finding out your rapist had given you a disease was more than any woman should have to bear.

Candice reached across the center console and grabbed April's hand. She squeezed it, conveying her support as they drove to the mall in silence.

ॐ

April sat in the passenger seat staring out of the window. She clutched her cell phone in her lap, wishing he would call. She needed him now more than ever. Not just as her man, but as her pastor. How could God do this to her? Had she lived such a horrible life that God was now taking out his wrath upon her?

She tapped the home button to make sure the phone wasn't dead. The screen illuminated and her heart sank. Maybe she should just call him. He had promised he would always be there when she needed him. She unlocked her phone and then locked it back. What if he rejected her? She couldn't handle that, so she tossed her phone into her purse and turned on the radio.

Shopping was a horrible idea. Every time she tried on an outfit, she had to look herself in the mirror. She felt disgusting.

Tears filled her eyes, and by the third outfit, she was a blubbering mess.

Candice heard sobs coming from the dressing room stall beside her. She quickly made herself presentable and rushed over. "Open the door!"

Silence.

It had gotten so quiet that April was holding her breath to quiet her sobs. Candice was so tired of April's *suffer in silence* mentality that she didn't ask again. She climbed under the stall door and shushed April when she started to argue.

"Why are you choosing to deal with this alone?" She embraced her, guiding her down to the small bench. "Talk to me or Sheena. You can even talk to Pastor Hawkins."

April broke down even harder. She hadn't cried that hard in years, not even when she was attacked. Oh how she needed Richard, but it was best that he wasn't around. He would probably be sickened with her and she couldn't take more of his rejection.

Candice held April tight, rocking and reassuring her everything would be all right.

April tried to relax in the comfort of her friend's embrace, but it wasn't enough. She needed her man. Nothing would ever compare to the peace she felt in his arms. His presence alone calmed her. "Please, just take me home."

Candice helped April back into her own clothes, gathered their things, and rushed her out to the car like she was shielding her from the paparazzi.

The ride was long and full of tears. By the time they pulled in front of her house, April's eyes were puffy and swollen. She was lightheaded from all the sniffling and her finger tips tingled from the lack of oxygen. Candice helped her into the house, but once inside, April shook her hands from her shoulders and ran upstairs to be alone in her makeshift isolation chamber. By the time Candice caught up with her, she was locked inside and wouldn't respond to pleas to open the door.

Candice didn't want to be forceful with her friend while she was hurting, but she definitely wasn't going to allow her to suffer alone. She did an about-face and went to find Sheena. Someone had a key to that door. If not, she was going to break it down just so she could sit at the side of April's bed and be that source of comfort.

She found Sheena and Paul cuddled up in the living room watching TV. "Hey." She kissed her brother on the head and plopped down on the couch next to him.

"Hey. When did you get here?"

"I just dropped April off. Something is going on with her and she's locked herself in her room. I need the key."

"What happened?" Sheena jumped up and was pushing Paul out of the way before he could respond. "Is it still that guy? Do you know who he is? What did he do to her?"

"Baby, calm down. One question at a time." Paul rubbed Sheena's back in attempt to soothe the anxiety emanating from her.

"I don't know who he is, but it's more than just him." Candice was not happy about telling her friend's business, but she had to do something. "She had a doctor's appointment today. She came out with a bag full of medicine and didn't want to talk about it."

"Oh God!" Sheena jumped up to go check on her sister, but Paul wrapped his arms around her waist.

"Wait a minute. You know how your sister is. If you bust into her room asking questions, she will shut down and you won't get anything out of her. I know it's going to hurt you to do so, but give Candice the key and let her take care of it." Paul saw the objection on her face and shut her down. "It's not about you, but about what your sister needs. I know you love her, but she needs Candice this time."

17

"A men." Richard ended his prayer and got up off his knees, feeling freer than he had in days. Who would've thought the sight of a naked woman would hit him so hard. But then again, April wasn't just any woman. It wasn't just her outward appearance that affected him, even though it was spectacular. She had an inner strength which rivaled that of an army of trained soldiers. Her intensity kept him on his toes. He had wanted to throw years of celibacy down the drain and give in to his fleshly desires, but his prayers had availed. Every time he picked up the phone to beg her to come over or hopped in his car to go get her, God stepped in and reminded him of the blessings that awaited him if he endured hardness and resisted temptation.

He was no longer bound by the image of the swell of her breast or the curves in her hips, but her essence still pumped through his veins. It was time for their separation to be over. A prior obligation to have lunch with his boys and their wives was keeping him from going to his woman, but as soon as he got the opportunity, he was going to get her. He hoped she would show up with her sister to lunch, so he could finally let everyone know—including her—how important she was to him. Knowing April, she'd probably avoid any place she knew he would be. He couldn't blame her. His silence when she walked out of his house probably broke her heart. Soon, he would soothe her broken heart and announce to the world her place in his life.

Richard finished dressing and rushed out the door. He wanted to make a quick stop to check on his mom, and then he would join everyone for lunch. He slid into the driver's seat of his Lexus GX with a smile. He turned the key in the ignition and Tye Tribbett's *He Turned It* instantly blared through the speakers. He raised the volume. God had definitely turned some situations around in his life. Just a few months ago, he was frustrated and on the verge of depression. Things were looking up, and the months he'd spent in agony were now a distant memory.

He arrived at his mom's house and used his key to enter. The sight that awaited him tore at his heart. "Hey mom." He sat on the coffee table in front of her and smoothed her wayward hair.

She must've seen the concern on his face. She adjusted her prone position on the couch, finger combed her hair, and cleared the phlegm from her throat before speaking. "Hey baby, I wasn't expecting company today."

"Yeah, well, you've been on my mind all morning. What's going on with you?" He saw her hesitation and refused to accept the excuses she had given him in the past. "Sister Lillian…" Calling her by her first name definitely got her attention. "I mean no disrespect, but what you fail to realize is I'm also your pastor. So, if calling you Lillian helps you open up and talk to me the way the rest of my members do, then I'll do it. Now, talk to me."

She sucked in a deep breath and exhaled. She closed her eyes to gather her thoughts. When she opened them, the tears started to flow. "Richie, I've made some mistakes in my life, but none of them as big as the mistake I made with Cole. He's my child and I let my hurt feelings stop me from being a mother." She stood and walked toward the bay window to watch the neighborhood.

Richard didn't follow. He wanted to wrap his arms around her and comfort her the way a son would his mother. Today, she was his parishioner and he couldn't.

"I should've never left without him, but I was so ashamed. How could I cheat on my husband like that in my home, with my son in the next room? I was unhappy, but I should've been woman enough to pack my things, get my son, and leave." Her shoulders shook as anguish overwhelmed her. Richard held his seat. It was time for some tough love.

"It's time for you to stop wallowing in the past."

"Wallowing in the past? How can you say something like that? I'm not foolish enough to believe that every marriage is made to last a lifetime, but motherhood is for eternity. I should've—"

"If everyone focused on what they should've done, their lives would be consumed with regret," he interrupted. He would apologize later for being rude and cutting her off, but he had to remain firm. He was having the hardest time being objective in the situation. On one hand, he agreed with her. Yes, she should've been woman enough to walk away without cheating; she definitely should've taken her son. But, what bothered him most were the lies. He hated being the only child, and not once in his thirty years had she mention he had a brother. On the other hand, the horrible values instilled into Cole were just a glimpse into the mind of his mother's ex-husband. Living with a man capable of such thoughts had to be torture.

"I assume you've repented." He paused for her response, and when she flashed him her famous *you're pressing your luck little boy* look, he continued. "Then, why condemn yourself for something God has long since forgotten?"

"Condemn myself?" She spun around with her hand on her hip. "My son can't stand the sight of me. Who can blame him? And then there's you."

"Me? What about me?" He couldn't explain why, but that hurt.

"I know you're judging me. You've lived a perfect life and never made a mistake."

His mind flashed to the things he wanted to do to April and he had to laugh. Innocent he was not. The things he had thought about that past week were mild compared to the things he'd actually done before becoming a pastor. Had she not heard the rumors about him? He laughed again. "You have got to be kidding me." He took a moment to rein his mind back into pastor mode. "No man is without sin, including me. How hypocritical would it be if I judged you?"

"So, you don't hate me?"

"Of course not. I have my opinions about the situation, but I know you did what you felt necessary. Anyone can say, after the fact, what should've been done. Stop fretting over the past and fix the present. Reach out to Cole and build a relationship with him."

"How can I do that if he won't talk to me?"

Richard shook his head. He knew Cole would make him pay for what he was about to do, but he learned a long time ago that it was easier to get forgiveness for doing something than it was to get permission to do it. So, instead of calling to get the okay, he opened his big mouth and said, "We are all meeting for lunch. Why don't you come with me?"

He held his breath, hoping she declined the offer, but when a smile spread across her face, he knew he'd have some explaining to do. Maybe being his mother's pastor wasn't such a good thing. If he had such a soft spot when pastoring his mother, how would he fare when pastoring his wife?

Lillian was dressed and ready within minutes. The sad, depressed woman that had greeted Richard when he arrived was now glowing with anticipation.

He held the restaurant door open for his mother, hoping things would go well, though he had a feeling things were going to end badly. He scanned the diners and spotted his friends. As he approached their table, his eyes locked on Cole's. The fury spreading across his face confirmed Richard's suspicions. Cole was pissed.

Cole stood up—his six-feet-four-inch stature just an inch taller than his brother's—and glared at the both of them. Without a word, he walked away. Lillian grabbed him by the elbow. Her soft touch halted his steps.

"Please don't leave." She placed her hand on his back. "I'd really like to get to know you."

There was only one other woman who could make his heart pound and she was at home in his bed. He wasn't ready to deal with his mother. If he was ever going to deal with Lillian, he'd definitely need Meme at his side. He turned his glare back to Richard. *So much for little brothers.* He would deal with Richard later. He had to get out of there before he lost control and finally told his mother what he really thought of her.

Cole's ride home was a blur. The more he thought about his mother and how she had shaken her responsibilities to shack up with some man, and how Richard—who he was beginning to trust—had violated that trust, his foot pressed harder on the gas. Within minutes, he stormed through his front door and slammed it shut.

Meme jumped up and looked at her guests, hoping they weren't as startled as she was. Cole walked into the living room and the look on his face spoke volumes. She hadn't seen him that angry since the day he found out she wasn't as perfect as he thought. That was the worst day of her life. It had led to all the injuries she was currently battling. He stalked toward her and her breath stalled in her lungs. Cole dropped to his knees in front of her and before she could say a word, his lips were devouring hers. She stroked her hands up and down his spine trying to soothe the beast raging in him. She wrapped her legs around him, locking him to her. She allowed her love to chase away his demons.

"Are you okay?" she mumbled against his lips.

"I'm getting there." He went in for one last kiss and then released her. "Why are you not in bed?"

She giggled and pointed behind him. "I have company."

He glanced over his shoulder and had to laugh at himself. "My bad."

"No need to apologize." She kissed his cheek before he stood and sat next to her on the couch. "Honey, you remember April and Candice don't you?"

"Yeah, how are you ladies doing today?"

"Good," they said in unison, still shocked that he was so taken with Meme he hadn't even noticed they were in the room.

April put on a good front, but when Cole walked into the room, her heart sank. His resemblance to Richard ate at her and all the progress she'd made flew right out the window. She still ached for him.

"Honey, are you okay? I'm sure they won't mind if we step out and talk for a minute."

"I'm good. Just had a misunderstanding with my little brother, but it's nothing I can't handle."

April's pulse slowed almost to a stop. She looked around for something else to focus on. She couldn't sit there and listen to a conversation about Richard. She would lose it and her secret would be out—a secret that she was now glad no one knew except Cole. She grabbed a magazine off the table, desperately needing to talk about something else. "We were talking about your wedding." She flipped through the bridal magazine for a page they had folded to show him. "Meme seems to like the idea of an outdoor wedding."

"She does?" Cole scooped her up and placed her in his lap. "Whatever she wants, she gets."

April watched as Cole inched in to kiss Meme and she cleared her throat to stop him, more so out of jealousy than embarrassment. She wanted someone to lose control over her. She wished she could go back to the woman she used to be: loving her freedom and not wanting to be tied down to one man. Now, she wanted a husband and family; however, the news she'd gotten from the doctor would most likely put a damper on that. She didn't need Cole and Meme sitting in her face, reminding her of what she'd never have.

Cole settled for nuzzling Meme's neck. Even that broke April's heart. She slammed the magazine on the table and stomped out the front door.

Candice stood gathering her and April's purses. "I'm sorry. Her and this mystery man that she refuses to talk about just broke up. I guess seeing you guys together is a little hard for her." She said her goodbyes and rushed out after April.

18

Richard climbed back in his car after dropping his mother off. He was grateful his friends hadn't called him out for bringing her. He shouldn't have brought her, but compassion had clouded his judgment. A rift between him and his brother was the last thing he wanted. Maybe he should've followed Cole out and apologized instead of letting him stew in his anger. With the way Cole could hold a grudge, they'd probably never reconcile.

He pulled his buzzing cell phone out of his pocket and read the text message.

Come by the house. We need to talk.

Without hesitation, he tossed his phone on the passenger seat and headed in that direction. Like a kid anxious to see the brother home from college, he couldn't help the joy he felt. He'd always wished for a sibling when he was younger. Back then, he would've even taken a sister. He just wanted someone who would be there when everyone else went home. Brent Meriwether was the only friend he had when he was a kid. They had grown apart when their fathers both started churches. Then, there were always other kids around, but he quickly learned some parents pushed their kids to be friends with him only because he was the pastor's son. Not really knowing who he could trust, he kept to himself until Marlon and Jaleel came along. He was well past the age of cops and robbers or building forts in the bedroom, but finally having a sibling meant a lot to him.

"Why didn't you tell me you broke up with her?" Cole answered the door without greeting him. His arms were folded across his chest; he was ready to cuss Richard out.

"What are you talking about?"

"She was just here and she's a mess."

"She told you we broke up?"

"Candice did. Now stop skirting around the issue. What was all that talk about God blessing you with something special if you were just going to kick her to the curb?"

"I appreciate your concern, but you better believe we are not broken up. This is just a misunderstanding that I plan on rectifying immediately."

"How did the misunderstanding occur?"

Richard wanted to tell him, if for nothing more than to prolong their conversation, but thought better of it. "Why are you all in my business?"

"The same way you were in my business by bringing your mother to lunch."

Touché. Richard bowed his head in defeat.

"All right then, spill it."

"It's simple. We were getting a little too comfy, so I distanced myself to get my head on straight." *Partial truth, not a lie.*

"Well, your distance is breaking that girl's heart. As far as she's concerned, you broke up with her. Now get in here, so we can figure out what you're going to do about it."

Richard made his way into the living room. Spotting Meme on the couch, he headed straight toward her. "Hey, baby girl. It's good to see you up and about. Are you feeling better?"

"I am. If I could convince Cole to let me go back to work, my world would be perfect."

"Not going to happen, so let it rest." Cole plopped down in his recliner.

She shook her head at him and turned her attention back to Richard. "Tell me what happened between you guys today. You were doing such a good job accepting each other."

"Your man has issues that he's refusing to work through."

"Keep running your mouth and you're going to get a real taste of what it's like to be a little brother when I bust you across the head."

"Cole," Meme gasped and threw her pillow at him. "Don't talk to the pastor like that."

"Your pastor…my little brother. If he pulls another stunt like he did today, I won't think twice about laying him out."

"Duly noted, but don't let the title fool you. This pastor ain't no punk."

Cole smirked and shook his head. "Is that so?"

"Most definitely."

"You guys stop. You're too old to be acting like this."

"Baby, he started it."

Meme rolled her eyes and stood up. "I'm going to bed. You guys behave." She gave Cole a quick peck on the cheek and he took full advantage, turning his lips into the kiss.

"What do I get if I behave?"

"I am still sitting over here." Richard shook his head in disbelief. Cole had come a long way. He was once a man adamant about remaining a bachelor, but Meme had walked into his life and turned it upside down. He went from hopping in and out of a different bed every night to climbing in to bed with the love of his life. He never looked so happy.

Meme chuckled and walked away. Cole's gaze followed the sway of her hips all the way out of the room.

"You going to be all right playa, or do you need me to leave?"

"Shut up, man. You know exactly how this feels." Cole got up and sat closer to Richard, so Meme wouldn't over hear their conversation. "Don't think for one second I bought that sorry excuse for why you backed away from April."

Richard smoothed his hand across his face to school his expression and leaned forward, resting his arms on his thighs. "I was sick and she came over to check on me. She took such good care of me that I was already feeling her more than I should have."

"I know exactly what you mean. That's how Meme got me."

"Man please, from what I hear, she had you hooked from the first time you laid eyes on her."

Cole tried to hide his smile, but failed. "Whatever man. What did April do that has you running?"

"I told you, I'm not running. I was sick and apparently threw up on her. While I was asleep, she decided to take a shower. As she was getting out, I came in the bathroom to throw up again. My God, she almost gave me a heart attack."

Cole was laughing so hard Richard couldn't finish talking. "What's wrong, baby boy? You can't handle that brick house?"

"Don't get it twisted. I can handle it. It took almost a week for me to convince myself not to."

"Get out of here. You should've hit that and asked God to forgive you."

"I told you before. Good things come to those that wait. I just had to get my mind right."

"Well, you better hope she takes you back."

"She has no choice." The look on Richard's face said it all. April was his.

Cole certainly understood that. Maybe that *take what you want* mentality ran in the family. "What can I do to help?"

He was going to say nothing, but thought better of it. "You can let me borrow Meme for a couple of hours."

"You're really asking for that beat down."

"Calm down. When are you going to realize I'm not like that?"

"I'm just messing with you." Cole laughed at the pissed off look on Richard's face. "If you didn't give in to April, I know for sure you're not like that."

"Good. Now like I was saying, I'd like to buy April something and a woman's opinion would help." It was Richard's turn to laugh at Cole. "If you could stop being so overprotective and let the girl out of the house, I'd really appreciate it."

Cole sat back and crossed his legs. "One hour and I'm going with you."

"You know, you're going to have to let go of what happened eventually."

"Yeah, I just can't lose her the way I've lost everyone else."

With that statement, Richard got a quick glimpse into the painful life his brother must've endured. He was four when his mother left. That alone must have been traumatic. Then, to have your father killed in an accident you should've been there to prevent. Not to mention how he had blamed himself for what happened to Meme. Richard definitely understood why he was being overprotective.

"I have no problem with you coming, but let's go now."

"I have to help her shower first."

"Man, don't be in there screwing around while I sit out here waiting."

Cole laughed as he walked away. Truth be told, he hadn't touched Meme in that way since before her injuries. He was afraid he would hurt her. Sure, he had touched her and pleasured her several times, but they had yet to make love.

He walked into the bedroom and she was lying on the bed watching TV. She had taken off her sweats and the swell of her backside hanging out her lace boy shorts hardened his body instantly. He shut the door and stood there taking in an eye full.

"Hey, did Richard leave?"

"No, he wants you to go shopping with him to pick something out for his lady friend. Do you feel up to it?"

"Pastor Hawkins has a lady?" She thought about it for a second and realized she couldn't care less. "You're letting me out of the house?" She hopped up off the bed and was pulling her sweats back on before he could answer.

"Relax before you hurt yourself," Cole laughed at her eagerness. *Maybe I am being a little over protective.* "Let me help you take a shower."

He went into the adjoining bathroom to warm the water. When he turned around, Meme was standing behind him, her body bare as the day she was born. Blood drained from his brain, pulsing into his manhood, and he stood dumbfounded by her beauty. His eyes scrutinized her perfection and lingered on her one imperfection. The wound on her stomach that normally reminded him of how she'd almost been taken from him and halted his sexual pursuits was no longer having its usual effect. Before he could stop himself, he lifted her onto the counter, devouring the parts of her that during the past few months he'd only allowed himself to dream of.

Meme moaned in pleasure and Cole mistook it for agony.

"Are you okay?"

"I've been okay. Now shut up and love me." She slammed her lips onto his and locked his head to hers, not allowing any objections. She was done waiting for him to accept the fact that she was okay. Her free hand unbuckled his belt and she almost gave him a heart attack.

"Baby, are you trying to kill me?" She was driving him to ecstasy. If he didn't take control, it would be a short trip.

She tightened her legs around him. She wanted and needed him more than he could ever imagine. He lifted her off the counter. The motion sent shockwaves through her body and she cried out in pleasure. Her body trembled like rolling thunder. The force was so powerful so potent they nearly toppled to the floor. They clung to each other letting ecstasy swirl through them.

Meme snuggled her face into his neck still vibrating with the aftershocks of their coupling. "Don't ever make me wait."

"Damn, Richard is waiting for us," Cole laughed. "I'm pretty sure he heard you screaming."

She didn't care. She ran her lips up and down his neck enticing him to forget about who was waiting. "One more time and then we can go."

She didn't have to ask twice.

Forty-five minutes later, they walked into the living room both ignoring Richard's smirk.

19

April woke from a sound sleep grasping for her ringing cell phone on the nightstand. She cracked one eye open, peering at the display. She hoped whoever was calling had a good excuse for waking her. Richard's name flashed on the screen, instantly clearing her grogginess. She sat up in the bed and answered the phone, trying to sound as sexy as the early hour would allow. A smile spread across her face when he told her he was outside and wanted her to throw on something and come down. In less than ten minutes, she was dressed, her teeth were brushed, and she was seated in his car.

It had been over a week since she'd walked out of his house. She had been sick ever since. Sitting next to him, she felt like a shy teenage girl who was finally getting some attention from her crush.

"Hey." He caressed her cheek, guiding her face toward him. "Good morning."

She looked up at him, her chest heaving with barely restrained emotions. Without second thought, she flung herself into his arms.

He wrapped his arms around her and held her tight. "I missed you, too." He hated to hurt her, but there was nothing else he could've done. Her glistening wet, naked body had haunted him all week. She had him was so messed up he'd called in a guest speaker to preach the previous Sunday's sermon. He didn't think he would be able to stand at the podium and speak, knowing April and all her glory was watching. He'd spent just about the entire service sitting in the pulpit searching the congregation for her. His heart sank into his stomach when he realized she hadn't come.

"This week has been hell without you. Don't hurt me like this again."

He felt the moisture on her cheeks and instantly regretted keeping his distance. Maybe he should've called. If she had missed him as much as he missed her, then he knew she had been suffering. The loneliness her presence had chased away came back in full force during their days apart.

He drove down to the pier and she was shocked when he pulled two fishing poles and a tackle box out of the truck. She had never fished a day in her life but decided to give it a shot.

She listened attentively as Richard instructed her how to bait a hook and cast the reel. April tried to look excited. Her stomach churned when he opened the container of worms. They wiggled and squirmed through the mud, but April kept a smile on her face. She tried to keep an open mind and even extended her hand to accept the worm Richard offered her. He asked her several times if she was sure, and like an idiot, she kept saying yes. The worm plopped down into her palm and she instantly lost all good sense. April screamed as loud as she could, irritating fellow fishermen around them. She hopped around in circles shaking and wiping her hand on her pants. Richard doubled over laughing. She didn't find it funny. She took her chair and fishing rod and moved to the opposite side of the pier.

Richard took a few minutes to review the situation. *Why is she mad? Why did she take the worm? Didn't she know how it would feel?* He watched her from across the pier and decided he didn't care about any of the whys. All he cared about was that she was upset and it was his fault.

"Love," he whispered as he stepped up behind her. His affectionate term of endearment caught her off guard. He could see the surprise on her face as she turned around. "Please don't be mad at me." He placed a hand on her waist and pulled her closer, rubbing his early morning stubble across her cheek. He freed her hair from the clip, allowing her silky tresses to fall around her neck. His fingers slid across her scalp as he ran his fingers through her hair.

April was in heaven. Leaning back against the rail of the pier, she tilted her head to fully enjoy his caress. The spellbinding rhythm flowed from her head to her toes and she begged, "Richard, please kiss me."

His gaze fell upon her lips and he wanted nothing more than to kiss them, but he couldn't. "I wish I could..." Before he could finish, April circled her arms around his neck and pulled him down to meet her lips. She moved quickly, not giving him time to object. He stood stiff and rigid. She lightly tapped his cheek, pleading against his mouth, "Honey, please, I need this."

Richard relented and gave her a small portion of what she wanted. He knew she was disappointed, but when it came to her, he was a ticking time bomb. He didn't want to set off the libido that he'd spent an entire week trying to contain.

"I wish I could have this with you all the time."

"I'm glad you feel that way." He pulled a ring out of his pocket and slipped it on her finger. He'd agonized over how to pop the question and decided fast and simple would be the best option. Their relationship was still so new and she was still terrified of the church finding out about them. He understood her reservations, but he had to have her.

She gasped and pulled away from him. "I can't marry you."

He knew those words were coming, but never imagined they'd hurt as much as they did. "Can you let me ask before you reject me?"

"I'm sorry, but I can't."

"Of course you can. I love you and you don't have to say it for me to know you love me."

"I can't." She broke free of his embrace and took the ring off. "Is love going to be enough when your congregation finds out I'm pregnant and blame you for getting me that way?" She choked on a sob. Finally letting her secret out wasn't as liberating as she'd thought it would be. The weight of her situation sent her tumbling to the ground and Richard was right there to catch her. He leaned her back against his chest and used the rail of the pier to help steady her.

He let her cry for a moment. His mind was processing what she had said. *Pregnant...by her rapist.* He had never felt such rage and malice in all his life. God be his strength if they ever found who attacked her. He reined in his emotions and focused his attention on her. He brushed her hair to one side and planted kisses on her neck. His kiss silenced her sobs. "I've waited a long time for you. Before we met, I dreamed of you. I saw your face just about every time I closed my eyes."

"You saw me?" She tried to turn toward him, but he stilled her with his lips to her neck. Her pulse accelerated beneath his kiss.

"When I walked into that hospital and saw you lying in that bed, my heart nearly stopped. You are mine. I'll walk away from this church before I allow what the congregation thinks to take you away from me. So, yes you will marry me?" He slipped the ring back on her finger and turned her toward him. For the first time, he allowed himself to let go and kiss her the way his heart wanted to. He forgot about his title and the repercussions of someone seeing them. His tongue caressed hers, sweeping the fullness of her mouth. His hands roamed down, grabbing her backside. He was getting carried away.

April squealed with delight and her body pulsed with desire. She slipped her hands between them and took the opportunity to caress the width of his chest. She went a step further and glided her hand beneath his shirt. His bare skin felt like heaven.

He spanked her backside and growled against her lips, "Behave." His hands dropped and he backed away from her, but his lips couldn't let her go. After three more lingering pecks, he forced himself to stop. "Excuse me for a second."

April watched him walk away. There was no doubt in her mind what the problem was. She was right there with him. She wanted him as much as he wanted her, if not more.

Richard stood a few feet away, trying to convince himself not to take her back to his place. He huffed in frustration and began quoting the same scriptures that had gotten him through the week. He heard the spin of a fishing reel and turned toward her just in time to see her smile triumphantly at her fishing line flying through the air then plunking down into the water. Her hair floated in the breeze, her nose and cheeks rosy from the chilly air. In that moment, he was more certain of her place in his life than he'd ever been about anything. He walked up behind her and wrapped his arms around her waist. His ring was still on her finger and he couldn't have been happier.

"Will you teach me what to do? I don't want to embarrass you."

"That's the great thing about serving God. He never calls you to do something without equipping you for it first. Everything you need is already in you. I told you God has a great work for you to do. Your dreams have even hinted at what's in store. You are my wife and God has given you everything you need to stand by my side." He smoothed his hands across her stomach and whispered in her ear. "As far as this baby is concerned, this is my baby. I will be at every appointment, there when it's delivered, and my name will be on the birth certificate. Your child is my child.

"Oh, Richard…" She went to turn and give him all the affection he deserved, but her fishing pole jerked so hard she almost dropped it.

She screamed while gripping the pole with both hands. Richard placed one hand on top of hers for support and guided the other to the reel. "Okay baby, pull the pole back a little and start reeling him in."

She did as she was told, but it was harder than it sounded. The flimsy pole bent and wobbled. She thought it would break, but she kept tugging and reeling as instructed. When her fish crested the surface of the water, she squealed and bounced around, forgetting all about holding the pole. Richard caught it before it flipped off the rail and finished reeling it in. April grabbed the fishing line and begged him to take a picture.

Richard laughed the entire time. Her diva pose with a fish dangling from her hand was more than he could take. He was glad she was enjoying herself. He loved to fish and couldn't see not being able to share it with her. Yes, she had flipped out over the worm, but he could deal with that.

He laughed as she tried to take the fish off the hook. The fish flipped and wiggled at the slightest touch. Every time it moved, April jumped and screamed. Richard placed his hand on top of hers and squeezed until the fish obeyed and then yanked the hook out.

"Thank you." April took the pole and went in search of another worm. This time, she knew what to expect. She gripped the worm so tight it didn't have an opportunity to squirm.

Richard was impressed. She baited her hook—clearly disgusted—and cast her line. He stepped up behind her, grazed his lips across her neck—his own fishing pole forgotten—and rubbed his hands on her stomach. The slow circle caress was almost erotic. "Are we really doing this?"

"Yes we are." She turned her lips to his and gave him a quick peck.

"Good." He turned her completely into his embrace, exerting the dominance she was so crazy about. "We have the city wide revival in three months. I won't be able to get away before then, but I want to get married right after that." He spoke against her lips, the intensity in his eyes holding hers. She nodded her consent, his power making her incapable of speaking. She braced herself for his impending kiss and was still unprepared for its potency.

Oh God... Where would she be? How entranced would she be if he hadn't held back all those times? Making love was out of the question, but oh how she wanted to. He had done so much for her the past few months that she wouldn't dare ask him to compromise his principles. That didn't stop her from wanting it. With every ounce of self-control she possessed, she broke their kiss. She gripped a fist full of the collar of his shirt, and between labored breaths begged, "Let's get married tomorrow."

Richard chuckled, "Do you love me?"

"More than I ever thought I could love someone."

"Then we can wait." He pecked her pouting lips and cradled her to his chest. "What we can do is throw a little dinner party and invite our family and friends."

"Ooh, I'll cook." Her eyes lit up and her mind was already spinning with menu ideas.

"You cook?"

"Just as good as my sister, if not better," April giggled at his shocked expression. "Come on now, Pastor Hawkins. Would the Lord bless you with a wife who couldn't take care of you?"

"Well, First Lady Hawkins…"

April gasped and placed her hand over his mouth. "Don't call me that." Hurt flashed across his face and she quickly clarified. "I'm honored to be your First Lady, but it makes me sound so old."

"Not as honored as I am to have you. So, First Lady Hawkins, you're just going to have to get used to it."

April brushed her lips across his cheek, "Anything for you."

Between the whispered endearments, soft kisses, and lingering gazes, they didn't get much fishing done. The sun had fully risen and they decided to call it quits. They swung by the store on their way to Richard's house to get everything she would need to cook. He was grateful for his secluded location and didn't have to worry about anyone they knew spotting them.

They carried the bags in together and put the groceries away. April plopped down in a chair at the kitchen table, yawning wide as her mouth would open. Her early morning wake-up call was finally catching up to her. Richard smiled and lifted her into his arms. He carried her through the living room into his bedroom. He kissed the objection off her lips and laid her on his bed. "I would take you home, but I'm not ready to be away from you. You sleep while I study." He kissed the crown of her head and gathered his Bible, concordance, dictionary, and several other books the average Christian knew nothing about and joined her on the bed.

April watched him, thinking this couldn't be good, but once his brow furrowed in concentration, he became so engrossed in his studying she thought he had forgotten about her. She crawled under the blanket and tried to get comfortable.

"It's hot in here. Why are you under the blanket?"

April smiled, happy that even though he was giving time to the Lord he still noticed her. "Take note," she glanced over her shoulder at him. "It could be as hot as hell and I'd still want a blanket."

"Stop cussing."

"I wasn't."

He could hear the smile in her voice and shook his head. *What am I going to do with her?*

20

April ran around mentally reciting her to-do-list and checking things off one by one. Everything had to be perfect—the table setting, the music, and especially the food. She was getting ready to drop a bomb on her family. Hopefully, she could ease their shock with a good meal. Time flew by. Any minute, the doorbell would be ringing and she still needed to get dressed.

All the food was arranged on the table. The aromas reminded her she had neglected to eat anything that morning. She'd been afraid to eat, fearing a bout of morning sickness would creep up on her. Her stomach cramped and the hunger pangs were just as gut wrenching as the vomiting. Her decision didn't seem too wise. She flopped into a chair at the dining room table, suddenly feeling as weak as if she hadn't eaten in weeks. She grabbed a dinner roll and shoveled it into her mouth, trying to hurry it down her throat to soothe her rolling stomach. Her head started spinning and she rested it on the table, fighting off the nausea that usually followed.

"Hey." Richard rubbed his hand down her back.

She turned her head toward him looking like a chipmunk—cheeks stuffed with bread.

"What's wrong?"

She lifted her head too fast and the sudden motion rocked her stomach. She clutched her mouth and took off running toward the restroom. Richard was right behind her. She spit the bread into the toilet just before she gagged and lost her stomach contents. Richard stroked her back until she finished and then ran her a warm bath.

"You've worked too hard this morning. I know you want everything to be perfect, but none of this matters if you're not a part of it." He kissed her forehead and walked to the door. "Soak for a few minutes, I will entertain everyone, break the news to them, and then come get you like we planned."

She looked up at him, barely able to hold her head up. He hated to leave her alone like that. She saw the look on his face and cut him off before he could speak another word. "I'm fine." She forced a smile, trying to convince him. If he thought for one minute she wasn't okay, he would call everyone and cancel. She wasn't having that. "Bring me a ginger ale and I'll be as good as new."

She waited until after he brought her drink to undress. As she stepped into the bathtub, the doorbell rang.

Showtime! She took a deep breath and lowered herself into the water. Her life was getting ready to change. There was no turning back. She hoped her family didn't lose their minds. The first group of voices was her ever-punctual sister and brother-in-law. She listened for little voices and heard none. She was glad they elected to find a sitter for the twins. The doorbell rang four more times, announcing all their guests had arrived. She figured it best to get out of the bath.

The clamor of multiple conversations filled the house and her heart thudded so fiercely she feared she might pass out. She took several deep breaths while pacing around the room. If she didn't calm down, she would wind up back in the bathroom throwing up again. Staying calm was a lost cause. The talking quieted and all she heard was Richard's voice.

"I invited you guys over because we are closer than I am with most of my own family. I'm grateful God placed you in my life and I can't think of any other group of people I'd want to share my good news with." He looked to Cole for support and his brows were raised so high in shock, he second guessed himself. "I've met someone," he fumbled and had to polish off his drink to wet his suddenly parched throat.

Every set of eyes in the room were on him waiting for him to finish.

"She means a lot to me and we waited to tell everyone until she was sure she'd be able to handle the backlash that's sure to follow. I wanted to tell you guys first, because whatever happens once the church finds out will be easier to handle if she has your support."

"Of course you have our support."

Richard looked at Sheena with skepticism, knowing she would be the main one to have a problem with him dating April. "I hope you really mean that. She's here. Just promise me when she comes out, you'll keep an open mind and hear us out before you get upset."

"Why would I get upset? I'm happy you've found someone to love."

"Okay… I'll go get her." The slight nod he got from Cole as he walked out of the room was the encouragement he needed.

He stepped into his room and April was on the verge of hyperventilating. "Come here."

She stepped into his embrace, instantly resting her head on his chest.

His presence calmed her and the kiss on her brow imparted a peace she still couldn't explain. "It's almost over." He reached into his pocket and pulled out her engagement ring that she'd insisted he hold on to until they told everyone. "I'm minutes away from being able to put this on your finger for good. Whether they're happy for us or not, this ring is going on your finger and we are getting married in three months."

She took one last deep breath and nodded that she was ready. He interlaced their fingers and led her out of the room. They walked into the living room and all you could hear was gasping like someone had sucked the oxygen out of the room. April stood there watching everyone, trying to put two and two together.

"April, you have got to be kidding me."

April looked toward Sheena and her heart dropped into her stomach. "Please be happy for me."

"Happy for you? This is my Pastor." Sheena stood and paced toward the opposite side of the room. "What happens when you get bored with the quiet life? Are you just going to kick him aside and go back to your old ways? I love my church and don't want to have to move because my sister broke the pastor's heart."

"I love him, Sheena. Do you think so little of me that you assume I can't love him?" Tears blurred her vision, but she refused to let them fall. She wouldn't give Sheena the satisfaction of seeing her cry.

"You don't love him, you're just obsessed with him. Didn't we already have this talk? You're joining the dozens of other women in the pastor's wives' club, claiming something that isn't for them."

"So, you talk a good game about believing God can work miracles, but when He actually works one you don't have faith enough to believe?" April wanted to march over and slap Sheena across the face, but Richard held firm to her waist. Every time she tried to move, he tightened his grip.

"The difference between her and this so-called pastor's wives' club is I love her." He'd had enough of Sheena's mouth, and the tears in April's eyes were pissing him off. He took the ring back out of his pocket and slipped it on April's finger while looking at Sheena. "I'd hate for things you say here to cause tension at family dinners."

He had barely gotten the words out before Candice and Meme were up on their feet screaming and rushing toward April. He stepped out of the way to let them have their moment and had one of his own with his boys. Sheena faded to the background, trying to figure out how her sister and Pastor Hawkins wound up in a relationship.

"Oh my God!" Meme embraced her squealing with excitement. She had helped Richard shop for the ring wondering what type of woman had won his heart and who she'd be forced to spend time with. "We are going to be sisters. We should have a double wedding."

"Oh no," Richard jumped into their conversation from the other side of the room. "Y'all are taking too long to get married. I'm not waiting that long."

"Didn't you tell me not to deny Meme the wedding of her dreams?" Cole slapped Richard on the back smirking at his eagerness. "Practice what you preach."

"No need," April smiled up at Richard. "I'm not one of those girls who've dreamed about their wedding since they were a kid. We can go to the courthouse and get married tomorrow if you want."

"Hold up!" Candice interrupted the conversation and marched over to Richard. "Are you the one that broke her heart and had her crying for days?"

"Yes, but it was a misunderstanding."

April saw Candice getting ready to tear into him and jumped in between them. "I have something else I want to announce, so please have a seat and then we can eat."

Everyone took their seats, but Sheena remained in the back of the room, leaning against the wall, arms folded across her chest. April tried her best to ignore her. She needed to unburden herself and there was no better time.

"A couple of weeks ago, I went to the doctor and received the worst news of my life. The animal that attacked me left part of himself with me and I'm carrying his child."

"Oh God!" Sheena was at her side within seconds. April wanted to reject her, but she had wanted her comfort since receiving the test results. She went to her and they shared a tender moment. Candice and Meme joined in along with April's cousins, Camilla and Delisa, and Marlon's wife, Latrice. They were a huddled bunch of tears and sniffles.

April absorbed the comfort before she continued talking. "Richard is going to raise the baby as his child." She looked at him, her heart swelling with love for him. "When the church finds out we are dating and that I'm pregnant…"

"They are going to assume he's the father." Cole looked to Richard, silently asking if he was ready to deal with that.

"Don't worry. We'll be there this Sunday and every one after that. We got your back."

"We will?" Cole looked at Meme like she'd lost her mind.

"Yes." She sat next to him and he conceded to her wishes.

Richard saw Cole nod and wanted to run around the room praising God. He knew the Lord would save his brother and those little steps showing progress increased his faith.

"Let's go eat." April brushed her lips across Richard's and then led her guest to the dining area.

Richard hung back and grabbed Cole by the arm. He waited until everyone was out of ear shot and took a minute to rag on his brother. "So, it's like that? I've been asking you to come to church for over a year and just like that you agree to go with Meme. I'm not feeling the love." He laughed and Cole punched him the arm. Richard laughed even harder. "I'm just saying, love has you pretty hemmed up."

"What about you? Love has you laying your title as pastor on the line. They're going to call you a sinner and abandon you."

"We'll cross that bridge when we get to it."

"There are so many other women out there. Are you sure you want the one relationship that can destroy you?"

"You have no idea how much I want her."

"Don't let your celibacy get you into something you can't get out of."

"There is so much more to it than that."

"All right, I got your back then."

"That's good to know. There's something else I need you to do for me."

"Anything, little brother." Cole tried to pat his head like he was six years old.

Richard wasn't having it. He swatted Cole's hand away and they stood in the hall tussling with each other until April called his name.

Richard straightened up and got back to what had been on his mind. "We are starting families and I really want us to be a part of each other's lives."

"No doubt." Cole gave Richard a fist bump and was about to seal it with a brotherly hug until Richard opened his mouth, speaking words Cole didn't want to hear.

"Then, I need you to work things out with our mother." They locked eyes and Richard saw the refusal before it ever crossed Cole's lips. "How can I enjoy my family when there is so much tension between you two? I couldn't even invite her over today, because I was afraid you'd walk out. She should be here to hear my good news."

"I hear you man, but it's easier said than done. You have no idea what my life was like after she left. All the moving around, an alcoholic father, being trained to use women..."

"I know it was messed up, and I'm not saying you have to welcome her with open arms. At least try to be cordial and able to stay in the same room with her without wanting to kill her."

"Richard honey, we are waiting on you." April saw the look on Cole's face and quietly backed out of the hall.

"I don't want to kill her. It just hurts too much to look at her." Cole stepped around him and followed April into the dining room.

Richard was right behind him. They tried to walk into the room looking normal, but tension was radiating off of them. April and Meme made eye contact, silently asking each other what was going on. They shrugged their shoulders and leaned in to question their men, both receiving the same response: a simple kiss on the cheek.

21

April arrived at Richard's bright and early before Sunday morning worship. He wasn't wasting any time going public with their relationship. He was set to make the big announcement during service and didn't feel comfortable not telling his mother beforehand. A small breakfast before service so they could meet was all it was, but for some reason she was more nervous than she was the day before.

Richard greeted her at the door with a kiss. Accepting his proposal and agreeing to go public with their relationship had unleashed something within him. He was more affectionate and passionate.

"Good morning," he whispered releasing her lips and trailing his mouth along the column of her neck. "I missed you last night."

"You did?" She circled her arms around his neck and leaned in to him.

"Yeah, I can't wait until we're married. I'll never have to let you go."

April squeezed him a little tighter. She could stay in his arms all day. Thinking about what she would face during the day, she definitely wanted to, but she refused to cower away. Richard was risking his reputation for her. She would withstand the ridicule for him. "I don't know what it is about me that's so special, but I thank God every day for giving you to me. If God never gives me anything else, He's already given me enough."

Richard swooped in for one more kiss. He made it a quick one. He felt himself getting to the point where he couldn't turn her loose. She totally understood and didn't complain when he backed away from her.

"I'll go cook breakfast before your mother gets here."

Richard watched her walk away and went straight to his prayer closet. They were in for a battle and he couldn't afford to be carnal-minded. He had to be fortified with the Spirit to combat the anger and negativity that might be slung at him after announcing his pending nuptials.

By the time Lillian rang the doorbell, his mind was where it needed to be. "Morning beautiful." He kissed her cheek and led her into the kitchen.

Lillian saw April placing food on the table and stopped mid-stride.

"Mom, this is April."

April's heart hammered away. The look on Lillian's face didn't make it any better. "It's nice to meet you." April extended her hand. Her hand hung out there and her heart dropped into to her stomach. Lillian just stood there staring at her. At least Sheena had voiced her objection and she knew exactly where she stood. With Lillian, the uncertainty was killing her.

"Mom..." Richard cleared his throat and Lillian stuttered out of her shocked stupor.

"It's nice to meet you as well." She shook April's hand, still trying to recover from being blindsided by her son's relationship. "Please forgive me, but my son and I recently had a conversation about relationships and he led me to believe he wasn't in one."

"I wasn't at the time, but when God does something, He does it quickly." Richard grabbed April's hand and flashed her ring.

Lillian might've fooled Richard with that smile and weak celebratory hug, but April knew the look of a pissed off woman. Lillian was definitely heated. April watched her take a seat at the table, her back as rigid and tense as her expression.

So much for a good relationship with my mother-in-law.

April sat at the table praying for Lillian to hurry and finish her breakfast. The woman did more talking than she did eating. April tried to join the conversation, but Lillian gave her one word responses like talking to her wasn't worth her time. Richard's phone rang and April braced for the confrontation that was surely coming. Richard wasn't out the room for two seconds before Lillian started in on her.

"I can certainly see why my son is smitten with you. I'll be watching you, and the first sign that you aren't what he needs, I'll shut this little romance down. His father and I worked hard to build our reputation. I will not sit by and let some random woman ruin it."

"Watch all you want, but interfere and you might be surprised at who is left standing on the outside looking in."

"Don't get too cocky, little girl. Beyond the obvious physical attributes, you have nothing to offer my son. When he realizes that, you'll be set aside like all the others."

"He loves me." April fought hard to keep her emotions in check. She wouldn't let Lillian see how her words were getting to her. "That alone should make me good enough for you."

They heard Richard's footsteps approaching and fell silent. He approached the table and they gave an awarding-winning performance. April was all smiles and pleasant looks, but inside she was fuming.

"There's an issue at the church that needs my attention, but you ladies enjoy the rest of your breakfast."

"Actually, I'm finished. I'll follow you out." Lillian grabbed her purse and headed for the door.

"You go ahead. I'll meet you there. I need to talk to April for a minute."

Inside, April was laughing her butt off at the astonishment on Lillian's face. *Me, one; Lillian, zero.* She tried not to gloat, but it was hard. Lillian strutted out of the kitchen and the soft click of the front door dissolved the tension that had built over the past hour.

"Don't think for one minute my mother has me fooled. She is territorial and overprotective. Stand your ground and don't let her bully you."

Her smile stretched from ear to ear and she stood there grinning like she'd won the lottery. There was nothing she could say, so she slung her arms around his neck and kissed him. She wouldn't worry him about the things his mother said. She could handle Lillian.

"Sorry I didn't get to finish breakfast. What I did taste was amazing. You keep cooking like this, and I'll need to step up my workouts."

"Don't worry. When I drop this baby, I'll put you through one of my workouts. I know what it takes to keep a body looking right."

You certainly do. Richard bit down on his lip to keep from blurting out the thoughts running through his mind. He silently backed out of the kitchen shaking his head at her sassy little smile and the seductive sway of her hips.

April pulled into the church parking lot excited and terrified all at once. She'd hurried to clean the kitchen, so she could get to church in time to get the seat Richard had instructed her to sit in. There were a lot of cars in the parking lot. She hoped she hadn't screwed up already. She'd never been to church that early and had no idea what was going on. She exhaled her tension and exited the car.

She walked into the sanctuary and was assailed by a self-appointed entourage. Candice, Meme, Sheena, Camilla, Delisa, and Latrice surrounded her and shuffled her downstairs in a cloud of good morning smooches. They unlocked an office and filed inside.

"If you are going to be first lady of this church, you will need a space to freshen up and make sure you are well put together before entering the church." Sheena took the lead on explaining what was going on. April was just shocked she was even there. "I feel horrible for how I reacted yesterday and wanted to make it up to you. After Paul tore me a new one for my behavior, I called Jaleel. He said this room wasn't being used, because the walls are too thin and you can practically hear everything that's going on in Pastor's office next door.

"I called the girls and we went shopping. Please accept this gift as my apology. The more I think about it, you are perfect for my pastor. He needs a spitfire woman who can hold her own against the throng of women after him, yet be soft and beautiful enough to excite him."

April patted the corners of her eyes, trying desperately to keep her tears from ruining her makeup. Between crying and vomiting, she had to reapply it twice before leaving the house and didn't want to do it again. Candice passed her a Kleenex and it was like waving a white flag to surrender to her emotions. The women surrounded her within seconds.

"Do you guys really think I can do this?"

"Of course you can." They were so caught up in comforting her that no one heard the door click open. Richard parted the circle and gathered her in his arms. He grabbed another tissue and patted her face dry. "Just remember, you're not auditioning to be my wife. No matter what happens—even if you choose to sit in a corner and not be involved in running the church—I'll love you no less." He soothed her with a quick kiss and then another to soothe himself. There were at least thirty church members he knew would withdraw their membership as soon as he broke the news of his engagement. Thinking of how many others would follow had his stomach in knots.

"Sheena called me down here this morning to approve what they'd done. I think it's perfect." He turned her around and leaned her back against his chest, so she could look around the office. "I'll have a door put in on this wall to adjoin our offices." He turned her around to face the opposite wall. "I'll knock this wall down. The office on the other side belongs to the choir director. He doesn't really need it. We'll build you a bathroom complete with a closet and shower." He bent close to her ear and whispered, "For the days you get a little sweaty at church."

He didn't have to explain his meaning. Her body warmed at the thought. She quickly turned around and planted her face against Richard's chest, so no one could see the heat in her cheeks. He chuckled and she pinched his arm. He laughed even harder. "I'm

sorry, but warning comes before destruction. You've been warned."
He let her go and walked toward the door.

"Behave," she barked at his back.

"You have three months." He turned back toward her and scanned her body, unable to conceal his desire for her.

"Ugh." Sheena hid her amusement behind a disgusted scowl. "I don't even want to know what you whispered in her ear."

"I heard him. He is no better than his brother." Meme shooed Richard out of the room. "Now go get ready, so I can help my future sister freshen up."

"Speaking of my brother, he was looking for you."

"I'm not speaking to him right now. He said he was coming to church. We pull up and he says he'll be waiting in the car for me."

"Baby girl," Richard shook his head, making a mental note to rag on Cole later. "When are you going to realize the hold you have on him? He's hiding in my office. Just remember, for him, being here means more than just coming to church. He's inevitably going to see our mother. He'll need you by his side when that happens."

Meme made a beeline toward the door, forgetting all about April. Richard blew April a kiss and followed Meme out.

22

April sat on the front row of the church for the first time in her life. Sheena sat on her left with Lady Lillian on the opposite side of her. On her right, her newly appointed personal security—who seemed more like a bodyguard—Deacon Carl. On his best day, he couldn't hide the thug life he used to live. She had rejected his offer to escort her upstairs. Richard quickly informed her she didn't have a choice. It was the only time since meeting him that his authoritative persona had gotten on her nerves. She was already on edge. A stranger's presence just made it worse. She sat as close to Sheena as she could without people wondering what was wrong with her. Besides Richard and her family, Deacon Carl was the only man who'd gotten that close to her since her attack.

She pulled out her phone and sent Richard a quick text.

Please tell him to move. I'm not ready to be this close to a strange man.

She watched Richard lift up his phone to read her message. His eyes shot to hers and he saw what no one else could see. She was afraid. He didn't hesitate to click on the radio in his ear. She heard a whispered *yes sir* come from Deacon Carl. Within seconds, he was repositioned to the seat across the aisle from her.

Any other Sunday, the church would be alit with praise. Sometimes—she hated to admit—she wished they'd hurry up, so she could get home early. That day, it seemed no one wanted to praise the Lord. It was barely thirty minutes into the service and the secretary got up to read the bulletin. Right after that, Richard would get up and give his announcement. She could handle Richard telling the church about their relationship. It was what she planned on saying afterward that had her worried. Her heart dropped into her stomach and she hoped morning sickness wouldn't send her running from the sanctuary.

She slipped her hand beneath Sheena's and entwined their fingers. She sucked in a long deep breath, trying to stave off the building anxiety. Sheena went to work. She signaled Delisa to take the seat next to April. Delisa slung her arm around April's shoulder and Sheena gripped her hand a little tighter. Inconspicuously, the two of them took turns whispering prayers and scriptures of encouragement into April's ears.

Richard stood at the podium while April closed her eyes to focus on calming down. All eyes were about to be on her and she didn't want them seeing her like that. He greeted the congregation and that same calm she normally felt when he spoke flowed over her. She opened her eyes and he was looking right at her. She answered the question on his face with a slight nod and he smiled.

"Those who've ever had to be single and serve the Lord will definitely understand what I'm about to say. I've been lonely." Sighs of sympathy resounded throughout the sanctuary, giving April hope for the best. "I've stood at this altar and performed wedding ceremonies and baby dedications, wishing it were me experiencing that type of joy. All I ever wanted was someone to love me. I stand here overjoyed to announce that the Lord has shown me favor. I'm getting married."

Shocked gasps echoed throughout the sanctuary, followed by dead silence. April held her breath. They weren't supposed to respond like that. She hoped they would be so happy he found someone that they wouldn't care she was some lowly no-name woman who had just shown up a few months before. Her girls behind her started clapping and their applause multiplied around the sanctuary, exploding into a standing ovation. They hooped and hollered their congratulations. April exhaled her relief. Richard calmed everyone and continued his speech.

"Months ago, I started having a recurring dream. There was this woman. I could see her face as clear as if she were standing in front of me. She looked vaguely familiar, but I couldn't recall who she was. I prayed for revelation. God was silent. He tested every bit of patience I had. I was at my wits end when He finally brought her into my life. I won't bore you with the particulars on how we met, but when we did, I nearly passed out."

Amid the scattered laughter, April heard Sheena's quick intake of breath and her smile spread a little wider. She undoubtedly had to be eating her words from the day before.

"So, without further ado, I'd like to introduce you to the woman who's stolen my heart and made me fall in love with her before we even met, April Walker."

The congregation applauded, but when she stood, the only ones left clapping were her family. She held her head high and strutted toward the podium like the diva she was once known for being. Deacon Carl rushed to her side to assist her up the few steps. She didn't have time to think about him touching her. She just needed to get to Richard's outstretched arms. His embrace melted away the rejection she'd felt when she stood. Lady Lillian made her way to them. Richard kissed her cheek and stepped out of the way for them to hug.

Lillian hugged her tightly—no doubt putting on a front for the congregation—and whispered into April's ear, "One point for you. Always keep your head up."

April put up with Lillian's farce and patiently waited for her to have a seat before telling Richard she had something to say. He didn't think twice to step aside and let her speak. She stood in the pulpit, grateful for her degree in Journalism and all the public speaking courses she had taken.

"I've never been one to get involved in gossip or spreading rumors. I feel it's important to get in front of them and cut them off.

Richard is such a wonderful man that he was willing to endure the rumors. I love him too much to let him."

Richard's arm clenched around her waist and he whispered, "You don't have to do this."

"You've done so much for me. Let me do this for you. It's best to be open and honest."

Richard conceded and stood firmly by her side while she continued.

"A few months ago, I met a man. I'll spare you the details, but he didn't like the fact I didn't want to pursue a relationship with him. He followed me home, attacked, and raped me in my front yard. Recently, I discovered that I'm pregnant with his child." April blocked out the shocked gasps and murmuring voices, choosing to focus on the group standing to support her. "Richard was willing to hold my secret and let everyone assume he'd conceived a child out of wedlock, but I couldn't stand by and let his reputation be destroyed. So, yes...I'm pregnant. It is not your pastor's baby. He is still very much the honorable man of God we all know and love." April buried her face into Richard's chest and relished in the comfort he willingly gave.

She heard the applause building, but when he turned her loose, the congregation standing on their feet honoring her was the shock of her life. She gracefully descended the steps and saw Lillian holding up two fingers, signaling two points. She sighed again and retook her seat, finally able to breathe freely. Their secret was out. No more hiding or sneaking around. As soon as church was over, she was going to make Richard take her to a restaurant for an actual date in the light of day.

Richard preached the sermon and left feeling a little less anxiety than he'd entered with. April's announcement was sure to minimize the amount of people leaving the church. He could handle the ones who left because they had their heart set on being first lady. However, losing members because they no longer trusted him was hard to accept. He made his way downstairs and radioed for Deacon Jaleel to hang back with Deacon Carl. He instructed him to give April twenty minutes and then bring her to his office. He rounded the corner to his office and wanted to fire every last one of his deacons for allowing Sister Johnson to get down to his office. She stood in front of his door holding some baked good she had made for him. He'd had enough of her nonsense and couldn't believe she had the audacity to come to his office after he announced his engagement. Richard didn't even acknowledge her. He walked past her, unlocked his door, and left her standing there with his deacons. He heard one of his deacons saying, "Why don't you take that pie to Lady April. I'm sure she'd appreciate the gesture," and couldn't help the laughter that rumbled out of him.

The minister finished the benediction. April stood and grabbed her purse, ready to head out on her date. She caught a glimpse of Cole and Meme making a quick escape before he had to see Lillian. She softly asked the Lord to send him peace and turned to head downstairs. She turned and was overcome with a crowd of people waiting to greet her. She shook hands with each one of them.

She tried her best to ignore the snide, condescending congratulations some offered and focused on the sincere well-wishes.

She saw Sister Johnson coming and braced for the hateful words that were sure to come.

"I baked this pie for Pastor Hawkins." She smiled sweetly, but April wasn't fooled. "I was instructed to give it to you."

"Oh, thank you." She reached for the pie thinking she might've misjudged Sister Johnson until she flipped the pan, slammed it against April's chest, and smeared apple pie all over her new suit.

Everyone around gasped, looking from April to Sister Johnson and back again. April stood stiff as a board, the gooey pie filling clinging to her chest.

"It's still warm. I baked it this morning." She turned and strutted away like it was just a normal day in the world of Sister Johnson.

They were all too stunned to do anything else but watch her walk away. April had never been more embarrassed. The commotion had caught the attention of quite a few people lingering about the sanctuary. She grabbed Sheena's lap scarf, covered her chest, and walked out as fast as she could. The deacons saw her coming and opened Richard's office door without asking any questions. He was laid on his chaise, muscles bulging around his wife beater t-shirt. She was so pissed, she couldn't even enjoy the sight. She dropped the lap scarf and didn't have to explain what happened.

"I'm sorry. I guess she's a little crazier than I thought." He stood and pulled her close, not caring about pie getting on his clothes. He touched his lips to hers and couldn't resist traipsing them down her neck. The sticky sweetness of the pie combined with her skin was heavenly. He trailed his tongue along her clavicle and twirled it down her chest lapping the gooey goodness until he reached the rim of her barely visible camisole.

"Richard," she moaned, secretly thanking Sister Johnson for being such a witch.

He paused, licking the remnant of pie from his lips and looking at her with such hunger she couldn't think straight. "I've never tasted a pie so good in all my life," he whispered, his voice gruff with a desire he definitely needed to work harder containing. He backed away from her chanting, "Three months, three months."

Three months, three months, April harnessed his words using them to calm herself. She closed her eyes and sucked in a slow deep breath, grateful he had made such an unpleasant incident fade into the background. Now she wanted to forego her earlier thoughts of going out for dinner and jump him right there in his office. She opened her eyes and he was sitting on the edge of his desk watching her.

"You okay?"

She shook her head at his knowing smile and turned to leave his office. "I'll be waiting for you to pick me up for dinner. Don't make me wait too long," She tossed back over her shoulder and marched out of his office.

Richard watched her leave and felt lighter than he had in almost a year. In a few short months, he would have a wife and a child, which was all he ever wanted. Every meaningless relationship, the loneliness, and emptiness had all faded with just the thought of April being his wife.

23

Richard's days seemed cluttered with pastoral duties. Before he realized it, four days had flown by and he hadn't seen April. She was so intertwined into his heart that his mind couldn't focus on the task he was trying to complete. Her face, smell, and kiss haunted him. If he didn't get it together, he would have to call in a guest minister to run the church until after they were married.

This is gonna have to be good enough.

He printed the sparse meeting agenda for the citywide revival committee and went to the conference room to wait for everyone to arrive. He stepped into the room and his pulse instantly accelerated.

April.

He rushed toward her, gathering her in his arms before she even realized he was there. "What are you doing here?" He captured her response in a kiss that made her want to forget about a wedding ceremony and sprint to the courthouse.

"I missed you." She smiled up at him and tossed her arms around his neck.

"I missed you, too. What are you doing here so early?"

"Well, I knew you had a meeting. I know you probably haven't eaten all day and won't be able to eat until after Bible class. Everyone else is coming straight from work and is probably in the same boat. So, I brought refreshments."

He looked down at the impressive spread of chicken wings, spring rolls, and vegetable trays and shook his head in disbelief. "You didn't have to do this."

"I know, but I wanted to." She hid her bashful smile and turned back toward the table she was setting. "Sit. I'll bring you a plate."

Her thoughtful gesture made his heart thump a little harder. She had stepped willfully into her role of taking care of him like she'd been doing it her entire life. There was no ulterior motive, just pure love. He stepped forward and reached for her, but thought better of it. Committee members were soon to arrive and might see them.

"Come home with me tonight."

She spun around, hoping she hadn't heard him wrong. She wanted nothing more than to be alone with him.

"You can have the bed and I'll stay on the couch. I just want you near me and to see your face when I wake up."

Her heart bounced into her throat, rendering her incapable of speaking. It was an innocent request, but her mind conjured up the most illicit images that sent her pulse racing. She wasn't where he was spiritually and didn't possess the strength to withstand the way he did.

"I…um," she stuttered, trying to break free from the sexual haze she'd succumbed to. All she could do was nod, trying to coax herself into behaving. She sat at the table watching him eat, wondering how she'd ever managed to live without him.

As attendees started arriving for the meeting, April stood and greeted each one, chitchatting while making plates. Richard watched her decorum and wanted to high-five the Lord for making such an excellent choice. They settled down to call the meeting to order and April tried to make her exit, but Richard made her sit.

The committee chairperson walked in, apologizing for being stuck in traffic. Richard froze right along with everyone else. Word had already spread about what she had done to April. He was shocked at her audacity. "Sister Johnson, please forgive me for not calling you, but after your behavior on Sunday, I didn't think one was warranted. You've been relieved of your leadership duties. Your behavior was not conducive to that of a leader or a child of God for that matter. Next time, I will relieve of your membership at this church."

She was flabbergasted. She stood there stammering for something to say. Her eyes cut to April, crucifying her with just one look. Richard raised an eyebrow, daring her to say something. She spun on her heels and stomped out of the room. April had won this battle, but the war was just beginning.

April crossed her legs and folded her hands in her lap trying to keep from bouncing around with joy. It was a small victory, but a great one. Sister Johnson and every woman like her had better recognize what time it was. Richard was off the market. She wouldn't be intimidated into leaving. She was there to stay.

♾

April sat on the front row during Bible class. She looked like she was paying attention, but she didn't hear a word Richard spoke. He got up to greet the congregation and smiled over at her. The simplistic act warmed her. She sat there fantasizing about him and the life they'd have together. She was so preoccupied with thoughts of him, she didn't realize he had finished teaching until he was standing in front of her and reaching for her hand. She grabbed his hand, hoping he hadn't been standing there long and let him lead her outside.

They rounded the corner to where she had parked and her eyes flew open. She let go of Richard's hand and rushed over to her car. She marched around the vehicle trying to muffle a scream. She looked at Richard and the murderous look on his face matched hers. All four of her tires were slashed.

This is how she wants to play? Then let's play. She unlocked her car to grab a few important things off the back seat and waited for Richard to finish speaking with the deacons before he led her to his car.

Richard huffed as he escorted her to his car; anger surged through him. There was only one person he could think of crazy enough to do something like that: Sister Johnson. He hated to kick someone out of the church. Even the most disturbed soul could be delivered. He had to help Sister Johnson see that even if April was out of the picture, she still wouldn't have a place in his life.

He looked at April watching the scenery pass by. The worried crease between her brows pissed him off even more. "You'll ride to church with me from now on."

She didn't respond, just sat there stewing in her anger. He tried to pull to the side of the road, but she stopped. "I'm fine, just pissed. It's going to take the power of God to keep me from punching her in the face the next time I see her."

"You're above that type of behavior."

She pinned him with a look that said otherwise. He couldn't help but chuckle.

"Okay, I feel you. Sometimes I want to knock a few people upside their head, but if I stoop to their level and go tit for tat, they've actually won. Maintaining my dignity and smiling in their face shows them there is nothing they can do to hurt me. Let Sister Johnson be Sister Johnson—alone, miserable, and no chance in hell at being with me."

"No chance?" She scooted closer to him and leaned her head on his shoulder.

"No chance." He kissed the crown of her head.

"How come you get to say hell and I don't?"

Laughter erupted from his chest. He laughed so hard her head bounced around on his shoulder. "It's all about the context in which you use it."

"So, I can't say Sister Johnson is crazy as hell, but I can tell her to go to hell?"

Richard pulled up in front of his house shaking his head. *What am I going to do with her?* He leaned forward and softly pecked her lips.

April stepped into his house and suddenly felt shy and unsure of how to act. In past relationships, a night at a man's house meant one thing, sweaty bodies slapping. What did Richard expect her to do? He grabbed her hand and led her to the sofa, so she could get comfortable. He removed her coat and went to light the fireplace.

"Richard?" She watched the little flicker of fire build and her desire for him sparked right along with it. "I'm nervous. Should we be alone like this?"

"Don't worry. I haven't had sex in five years. I'm not about to give in now, but I am going to kiss you and hold you." He demonstrated his intent, and in spite of the blazing flames in the fire place, chills shot up her spine. "Can you handle that?"

He removed his tie and shirt and stretched out along the couch. He pulled April down with him. She loved the way his undershirts fit him and swore to buy him an entire box as a wedding present. She fit perfectly between his legs and across his chest. She laid her head flat against him, marveling at how his heart beat matched her own.

"Promise we'll have lots of moments like these once we're married?"

"I promise." His hand slid up her spine to her neck to guide her mouth to his. He took his time savoring her lips. She moaned into his mouth and it unleashed something inside him that he had prided himself on being able to contain. His hands roamed down her back to her waist and gripped her back side. Her eyes flew open in shock. She was helpless to ward off the onslaught of passion consuming her.

Oh God! Her mind pleaded for her to stop him, but her body was prisoner to his assault. She'd been kissed many times, but never had her body been weakened by a man's caress.

After their kiss ended, she trembled against him. He held her close and whispered in her ear, "That was just in case you doubted whether this church boy can fulfill you."

She smiled up at him—still panting—and wondered why he seemed so unaffected. The fact that he could take her to such pleasure and maintain control excited her. She'd never admit to wondering if the sexual part of their marriage would be fulfilling, but he had certainly put those thoughts to bed.

"Give me something else to focus on before I rip through your clothes."

He laughed, but saw the truth in her words. He'd almost taken her to a place of no return. He helped her roll over to rest her back against his chest, hoping the less intimate position would calm her.

They sat enjoying the warmth of the fire in silence. She lifted her arms over her head and rested them across his chest. He stroked his fingers up the length of them. The slow, hypnotic rhythm calmed her.

"Baby, I was thinking. Maybe we could get married a little sooner." His hands were still on her arm and she rushed to finish before he got the wrong impression. "In three months I'll be fat."

"You know I don't care about that."

"Yeah, but I do. What woman wants to be bloated on her wedding day? We could have a nice, small ceremony with family and close friends, fly away for the weekend, and not miss a beat. We wouldn't have to wait three months to enjoy more moments like this. I can plan everything in two weeks."

Richard didn't have to think about it. If she wasn't concerned about a big wedding with hundreds of people, then he wasn't either. He opened his mouth to answer her and the doorbell rang. He shrugged his shoulders at the question written on her face and went to answer the door.

He checked the peephole and couldn't believe his eyes. He ran the face through his memory and couldn't come up with a name, but knew she was a member of his church. *Church member or not, she'd better have a good reason for standing on my doorstep,* he thought. He snatched the door open, letting his face show his annoyance. "May I help?"

She rushed past him, catching him off guard. He stumbled back, barely keeping himself upright. He chased after her, praying to God he didn't kill her when he caught her. She flung her coat off, catching him in the face and cut into his living room before he could reach her. He snatched the coat off his head and marched in behind her. She stood in his living room just as naked as the day she was born. Richard stopped mid-stride and almost swallowed his tongue he was so shocked. He looked to April and could practically see steam coming from her head.

"How can you choose her?" Tears flooded the intruder's cheeks. Her soft, wounded voice was the only thing that kept April from beating her down. "I've loved you for four years."

Richard was speechless. He stood there staring at her trying to figure what he'd done to her, Sister Johnson, and the dozens of other women who had staked their claim on him to make them believe he had feelings for him. He didn't even know the woman's name, yet there she stood professing to have loved him for years.

April stomped over, grabbed the woman's coat, and threw it in her face with as much force as she could. "Get out of here!"

"Is it because she'll sleep with you? I can give you what you need."

"Lady," April stepped into her face so close she stepped on the woman's foot. "You have no idea who you are messing with. I suggest you get the hell out of here while you can still walk out."

"April…" She spun around and silenced Richard with a look that threatened to cut him if he said another word.

The woman stepped around April—taking advantage of her distraction—and latched on to Richard. She flung her limbs around him, pinning his arms to his side. She bucked against him, fighting off his attempts to get free. She tightened her arms around his neck and legs around his waist, clinging to him like her life depended on it.

April had reached her limit. Richard was being too passive. She understood his not wanting to hurt a woman, but she was not bound by the same constraints. She grabbed a fist full of the woman's hair and yanked so hard hairs snapped from her scalp. She had no choice but to let go of Richard. Her arms flailed, slapping April across the shoulders and face. April didn't let that stop her. She tugged until the woman's feet cooperated and followed her to the front door. April tossed her onto the porch not caring who saw her.

The door slam echoed throughout the house. April stood there silently staring at the door, trying to process what happened.

Is that what everybody thinks…I'm sleeping with him?

She didn't know why she had allowed the words of a woman who was obviously delusional to affect her, but she couldn't help it. Maybe the woman was justified in thinking she had a place in Richard's life. She did, after all, know where he lived and felt comfortable enough to come without her clothes on.

I've loved you for four years. Those words replayed through her mind and April's heart sank. Was it possible that Richard had lied to her, misrepresenting the man he was? Did he string that

215

woman along and then toss her aside for the next best thing? That kind of heartbreak would drive any woman insane.

"April baby, I'm sorry." He reached for her and she backed away.

"Yeah, I know." She shook her head and marched off to gather her things. She needed to get away from him, so she could think. She came back to the door and he was blocking her exit.

"If you think I'm going to let you walk out on me again, you really don't know me."

"Richard, please move."

"Some lunatic barges her way in here and you're just going to take what she says and run with it instead of having faith in the man that's shown you his character time and time again."

She turned her head away, too ashamed to let him look in her eyes.

"It's about to get real at the church." He stepped toward her again nuzzling her neck and backing her up against the wall. "She may not be the only woman acting crazy. You can't tuck tail and run every time." Without second thought, she dropped her things to the floor and jumped on him wrapping her arms and legs around him silently pleading for him to forgive her.

"She was all over you." Her strangled voice was barely above a whisper. She kissed and touched him everywhere that woman had, trying to erase her scent. "What if I wasn't here? Would you have been able to get rid of her?"

"I hope so. If not, I would've called the cops."

"I'm sorry for overreacting. I've just never seen a woman so hurt over a man she never had. She looked as tore up as I did the week we weren't together."

"I hear you, but I love you. That should be enough to keep all those crazy thoughts out of your head."

"Sorry." She shook her head, looking around the room trying to come up with the words to explain what had gotten in to her. "I never had a man that I cared enough about to get jealous over." She shrugged her shoulders and hoped he understood.

"I hear you." Call him crazy, but he loved the fact that she had never been tied to one man. It meant he was the only one to penetrate her heart. She might not have been pure in the physical sense, but her soul was a virgin to love and he was her first. "Can we act like she never showed up and continue with our evening?"

She nodded against his shoulder and he carried her back into the living room. He stretched back across the sofa, admonishing himself to keep his hands and lips to himself. That kiss had tried every last ounce of his control. His abstinence wouldn't survive another. Maybe getting married in two weeks wasn't a bad idea.

"So, our wedding…how would you plan it?"

"My favorite color is purple, so I'd definitely go with that. Your tux would be gray, my dress simple and elegant, but definitely not white. We'd have only a maid of honor and a best man. The ceremony would be held At Sheena's, as well as the reception."

"Sounds nice already."

"Yeah, it does." She scooted up his body to connect their lips and he placed a finger to her lips, halting her pursuit.

"Let's do it."

"Really?"

He nodded and a smile spread so broad across her face that he couldn't help but smile back. Before he could do or say anything else, she rolled off his chest to the floor and was digging through her purse for her phone.

For over an hour, he listened to her make call after call. The more she talked, the more animated she became. Her arms flailed around as she spoke. He had never seen her so excited. He felt joy emanating from her. He had never been happier.

24

April pulled up in front of Cole's house, praying he had gotten over his over protectiveness and would agree to let Meme join her for lunch. She hadn't even made it out of the car before Meme rushed out the door and hopped in the passenger seat.

"What's wrong?"

"He's not home. He's out playing ball with your man and his boys."

April shook her head and pulled away from the curb. "He's going to be pissed when he gets home."

"I know, but maybe he'll see I'm fine on my own. Vanessa is in jail. Sahara is dead. No one else wants to hurt me. I'll be fine."

"I agree, but you have to understand where he's coming from. He pushed you away and right into the trap of a lunatic. You could've died."

"But I didn't. God spared my life and I want to live it, not stay locked up in the house worried about what could happen."

"All right, you just make sure he knows this was all you. I don't want my future brother-in-law mad at me." Silence settled over the car and April thought maybe she had offended her. She opened her mouth to apologize, but Meme turned to her with hurt etched on her face.

"I don't think Cole wants to marry me."

"Why would you say that? I've never seen a man more obsessed with a woman than Cole is with you."

"I know he loves me and wants me. Until me, he was dead set against relationships. I think he likes the relationship but doesn't want to be legally tied down. I'm trying not to be, but I'm so jealous of you right now. You're getting married before me."

April patted her hand to silence the anguish she heard in Meme's voice. "All I can say is talk to him. Try to see things from his perspective. It must be difficult to suddenly want something you'd never even thought of and have no idea how to obtain it. Have you tried setting a date?"

"I asked him what season he wanted to get married in. He said he didn't care." She blotted tears from the corner of her eyes and April fought hard to hold in laughter.

"Girl, that doesn't mean he doesn't want to marry you. It means he doesn't care what season it is as long as he's marrying you. I don't know Cole that well, but I'm a journalist. We are nosy and very observant. He is a brutish, brooding, big baby. He will chop a man off at the knees, kill him with a simple look, and then come home and curl up in your lap. He'll move heaven and earth for you."

She pulled the car into a parking space and turned her full attention toward Meme, explaining what she had in mind to propel Cole into action.

They walked into the restaurant, both giddy over things to come. They had a lot of work to do and a short time to do it. Meme was so excited, she didn't see who they were meeting for lunch until they were almost to the table. She turned toward April with a facial expression that asked if she was crazy.

April answered her unspoken question by saying, "We are going to be family and I want it to be a happy one." She kissed Lillian's cheek, took her seat, and waited for Meme to do the same.

"April, I appreciate what you are trying to do, but I shouldn't be here. Cole will be beyond pissed when he finds out I had lunch with his mother."

"Who's going to tell him?" April perused the menu, giving Meme time to process the situation. She slid into her seat and April smiled at the small victory toward helping her soon-to-be brother find some peace. She looked at Lillian and bit back her laugh. *Guess that's three points.*

The appetizer had barely arrived when Meme's phone started buzzing like crazy. She checked the screen and her wide eyes shot over to April, imploring about what she should do.

"That's all you. I had nothing to do with you breaking out of prison." She laughed and Meme playfully punched her arm. "You better answer before he sends out the search and rescue squad."

Meme rolled her eyes, sent his call to voicemail, and sent him a text instead. She flashed April the screen, showing her the message she was sending. April almost choked on her water.

April drug me out to lunch. Be home soon.

Not even a minute later, April's phone buzzed with a text. She shook her head and flashed Meme the screen.

Take her home before my brother has a heart attack. See you when you get here.

They hurried and finished their appetizers, had the entrees boxed, and rushed out the door. If Cole wanted to end their lunch, then they would just have to finish at his place. April smiled at her plan, turned to Lillian, and instructed her to follow them.

Meme almost swallowed her tongue. She stood outside the car refusing to get in until April changed her mind.

April revved her engine, threatening to leave Meme if she didn't get in. "Trust me, this will be good." Meme flopped into the car rolling her eyes and cursing April under her breath. April pulled from the curb, checked her rearview mirror, made sure Lillian was following, and prayed her actions didn't blow up in her face.

৩✖৩

They walked through the front door and April's heart climbed into her throat. Meme led them into the living room and went straight to Cole's lap. April went to Richard's, giving both men time to process Lillian being there. April and Richard watched

Meme rubbing Cole's chest and whispering in his ear trying to calm the beast threatening to break free. Lillian ignored his homicidal look and made her way to the armchair.

"April invited me to lunch and surprised me by bringing Meme along."

"Get out!" Cole barked making everyone in the room jump.

"Shhh." Meme coaxed his face toward her and connected their lips. If things got out of control, she had a few choice words waiting for April.

"You have every right to hate me." Lillian picked at an invisible piece of lint on her skirt. "I don't deserve your forgiveness, but you certainly deserve the peace that comes with forgiving."

"So, now you're concerned about what I deserve? At four years old I deserved a mother, but you were too busy running behind some man to care. Don't sit here acting concerned for my wellbeing."

"Is that really what you think, that I didn't care about you?"

April and Richard sat back watching everything play out like it was a movie. April marveled at how Meme's caress soothed Cole and wondered if she could have that same effect on Richard.

"Cheating on your father was horrible, but I will not apologize for falling in love. I loved your father, but he didn't know how to love me back. I should've divorced him, but you needed a father, so I stayed."

April's eyes nearly popped out of her head when Lillian got up and sat next to Cole. If nothing else, Lillian was ballsy. Cole looked so pissed he scared April, and she was clear across the room.

"He fronted me about cheating and called me every degrading name in the book. I was ashamed and I was angry."

"Angry? You were angry? You had no right to be!" Cole lifted Meme off his lap and placed her on the other side of him.

Richard did the same and went to sit on the coffee table in front of them.

"Do you know what life was like without a mother? Or, what it was like living with a father who turned to alcohol to cope with losing the only woman he loved?"

"He didn't love me. You were too young to see how things really were. He was so verbally abusive. I just wanted to be loved. No matter how wrong it was, I found love."

"And left me in the process." His chest deflated in defeat. Cole had lost the fight in him and his anger turned to sorrow.

"Yes I left, but I came back the next day. You were gone." She touched her hand to his cheek. He didn't budge and she lost her composure. Emotion strangled her voice and the tears she had been holding back streamed down her face. "I walked around that house calling your name. I went to your room and all your clothes and toys were gone. I lost it. I checked under beds, in cabinets, and in the backyard, because I refused to accept that you weren't there. I spoke with the neighbors, called your father's family, and no one had heard from him. I searched for months and stressed myself so bad I nearly miscarried Richard. I was hospitalized, but as soon as I delivered him, I was right back at it until I left him in the store while I was out putting up flyers. I was driving myself crazy looking for one child and neglecting the other. I asked God to help me find peace with the fact I'd never see you again. I'm sorry. I'll never have the words to explain how much..."

Cole rose to his feet, his six-foot-four-inch stature towering over everyone. He didn't utter a word, he just turned and walked out of the room. Meme jumped up and followed behind him.

Richard moved to comfort his mother, but April jumped in front of him. "I'm sorry. This is my fault."

"Don't be sorry. I got to touch my baby again. It's more than I ever hoped for. He may never forgive me, but at least he knows the truth. I need to apologize to you." She patted April's hand and stood to leave. "You're exactly what my son needs." April escorted her to the door hoping she was right and praying she hadn't made things worse.

ၐﻬ

"It's okay to forgive her." Meme walked up behind him, wrapped her arms around him, and rested her head against his back. "Let's start our new life together free of all the hang-ups from our past."

"I don't know how. I've hated her for so long. That's all I know how to do."

"It's easy. Try to put yourself in her shoes. It looks like she's tortured herself for years imagining what your life was like without her. Do the same. Could your father have been difficult to live with? Verbal abuse can be just as damaging as physical. And, when you're done considering all that, remember, she came back for you."

"I'll try as long as you promise me something." He turned toward her and lifted her into his arms. Instinctively, her legs wrapped around his waist and arms around his neck.

"Anything for you."

"Tell me where you're going before leaving the house. I know I've been keeping a tight leash, but I still have nightmares of you being limp in my arms with your blood all over my clothes. When I came home and you weren't here, my mind went back to that day."

"I promise, but I'm going back to work and back to life. I'm better now. You can't keep me locked away." She rested her forehead against his and he quickly found her lips. He unleashed his tension with that kiss. *She's right*, Cole conceded.

"I love you."

"I love you, too."

25

"Are you having strippers at your bachelor party?" Richard almost cut himself while shaving. His eyes flashed to April's reflection in the mirror and he had to laugh at her nervous fidgeting.

"Are you having them at yours?"

"Richard," she whined, throwing a two-year-old temper tantrum and plopped down on the toilet. "Don't make fun of me."

"No, I'm not having strippers, but a little lap dance sounds nice." He gathered her in his arms and molded her against him. "This time tomorrow you'll be my wife and we'll be alone in our Vegas hotel suite. A lap dance would set things off nice."

Just the thought of revealing herself to him set her on edge. She suckled his bottom lip and moaned, "You have no idea what type of woman you're marrying."

"I know exactly who you are and just thinking about it had me taking cold showers all week."

"Mm, a shower with you sounds really nice."

"I'll be sure to add it to my list of things to do tomorrow night." He groaned into their kiss, intensifying the passion until he felt her trembling against him.

"I have a few things on my list, too." She was tempted to show him a few, but was saved by the ringing doorbell. She trailed behind him, traversing past the boxes filled with her things they'd moved in earlier that day.

She stood behind him looking at the men who had come to pick him up and couldn't help the whine that came out of her mouth. "Baby, don't go. Let's stay home and watch a movie together."

He turned back toward her and kissed her passionately as he had done before. He didn't care who was watching.

"Come on, playa; you got a lifetime for all that." Richard shook his head at Cole and the roar of laughter behind him. He tried his best to fight off the arms pulling him away from April. They pulled him out onto the porch and practically carried him to the car.

Paul stayed behind, looking at April and shaking his head. "Whiny baby, just like your sister."

April laughed as he backed away to join his friends. She rushed into the bathroom to put the finishing touches on her outfit before her own ride showed up. She snapped a couple bathroom mirror selfies and sent them to Richard.

Are you sure you want to let all this out for a night on the town by herself?

He replied back almost instantly, *Behave or I'll add a spanking to my list for tomorrow night.*

Mmmm, don't threaten me with a good time, she added a winking face and powered her phone off.

Her doorbell rang and she dropped the phone into her clutch purse. In spite of how she tried to get Richard to stay home, she was excited about her night out with the girls. She hadn't partied since the night she was raped. She was ashamed of the places she had been and things she had done, but those things were now behind her. She was anxious to see how the other side partied.

She opened the front door and was greeted with a loud, "Hey girl."

Their excitement amped her up even more. Her response was just as exuberant. They rushed her out to the limo in a whirlwind of smooches. April relaxed back into the plush leather seat trying to keep her mind off Richard and enjoy her night.

They pulled up to a salon and she tried to hide her disappointment. She didn't know what to expect—certainly not a party like she was used to—but sitting around a salon wasn't it. She stepped through the doors feeling like her leopard-print, peep-toe pumps would've been best left in the box. They walked through the salon and into the spa area, opened the door, and loud music bum rushed her ears. Waiters welcomed them with flutes of champagne. April's mouth dropped open as she watched her sister and the super spiritual clique grab a glass and bop to the music as they made themselves comfortable in spa chairs.

"What? We do know how to let our hair down on occasion." Sheena tossed her purse to the side and dug into the platter of hors d'oeuvres sitting next to her.

"You should've seen your face when we pulled up," Meme giggled, and passed April a glass. "Sparkling cider for the mommy-to-be."

Yeah, let's take real good care of my rapist's baby. April rolled her eyes and shook off the negative thought. She grabbed the glass and joined the other ladies. Camilla, Delisa, Latrice, Candice, Sheena, and Meme had outdone themselves and definitely exceeded her expectations.

❧

Richard leaned against the wall next to Cole with his pool cue between his legs supporting his outstretched arms. "What's up, playa? Why you standing by yourself?"

"I have to be losing my mind," he laughed and rubbed his hand across his face. "There's a bar and I don't want a drink. Beautiful honies over there trying to catch my eye and all I can think about is Meme."

Richard looked over at the women Cole was referring to. Apparently looking in their direction must've been invitation to join them. They strutted over with their intentions written all over their face.

"What are you fine brothers doing out alone tonight?"

Paul, Tim, Jaleel, and Marlon flashed their wedding rings and kept right on shooting pool.

They turned toward Richard and Cole like a pack of vultures swarming over their next meal. "What about you two? I don't see any rings."

"This is my bachelor party." Richard tried to be diplomatic, but the hungry look in her eyes was turning his stomach.

"And I'm engaged."

She trailed her finger down the middle of Cole's chest." Good, means there's still time."

Cole grabbed her wrist and gave her a look that would've made a smarter woman back off.

"Ooh, I like it a little rough." She smiled and leaned into him.

"Well, I don't like it trashy." He let her go and walked away without giving her a second thought.

"Sorry." Richard stepped around her to join his boys.

"What about you? Down for a little fun tonight?"

"We aren't really here for that tonight. Thanks for the interest though. Next time you think about approaching a man, consider this: men are predators. When his food is tossed at him, it'll tame him and diminish his natural animal instincts. When he has to hunt, stalk, and chase down his prey, it makes the reward of the catch all the more satisfying and keeps him at the top of the food chain. Anything worth having is worth the pursuit it takes to obtain it. Know your worth and make him work for it." He walked away even more grateful that he didn't have to deal with the dating scene. He joined the trash talking at the pool table.

"Glad you decided to join us," Tim laughed at Cole. "Standing over there like someone stole your puppy."

"I thought I had it bad." Richard shook his head at the sappy look on Cole's face.

"Y'all keep laughing. You didn't see what Meme looked like walking out the house."

"April sent me a picture. I almost made y'all turn back around."

"Man, Sheena had on these heels," Paul exhaled in frustration as he brought his soda to his mouth, quickly silencing obscene thoughts from spewing out of his mouth.

"Eight ball, corner pocket." Tim aimed up his shot and the conversation paused. The angle was impossible, but Tim had shown them he wasn't an amateur like the rest of them. The cue ball sailed across the table, sure enough knocking the eight ball into the corner pocket.

"You know…" Cole put his stick back into the rack. "I know where they went tonight." They all turned to him shaking their heads. "What? Nothing's happening up in here that we want to be a part of. I'm not down for getting beat all night. I say we pay them a little visit."

Richard looked around, his vision clouded with cigarette smoke, men-hungry women salivating at him like he was a rib eye steak, Tim racking up for another game, and the music was horrible.

Yeah there is definitely some place I'd rather be. He laid his pool stick on the table. One by one, his boys followed suit and marched out behind him.

ço∞ɔ

"April, girl you are crazy," Delisa hollered and threw her head back laughing. To say they'd been a little liberal with the champagne was an understatement. For a group of women who didn't drink on the regular, two flutes had resulted in the group of them falling out of their seats laughing at April.

April strutted around in her four-inch heels sucking her stomach as far in as her baby bump would allow. She sucked her cheeks in and stuck out her breasts, bouncing them around to accent each word she spoke. "Praise the Lord, Pastor." She sashayed around switching so hard it appeared she would likely break a hip. "I baked you another pie, because that's the only way I can get you to notice me." She patted her breasts, making sure they were firmly in place and high enough for the world to see.

"Girl, I still don't know how you walked away so calmly after she threw that pie on you. I would've snatched her bald."

"Candy sweetie, that isn't a lot of snatching."

The room erupted with laughter. They were high fiving and cutting on Sister Johnson so bad they grew weak. The stylists and manicurist had given up on trying to provide services and just joined the party.

"Okay Meme, break it down for me again," Wayne, the salon owner, joined in the fun. "Please explain this crazy family circle y'all got going on."

"It's simple, sweetie. Sheena and April are sisters. Camilla and Delisa are sisters, and they're cousins. Sheena is married to Paul whose brother, Tim, is married to Camilla. Delisa is married to Jaleel who is my cousin. Latrice, you know, is married to my brother. Now I am engaged to Cole who happens to be brothers with Richard. He rounds out our family circle by marrying April, which brings us right back to the beginning."

I guess we do complete the circle, April laughed to herself. She didn't know how many times she had laughed at Sheena and Camilla for being biological cousins and sisters by marriage. She'd messed around and got herself involved in the same circle.

Don't talk.

Just listen.

Jodeci crooned through the speakers. The ladies screamed and flooded the center of the room like they were at a live concert

"Turn that up." April threw her hands in the air, closed her eyes, and let the song take control. The sway of her curves flowed with the rhythm. She felt loose like she'd been drinking.

Sorry I left you,

Left you cryin'.

But since you've been gone,

I've been all alone.

'Cause all of my tears,

You know they left me drownin'.
Please, baby I'm beggin'
For you to stay at home.

Male voices entered the room singing the lyrics. April spun around to see what was going on. Richard walked in leading a pack of brothers singing so off key they would make dogs howl. April nearly broke her neck trying to get to him. He cradled her in his arms, pressing herself against the length of him. Presumably, the other men followed his lead, but he had tuned them out. Their bodies rocked in a slow, hypnotic dance, hinting at what was to come in less than twenty-four hours. She was putty in his hands, pliable for him to do what he pleased.

"What are you doing here?"

He didn't bother to answer, he simply showed her. She consumed his every thought, sent his pulse into overdrive with the slightest touch, and completed him so perfectly it seemed as though the Lord gathered all of his lacking qualities and poured them into her. That's why he was there. He couldn't get enough of her. He wrapped his hand in her hair, tugging it back to expose the smooth column of her neck.

"Are you ready to submit to me?"

The vibration of his voice resonated throughout her entire being. His dominance weakened her, and she clung to him for support. She was too far gone under his spell to respond. His lips trailed up her neck and along her jawline in pursuit her lips. He moved in for the kill—to taste the sweetness of her mouth—but by the grace of God, the song went off. The faster tempo did nothing to dissipate the haze surrounding them.

She watched him walk away. Her chest heaved, signifying that she was in fact ready to submit. She would bow to him, kneel before him, and cater to his every need.

"I know this isn't the same April that told me to sex Cole out my system and keep it moving."

April spun around to Meme's smirking face. "Pastor Hawkins is putting it on you. Look at you, can't even speak." She laughed and guided April to the spa chair Richard was sitting in. "It's okay. Look around you, just about every woman in here has met her match." April climbed onto Richard's lap and did just that.

Until she had met Paul, Sheena used to be so holy a man couldn't get near her. Delisa was as wild as April once was and Jaleel wore her down to the point that she couldn't live without him. Then, there was Camilla whose heart beat so strongly for Tim that fate led them back to each other. Latrice had succumbed to love during one of the most horrifying times of her life. Lastly and most astonishing was Meme who had sworn off all men, but one encounter with Cole changed all that. Yes, it was unquestionably okay for her to have fallen for Richard the way she had. He was all she ever wanted. All the resistance to relationships and hopping from man to man was just her heart rebelling against being subjected to the wrong men.

April leaned back, kicked off her shoes, and finally sank her feet into the basin of hot water as Richard's arms slid around her. She was in heaven. The world would be perfect if her best friend would find someone. She scanned the room and found Candice sitting alone in a corner. The look on her face and the champagne glasses in each hand said it all. She was lonely and a room full of couples was the last place she wanted to be.

26

The incessant knocking on her door was driving April insane. She just needed thirty more minutes of sleep. She had tossed and turned for hours. She was as anxious as a kid on Christmas Eve. It was her wedding day and she was marrying the man of her dreams. He was the only man who had ever challenged her to be a better person and had loved her without trying to take her to bed.

That thought propelled her from the bed. She stumbled across the room trying to shake off the grogginess and snatched the door open. She smiled at the woman standing before her and enveloped her in a hug that left them both sniffling. Two weeks had gone by so fast. It was the day that would change their lives forever.

Before they could dwell on it too long, they were caught up in a flurry of stylists, estheticians, and manicurists, most of whose services should've been done the night before but was delayed by an influx of lovesick men. They allowed her a quick shower before they went to work. Within three hours, April was slipping into her wedding gown. She was going to settle for something simple since it was such short notice, but Sheena spared no expense. From the dress to the decorations to the food, Sheena had gone all out. "It doesn't have to look like a backyard wedding," is what she'd said. April looked out her bedroom window over all the activity buzzing about. Sheena had definitely stayed true to her word. The yard was transformed to a garden oasis filled with every white flower imaginable. Strewn in among them, the most beautiful African violets she had ever seen. Cherub fountains sat on opposite sides of the floral wedding arch. The small section of seats for her guests was starting to fill up and the butterflies in her stomach took flight. She took a deep breath, praying morning sickness didn't visit. She then asked everyone to leave the room.

Any minute, her father would be up to walk her down the aisle; it was all becoming real. She would soon be Mrs. Richard Hawkins. She fought off the doubt that she couldn't handle it and let her heart take control. She loved that man more than she ever thought possible. From the day they met, she had been enamored with him. The circumstances under which God had brought them together left no room for doubt on whether she was his.

There was a knock on the door and she turned to the only woman left in the room.

It's time, they silently spoke to each other through exchanged glances and answered the door together.

Richard stood holding his breath at the arch between his mentor and his brother. All morning he had battled the thought that April wasn't going to show up. She was going to think about him, all the drama and responsibility that came with his position, and run. He pulled himself together and focused on her heart. She loved him and would take on the world for him. She'd said as much and it showed in her dedication to his ministry.

Right on cue, the wedding march began to play, their guests stood, and the French doors opened. April stepped through the doorway forcing herself to stay put for the photographers as rehearsed. She locked eyes with Richard and wanted nothing more than to do away with all the rigmarole of a ceremony, run to him, say *I do,* and be his wife. She looked back to the woman waiting behind her and signaled her to step forward. Meme entered the garden wearing a gown just as beautiful as April's. April smiled at all the shocked gasps and stepped aside, allowing her a moment with the cameras.

Cole sucked in a breath and looked at Richard questioning what was going on. Richard touched a hand to his back and turned to him to explain, but the tears he saw stirred his own.

Marlon took his place next to Cole as best man. "When a man possesses a woman and allows her to possess him in return…when he dedicates his life to loving her and ensuring her safety, she should be his wife. Don't you think it's time you married my little sister?"

Cole looked to Meme and the tears he had fought back trickled down his cheek. She had held him captive from the day they had met. His desire for her had never dwindled. His answer was easy. He nodded and held his breath as she made her way toward him.

April tuned Meme and Cole out and followed her heart to Richard. She reached the spot where she was supposed to pause and wait for him to come get her. Her father had to grip her arm a little tighter to keep her there.

"Take good care of my baby girl."

"I plan on it, for the rest of my life."

She watched them shake hands and anxiously held her breath. *Touch me, hold me*, she thought. His hand brushing her shoulder felt like heaven and she couldn't help the tear that escaped her eye. He kissed it from her cheek and led them to their future.

Sheena had put so much time and effort into making everything beautiful, April didn't care about any of it. The flowers, the music, and the dress were all overshadowed by seven words. "I now pronounce you husband and wife." As the minister spoke those words an unspeakable joy flowed over her. She flung her arms around Richard's neck—not waiting for permission—and planted her lips on his. He returned her kiss with just as much passion as she gave and had to be patted on the back to turn her loose.

Richard checked his watch for the fifth time. He wanted to pat himself on the back for scheduling their flight to depart just hours after the ceremony. He had thirty more minutes of pretending he was having a good time before they had to change clothes. He appreciated all the trouble everyone had gone through to make the day special, but all he could think of was being alone with his wife—holding her, touching her, and making love to her for the first time.

Her gown flowed across her curves, tempting him as she walked down the aisle toward him. He had schooled his face into an impassive expression, but his heart pounded ferociously. He was lucky to have made it through his vows. He was brain-dead and didn't know how he had managed to string words together.

He watched everyone dancing, having a good time, and enjoying the food. He had barely touched his plate and hadn't gotten out of his seat since he danced with April. His eyes followed her as she moved about the yard talking and laughing. She was his. All the loneliness was over. God had blessed him with an amazing woman to spend the rest of his life with. She looked up and caught him staring. She blew him a kiss. He caught it and planted it against his chest.

Fifteen more minutes. He checked his watch again and stood to go say his goodbyes. He found Cole and Meme huddled up in the same corner they'd been in since the first dance. "Are you going to let her come up for air long enough for me to say bye?" He stood there shaking his head, waiting for them to acknowledge his presence. He finally tapped Cole on the back of the head. "Come on now, playa, she's your wife now. She's not going anywhere."

Cole pulled back to look at her. "I know. Today is the best day of my life. I just hate you felt you had to surprise me like this. I would've married you while you were in the hospital, but I didn't want to steal your perfect wedding."

"It would've been as perfect as today simply because you were there." Meme rested her forehead against his. She couldn't believe she was finally his wife. Having him made all the hell she'd been through worthwhile.

"Well, I'm gonna let you get back to whatever you're over here doing. I just wanted to say bye before we head on out."

"You're leaving? You mean we don't have to stay?" Cole set Meme aside and jumped to his feet.

Richard grabbed him by the arm before he could rush off. He laughed, whispering for Cole's ears only, "What are you rushing off for? It's not like you haven't been doing the dirty deed all this time anyway."

"Yeah, but like you pointed out, she's my wife now. I'm surprised you're not somewhere ending your hiatus as we speak."

Richard laughed and shook his head. There was so much he could say but left it alone. "Well, I heard Marlon blessed you with a trip to Paris. Be safe and do some sightseeing," Richard paused mid-sentence and watched their mother approach.

"Congratulations, I'm so happy for both of you."

He accepted her hug and kiss, and held his breath as she turned to Cole.

Cole leaned forward and pecked her cheek. "I promised Meme I'd try, but I can't really promise you anything." He grabbed Meme's hand and walked away leaving Lillian a blubbering mess.

Richard tried to comfort her, but she shooed him away. "Get out of here and enjoy your new life."

He passed her a handkerchief and went to find April.

April felt him behind her. His presence stole the words from her mouth and she turned toward him, leaving Candice wondering what she'd been about to say.

"Hi." She leaned into him, instantly wrapping her arms around his neck.

"It's time to go." He led her around the yard to finish saying their goodbyes and they escaped up to their room to change for their flight.

He shut the door behind them and turned to her while removing his tie. He tossed it aside along with his jacket and stepped toward her. Her hands went to his waist and he grabbed her wrist. "You do that and we'll miss our flight."

She ignored his warning and unfastened his belt. Slowly, she eased his zipper down and her hand crept past the elastic waistband of his briefs. Her fingers grazed his flesh and the whoosh of oxygen leaving his body brushed across her cheek.

"Keep it up and you'll get what you're asking for." She kept at it, weakening his resolve to wait until they made it to their hotel.

His hands found the zipper of her dress and he forced some restraint, so he wouldn't rip it off. It folded down at the bodice revealing her bare breast. She should've been afraid of the growl that rumbled out of him, but it didn't deter her. He gripped a handful of her fleshy mounds and lowered his head to it. She threw her head back moaning in anticipation and nearly jumped out of her skin when someone banged on the door.

Richard watched her back away from him, stuffing herself back into her dress and wanted to strangle whoever was at the door. "Who is it?" He rolled his eyes at the laughter that responded, adjusted his clothes, and snatched the door open.

"My bad, little brother. I didn't mean to interrupt the festivities." Meme punched him in the ribs and gave him a look that shut him up.

"I thought you left."

"We're trying to, but Sheena is trippin'. We have to leave at the same time. So, if you don't mind…"

Richard slammed the door in his face. Cole's laughter vibrated through the door. "I guess I owe you one. Just don't make me wait too long."

"Can you wait a couple more hours?" Richard turned to April, totally understanding the look on her face.

NO! "Of course."

Richard kissed the crown of her head and went to retrieve their clothes.

245

Cole and Meme were waiting for them at the bottom of the stairs. April descended with the newfound grace of a queen trailing behind her king. They led the way to the front door. They stepped out onto the porch and were assailed by a cloud of bubbles. Page and Paul Jr. stood on each side of the door cranking handheld bubble blowers and having the time of their lives. Their families were lined up cheering their well-wishes.

April thought she'd cried enough for one day, but she misted up again. She hugged her parents, thanking them for putting up with her drama and never giving up on her. She thanked Sheena for organizing such a beautiful ceremony, posed for parting photos, and allowed Richard to lead her away.

Richard made her sit on the opposite side of the limo. If he touched her while confined to such a small space, he wouldn't be able to stop. He didn't want to get arrested for sexing his wife in front of the airport. He didn't fare any better sitting next to her on the plane.

"You smell good enough to eat."

"I taste even better," she shot back at him, daring him to sample her.

He inhaled a deep breath and rested his head back against the seat. April pulled out a magazine to read on the short flight. She crossed her legs and ran her foot up the back of his calf. She turned the page and smoothed her elbow along his forearm. She rested her palm on his thigh and twirled lazy circles just above his knee.

Richard leaned toward her whispering in her ear, "I'm going to make you pay for every single touch. I have five years to make up for. I suggest you get some rest while you can."

Her hand stilled and she did nothing to hide the rush of heat that coursed through her.

Richard sat back and followed the flight attendant's instruction to fasten his seatbelt. April was too flustered to comprehend what was being said, so he reached over and buckled it for her.

ల%

She had left the planning of their getaway up to Richard. When they entered the suite, she was so glad she had. Candles were already burning, African Violets trailed from the entrance to the bath, where the tub had already been filled. He led her there, slowly tugging at the buttons on her blouse. He undressed her and took a moment to admire her body in the candlelight's glow. His eyes roamed the places he longed to touch.

"Richard," she moaned, but he silenced her and helped her step into the water. She was on fire and if she sat there too long, she would boil the bath water. He had planned to let her bathe alone, but couldn't resist joining her. He held her eyes as he disrobed. She scooted to the rim of the tub anticipating the big reveal.

She kneeled before him as he joined her. She raised her hands and trailed them down the rippled contours of his abs, worshiping his perfection. He kneeled with her and pulled her toward him as he reclined back. His hands were everywhere and his lips not too far behind. The slight nip of his teeth sent her into overdrive. She straddled his lap vowing to let him take it slow the next time. Right then she desperately needed to connect with him. The ferocity of their love making sent water splashing over both sides of the tub. She opened her mouth to moan, scream, curse him out, or something, but didn't have the oxygen to do so. She collapsed against his chest and rode out the wave.

"What was that?" she panted once he'd calmed.

"Did I hurt you?" He searched her eyes for the truth.

"I enjoyed every minute of it. You just shocked me."

He raised an eyebrow at her and tapped her backside. "Let's go to bed and I'll do more than shock you."

She stood and stepped out of the tub, swaying her hips for his enjoyment as she walked toward the door. She looked back over her shoulder and barely above a whisper asked, "What do you want me to do?"

Her voice quivered and he loved it. He rose from the tub and stalked toward her. "Lay across the bed, face down, no peeking or I'll blindfold you."

His weight dipped the bed and April held her breath in anticipation of his next move. Hot oil splashed along her spine, tingling as he smeared it along her skin awakening every nerve from her shoulders to the soles of her feet.

"Most men fail to realize that making love is an art form. It takes preparation. No painter puts brush to canvas without first prepping his palette." He rolled her over and trickled more oil. He traced the path of oil with his finger and the tingling that ensued made her squirm with need as if those desires hadn't been quenched moments ago. "It takes paying close attention to detail and being able to see what the average eye doesn't. Most importantly—" His fingers ventured between her thighs and parted them for his entrance, "It takes being able to manipulate your material into doing exactly what you want it to do." Her back arched off the bed and she called on God for help. There was no reprieve. She reveled in the slow, glorious rhythm he'd created. Her eyes rolled back as the same crescendo built inside her. She whined his name begging for mercy, but he was relentless. She dug her nails into his back and gave into the release.

"My God," April panted as he rolled her over to rest upon his chest. "What have I gotten myself into?"

His laughter rumbled through his chest and against her cheek.

"Oh, that's funny? Let me get a nap and we'll see if you can take it as well as you can dish it out."

"So, you need a nap?"

She could hear the smile in his voice and she would definitely make him pay for being so cocky, but she needed sleep first.

27

Every morning after their wedding, April woke up to Richard working her body into a masterpiece. They had returned home after the weekend, but stayed secluded up in their bedroom connecting so deeply their hearts were in perfect sync. Each time was better than the last. She realized she had never made love until him. Even when he delved into his suitcase, pulled out handcuffs, and shackled her to the bed, he was still attentive, intense, and wonderful. That morning was no different.

"I love you so much,"

"I love you, too," she purred back, still reeling from their lovemaking. "Let's not leave the house today. Cancel your meetings and let someone else teach Bible class."

"It's not that easy, but I promise after this revival, I'll take you anywhere in the world for two weeks. I've already instructed my secretary to block off the days on my schedule. You pick the place and I'll work on everything else." He rolled out of bed and went into the adjoining bath.

It sounded nice—two weeks alone with him—but she was totally unprepared for the emotions surging through her. She knew he was a pastor and was obligated to do things, but that didn't prepare her for the jealousy she felt over having to share her husband with the church and his responsibilities. They had just gotten married for crying out loud. It hadn't been a week and already he was rushing out to some meeting.

"Will you shower with me?" He stepped back into the room waiting for her response.

She rolled over and turned her back to him, angry over the tears swelling in her eyes.

"Hey." He peeled the covers off her shoulders and climbed back into bed with her. "I'll cancel, we'll go back to Vegas, and disappear for however long you want. Just don't cry." His fate was sealed. Those tears wrapped him so tightly around her finger. He couldn't breathe until they were gone. He wiped them with the pads of his thumbs and then reached for his phone on the nightstand.

April grabbed his wrist. "I can't stand in the way of you being great."

"I don't want you to feel like you come second to the church. I'll walk away from it before I let that happen."

"I'll never make you choose. I just have to find a way to get more involved, so that it feels like our church." She rolled out the other side of the bed hoping he would follow. She was trying to be the woman he needed at his side, not the baby pouting until she got her way. "I was thinking maybe I'd join the choir." She yelled back into the room as she turned on the shower.

That certainly got his attention and he was in the bathroom within seconds. "You sing?" As the words came out his mouth, he recalled the day she sang to him while he was sick.

She opened her mouth and gave him a little sample.

His jaw nearly hit the floor. It had been a long time since he'd heard anyone sing like that. "You're definitely joining the choir."

He helped her into the shower and wasted no time with their customary love making. He couldn't shower without washing her and couldn't rub soap all over her body without getting aroused. He had talked himself off the ledge of sexual arousal for five years and refused to do it with his wife, so making love in the shower was unavoidable. April didn't complain one bit. Nearly an hour later, he carried her limp body out of the bathroom and laid her across the bed. She watched him get dressed and then mustered up all her strength to put on a robe and walk him to the door. She kissed him goodbye and turned around to face all the boxes still cluttering their house.

Richard pulled up to the church feeling like a new man. He was early for his meeting, so he took a minute to walk the grounds of the church his father had built. It had been merely a week since he'd last been there, but life seemed so different. He had a wife to consider and couldn't keep the same hours as before. He remembered what April said the first day they met about him being available twenty-four hours a day and decided it was time to make some changes.

He stared out over the garden one of the mothers of the church had talked him into building. Many of them lived in senior citizen housing and didn't have yards to accommodate a garden, so he built them one on the church grounds. He smiled at the laughing and talking he heard coming from that direction and headed toward the church daycare.

He stepped lightly past the classrooms not wanting to interrupt whatever activity was taking place. He stopped at the nursery and gazed in on the babies. Most of them were in the cribs—presumably sleeping—but there was one little fighter lying out on the mat. Richard watched him kicking, stretching, and trying with all he had to reach the ball in front of him.

"We put toys in front of him to motivate him to crawl."

He turned with a smile and greeted the daycare director.

"Glad you made it back safely, Pastor." She glanced down at the ring on his finger. The look that flashed across her face made him regret coming in there. "I was hoping it wasn't true, but seeing that ring hurts more than what I thought it would."

"Sister..."

She lifted a silencing hand and looked away trying to blink away the moisture in her eyes. "I kept my distance to keep from being lumped into the pastor's wives club, but I silently hoped you'd see how great we could be together."

Richard stood there trying to keep the shock off his face.

"I just knew the Lord sent me here to be your wife. I guess that makes me just as insane as the dozens of other women who've been chasing after you."

"I'm sorry, but there is no doubt in my mind that I picked the right one."

"She's beautiful and I'm happy for you, but..."

He held his breath for the *but*.

She struggled with her words, obviously conflicted. She draped her arms around her torso as if warding off a sudden chill. "As much as I love it here, I can't stay. Consider this my two-week notice." She walked away without even giving him an opportunity to respond.

Her words hit him in the gut and he watched her walk away with a sense of dread overwhelming him. *So it begins.* The fall out, mass exodus, and abandonment was inevitable. He had to face reality. Some of his members had ulterior motives that he had just cut off at the pass. He had eliminated their need to maintain their membership with his church. He sucked in a breath struggling to absorb reality and retreated to his office to find solace.

He dialed April's number, desperately in need of the peace her voice brought.

"Hey baby," she purred through the phone and he sighed at the instant relief. "Your meeting's over already?"

"It hasn't started yet."

"Who are you meeting?"

"The man who married us, Pastor Meriwether. He was good friends with my father and really stepped in to help me adjust to running this church after he passed. His son and I were tight as kids. The citywide revival is his baby and he selects a different church to host it each year. So, we're just going over some particulars for the service."

"Is there anything I can do to help?"

"Actually there is. I'd love for you to lead a song with the choir." The line went silent and he had to bite his lip to keep from laughing. He could picture her rolling her eyes and on the verge of telling him, *hell no.*

"What are you going to give me if I do?"

"Ooh." He licked his lips and leaned back in his chair. "One good deed does deserve another."

"Yes it does."

"What do you want?"

"Oh, so many things," she moaned across the line and his body instantly hardened. "But, something involving oil and handcuffs might persuade me to get up there and sing my little heart out."

He nearly bit a hole through his lip trying not to disgrace the house of the Lord by speaking the things floating around his mind. "You like being restrained?"

"Very much."

There was a knock on his office door and he hated to end the conversation. "I'll call when I'm done. Be showered, naked, and lying face down in the middle of our bed when I get there." He ended the call, struggling to get his mind focused on what his meeting was about. Her tortured moan as he hung up didn't make the situation any better.

"Come in." He coughed to clear the arousal from his voice and stood to greet Pastor Meriwether.

"How's married life treating you?"

"Better than I ever imagined." *Even better when this meeting is over.* He shook those thoughts from his mind and pulled out his agenda.

"I don't say this often enough, but I'm proud of you and I'm sure your dad would be, too. You could've followed the path Junior did, but you chose to stand and serve the Lord."

"Thank you. How's he doing?" Brent was a touchy subject and Richard was surprised he'd brought him up.

"Better. He'd been in the streets, running with the wrong crowd, and not wanting to hear anything about the word of God. One morning a few months ago, I woke up and he was asleep on my couch. He moved back in and has been going to church ever since. Modern-day prodigal son returned home."

"Man, that's good to hear."

"You should call him. He could use a friend right now."

"Say no more."

"Good, now let's see what you've planned so far."

They spent the next two hours going over plans for the revival. Pastor Meriwether expressed how disappointed he was with the previous year's revival and wanted to make sure Richard didn't fall into the same pitfalls of poor planning, budgeting, and hospitality. When the meeting was over, he had another reason to be proud. He'd taken care of business and had everything planned out with a little over two months to spare. Richard didn't have time for pats on the back or more small talk. He had a woman to get home to. He sped home and wasted no time persuading her to do as he wished.

28

April woke up from a sound sleep and sat on the edge of the bed. She quietly tipped out of the room trying to not wake Richard. She lay on the couch and placed her hand on her stomach wondering if she was tripping or if she had in fact felt the baby move. She felt it again and the sorrow that fell on her nearly suffocated her. There it was, the reality of her situation. Why didn't she get an abortion or take the morning-after pill? She blamed her parents and her unrealistic Christian upbringing. Pro-life meant pro-torture. How could any woman be expected to mentally survive nine months of reliving their rape? With every time she threw up, every pound she gained, and every doctor's appointment, she was forced to remember what happened. Having to deal with part of her rapist moving around inside of her was too much.

She enfolded her arms around her burgeoning belly wanting desperately to pray but unable to find the words. God could've prevented such an atrocity from happening to her. Wasn't the rape itself punishment enough for the life she'd been living? Did He have to create a life from it? Then again, if she'd been living for the Lord, the entire incident would've never happened. That thought intensified her despair. She could no longer keep her sobs quiet. She muffled them with her hands, but it was no use. She heard the bed creak and tried to dry her cheeks with the sleeve of her robe. Tears fell as fast as she dried them. When Richard stepped into the room, she gave up trying.

"Hey, what's wrong?" He kneeled in front of her and embraced her.

"I can't do this anymore."

Her strangled words slapped him across the face and his hands froze in mid-air as he processed what she said. "Has it been bad?" He tilted his head in confusion struggling to come up with one incident that could lead to her feeling that way.

"It's the hardest thing I've ever had to do." Her sobs spiraled out of control and she bolted to the bathroom to catch the nausea she felt rising.

Richard's heart shattered as he watched her run off. He followed her to make sure she was all right. He sat next to her rubbing her back and didn't protest when she climbed into his lap. He rocked her until she calmed and then laid her across the bed. She drifted off to sleep and he went to lie on the couch.

He laid there for the rest of the morning trying to figure out where he'd gone wrong. Maybe he'd jumped the gun. Things never worked when he stepped out of God's timing. She was for him.

There was no doubt about that, but what had gone wrong? He remembered Sheena's fear of April getting bored with him. Maybe she was right. Maybe he didn't measure up to her past partners. Maybe his sexual proclivities were too much for her. He fought off his emotions as best he could, but one tear slipped out and he thought it best if he was gone before she woke up. He wouldn't pour his heart out and beg her to love him.

He dressed in the dim light of the sunrise careful not to make a sound. She looked even more beautiful in the natural light. She was still wrapped in her robe which was slightly parted, revealing the swell of her breast and the crease between her thighs. He ached to touch her and make love to her like he had every morning. He backed out of the room. He would honor her wishes. She wanted out. He'd let her out.

He drove to church trying to build up the mental strength to make it through Sunday morning worship, knowing he was losing the love of his life. His phone vibrated and he contemplated sending her call to voicemail. "Hello?"

"Hey, where are you? I reached for you and you were gone."

"I had to leave, but I'll send Deacon Carl to get you."

"No, I'll drive myself."

"Relax, Carl is a good brother. He won't hurt you."

She opened her mouth to beg him to come back for her, but her words were interrupted by the soft click of the call ending.

What just happened? April climbed out of bed trying to shake off the apprehension that flooded the room. She went to her closet to find an outfit. Every last one of the suits she'd recently purchased clenched tight at the waist. She took a deep breath, willing her hormones to subside and not send her into an emotional tizzy over an outfit. She settled on a navy suit with a longer jacket that would conceal the open zipper on the back of the skirt. It didn't look too bad if she left it unbuttoned. All the fuss over her clothes barely left time for a quick shower and application of make-up before Deacon Carl arrived.

They arrived at church and she went directly to Richard's office. His leaving without speaking to her still wasn't sitting well with her. She poised her hand to knock on his door and thought better of it. He had a job to do and she didn't want to distract his mind from delivering God's word. She went to her office instead and sat there wondering if he'd even notice if she didn't go upstairs. The way he was acting, she wondered if he even cared.

The baby kicked again and she took several deep breaths to hold back the tears that wanted to follow. "Oh God, be my strength."

She heard talking coming from Richard's office and stood by the adjoining door hoping he invited her in. He didn't. He encouraged and prayed for the deacons and other ministers. She stood there supporting everything he said. The last words he spoke broke her heart.

"Carl, get April. Make sure she's ready to go up."

She met him in the hall, so he didn't have to bother. Richard stepped out of his office and in spite of how confused and angry she was at him, he still took her breath away. He strode toward her—

261

power in his stride and crooked a smile taunting her—and stroked a finger under her chin.

"Beautiful, as usual."

"All for you." She didn't have time to analyze the look he flashed her. Deacon Carl hurried her along behind him. The congregation greeted them with a standing ovation. They stood there soaking it in. Before taking his place in the pulpit, Richard turned to her with hurt in his eyes. She silently pleaded for him to tell her what was going on. He simply kissed the crown of her head and signaled Deacon Carl to escort her to her seat.

Richard stepped into the pulpit and his heart sank. As the congregation settled, he couldn't help but notice all the vacant seats. His heart dropped into his stomach. He looked to April and couldn't believe what he had risked for someone who didn't really want him. When she decided to leave him, his days as pastor would be numbered. The board wouldn't hesitate to call in another minister. He swallowed that truth and grabbed his Bible. God had given him a word and he was ready to give it. He didn't even care that service had just started.

He preached the people happy. They danced in the aisles and cried out to God, his rushed nuptials seemingly forgotten. April sat there the entire time watching him with a blank expression on her face. He spoke into his ear piece and exited the sanctuary. Moments later, Deacon Carl tapped her on the shoulder.

"Pastor said for you to do the benediction. Then, I'm to drive you home."

She turned to him, expression never changing, "You do it." Before he could even respond, she was on her feet trailing behind Richard.

She pushed past the deacons standing in his doorway and looked him straight in the eye, "I'll be waiting for you in the car." She pinned him with a look that warned him to say something contrary and she'd turn his office out. She accepted his taut nod and marched out without another word.

She sat fuming in the car. The warm leather seats didn't help the fire raging through her. *How dare he dismiss me?* She sat there for a full fifteen minutes before his entourage appeared in the doorway. If he thought she was going to bow to him the way everyone else did, he had another thing coming. A spark of the fire that blazed through her before her attack returned and she'd make him regret the day it did.

Richard climbed into the car and smoothed his knuckles along her cheek, stifling her volcanic eruption. "Sorry, I didn't think you wanted to wait around for me."

April watched his every move. There was something he wasn't telling her. Maybe he was finally realizing she wasn't the right woman to be by his side. Maybe he was disappointed over her feelings about the baby. Something definitely wasn't right.

Guess the jokes on Sheena, All that talk about April getting bored and breaking Richard's heart was for nothing. He was the one who looked like he wanted out. April leaned back in the seat trying to hold it together until she got home and could fall apart in peace.

29

She lay awake every morning for about a week pretending to be asleep while her husband escaped their bed. He had made a habit of leaving just before the sun rose and not returning until hours after it set. Each time, it broke her heart a little more. She tried to regard him with the same nonchalant attitude she had used toward others in her past. The problem was she hadn't loved any of them. Her heart beat so strongly for Richard that his distance made her physically sick.

She couldn't take his abandonment another day. She rose and showered before his alarm went off. She didn't bother dressing quietly. She wanted him to wake up and feel the pain of her walking out on him the way she had.

"Where are you going?"

She paused in the doorway, hating how weak she was for him. She had lived her entire life ensuring no man would ever have that much power over her. The sound of his voice addressing her after days of silence was as solemn as the deaf hearing for the first time. Her eyes fluttered closed and her mouth slightly parted as his words caressed her.

She should've kept walking, but the sound of his footsteps shuffling across the carpet toward her rooted her to that spot. She felt his heat behind her and yearned for him to touch her.

"Where are you going?" He raised his hand to caress her shoulder and turn her attention toward him, but dropped it back to his side. He was unsure if she wanted his touch. He couldn't tolerate her rejection. He waited for her response. There was nothing. He backed away, accepting the fact that it was over. "Be safe." He backed away and locked himself in the bathroom.

April clamped her hand over her mouth until she heard the bathroom door click shut. She couldn't utter a word without her anguish breaking free. She had no idea where she was going, but she knew she couldn't lay there while he left. She couldn't take his indifferent attitude toward her. Maybe it was best if she moved back in with Sheena. She grabbed her purse and headed there, grateful that she had kept her key.

Richard cried. He thought he would never experience anything more painful than losing a parent, but losing April was right up there. He didn't want to lose her, but couldn't force her to love him. With that sad truth, he let the last tear trickle down his cheek. He resolved to handle the situation the way he did all others. *God will work it out.*

It was hard, but he managed to get dressed and make it to his first appointment of the day on time. He followed up on the promise he'd made to Pastor Meriwether to reach out to Brent. Richard had fond memories of them cutting up on the church pews, getting pinched, and being slapped on the back of the head. After their dads branched out and started their churches, their mothers tried to get them together, but time was limited. Richard still considered him a friend, but during middle school, Brent stopped buying in to the whole Christian lifestyle. He got into some things Richard didn't agree with. That was the end of their friendship. The things he'd heard about Brent down through the years were shocking but expected. It was certainly good to hear the brother had returned to the Lord.

"What's up, my brother?" Richard stood as he approached and greeted him with a shoulder hug.

"What's up, man? Long time no see."

Richard reclaimed his seat, not wasting any time beating around the bush. "I hear you finally decided to give your life to Christ."

He dropped his head in obvious shame. Richard watched his every move, trying to gauge his sincerity. He would welcome an old friend back into his life, but he didn't have time for foolishness.

"You can get to a point so low in your life that you realize God is the only way to go. For years, I lived in despair. Rock bottom there is pretty close to death. I did something..." He sucked in a deep breath and brushed his hand across his close cropped hair, seemingly trying to wipe away his thoughts. "Let's just say I messed up and I'm trying to make it right."

"I hear you." Richard relaxed back into his chair deciding to take a chance. After all, forgiveness was the foundation of the church. "Sounds like you're headed in the right direction."

"I'm trying. Enough about me, what's this I hear about you being married?"

"Yeah, I'm something like that." He took a huge gulp of his water hoping Brent wouldn't press for more.

"And…"

"And, she's perfect. You should've come with your dad to the ceremony."

"I thought about it, but I've been trying to keep a low profile, stay out of trouble, and serve the Lord."

"Guess I can't fault you for that. You can meet her at the citywide revival." Richard swallowed back the anxiety that constricted his throat with a few sips of his water. Would they even still be together at that time? That thought messed him up for the rest of breakfast. He sat there trying to be attentive in conversation, but after having to ask Brent to repeat himself several times, he asked for the check and said he wasn't feeling well. He fumbled through the rest of his meetings in the same manner. When he arrived home that evening to an empty house, he couldn't help but wonder if she was ever coming back.

April drove aimlessly around the city until the mall opened and then shopped for hours, frivolously spending money to make herself feel better. She opted to be alone instead of at Sheena's house. Her sister was nosy and she didn't feel like being bothered with a bunch of questions. The unease that usually crept up on her with the setting of the sun was more intense than usual. She preferred to be safe in the confines of her home at night, but didn't want to sit at home listening to the silence mock her broken marriage.

She turned the key in the ignition and backed her car out of the parking stall. She didn't want to go home and couldn't go to anyone else's house without them asking questions, so she went to the only other place where her presence wouldn't be questioned. She had no idea what was going on there, but couldn't help the tiny spark of hope that flared at the prospect of Richard being there. She entered through the private entrance of the church and went straight to his office. The door was locked and the chasm in her heart ripped a little wider. She stood in the dark hallway wondering where she should go from there. She heard music coming from upstairs and on autopilot followed it.

April stood just outside the sanctuary listening to the choir rehearse. The sound of their melodic voices helped to ease her angst. She took a deep breath and walked inside. It was as good a time as any. She desperately needed something to take her mind off of Richard. Singing would do the trick. The door banged loudly announcing her entrance and almost instantly a voice came over the microphone.

"Rehearsals are closed."

"I was hoping to join the choir." April hedged a little further into the sanctuary.

The director spun around, shock and apology written all over his face. "Lady April..."

She waved at the forty-plus sets of eyes on her and made her way to the choir stand. She shook the director's hand and prepared to have a seat.

"Actually Dedrick, didn't Pastor say, no new members until after the revival? He doesn't want people joining the choir just to be seen."

"Oh, okay." April hopped back to her feet and retraced her steps. She silenced Dedrick with a raised hand. "No new members means, no new members. I don't expect special treatment." She could hear him reprimanding the sister, demanding she apologize. April didn't have time to wait. She felt so humiliated and hurried back to her office. She heard footsteps closing in on her and wanted to run away, but her heels and swollen belly made going down the steps difficult. She was two steps from the bottom when the woman caught her. She paused to allow the apology but was met with a shove to her shoulder instead. She stumbled down the last few stairs, her ankle twisted, and she buckled to her knees. The impact sent pain searing through her abdomen. She kneeled there panting and clenching her side as the woman stood over her leering at her like she was about to pounce.

"If you knew what's good for you, you'd go back where you came from."

April sucked up the pain and clamored to her feet. The woman backed away, allowing her warning to register. April wanted to teach her that she wasn't one to be messed with, but her cramping stomach kept her in place. Once she was sure the woman was gone, she made her way to the car. Her first thought was to go to the hospital to check on the baby, but she quieted that voice and drove home, ignoring the tiny hope that falling down the stairs was God's way of setting her free from her current situation.

That hope was short lived. By the time she arrived home, the pain had eased considerably. She walked through the dark house hoping Richard was home. She didn't care how he felt about her, she loved him. All she needed was for him to wrap his arms around her and she'd be okay. The only light in the house illuminated from their bedroom. She headed in that direction.

The sight of him relaxing against the bed—chest bare and body etched to perfection—halted her steps. He noticed her standing in the doorway and trapped her in his gaze. He slid to his feet and stalked toward her. His domineering frame made her breath catch in her throat.

He touched a finger to her chin, lifting it until her eyes met his. Instinctively, her hands went to his chest, the contact scorching him just as it had the first time she'd touched him.

She searched his face silently imploring him to end her torment and out of desperation finally asked, "Do you regret marrying me?"

"No! I love you." He caressed her cheek and threaded his fingers through her silky strands at the nape of her neck

"You've been so distant." She shuttered at the intimate contact, barely managing enough breath to speak.

"Thought I was giving you what you wanted."

"Why on earth would I want that?"

"What do you want?" He wrapped his arms around her, no longer able to resist feeling her flush against him. "You said you can't do this anymore."

"I wasn't talking about you." Her voice—barely above a whisper—brushed across his cheek and she pulled away before he could ask questions.

He followed her and gripped her waist before she could escape into the bathroom. He had waited too long and had been hurting far too much for him to allow her to make that statement and not demand an explanation. He was expecting to have to persuade her to open up, but she spun on him, wasting no time putting him in his place.

"Do you really think so little of me that you'd assume I could vow to love you and then be done with you days later? I love you."

"You do?"

"Yes." Her soft spoken response wisped past her trembling lips. "I was talking about the baby. I don't want this baby." She crumbled under the weight of her confession, covering her mouth to muffle her sobs. He was right there to catch her. "Every day, this pregnancy reminds me of what he did to me. He attacked and beat me until I was unrecognizable. He stole my dignity, my peace, and my love for life. That night on the couch I had just felt the baby move for the first time. Part of him is living inside me and I'm expected to be happy about it. I don't want this baby!" She slapped her hand across her stomach unleashing all her anguish.

His heart broke for her.

Sobs shook her body and Richard wanted to kick himself for causing her more distress than what she was already handling. He cradled her between his legs and rested her back against his chest.

What could he say? He smoothed his hands across the areas she had slapped, hoping his love for her showed with each caress. He tried to hone in on her pain, but he couldn't. He loved the baby already. He had looked past her attacker and saw her. The baby was a part of her. To him, that overshadowed everything else.

"I should've taken the morning-after pill or got an abortion." She angrily swiped at her wet cheeks and wrenched herself from his arms switching from sorrow to rage in an instant. "The doctor came in to discuss my options and my mom started talking that 'before I was formed in my mother's womb the Lord knew me,' nonsense and I backed down." She flopped onto the floor sobbing into the carpet. Richard unfolded her legs from under her and laid her on her side, and then he stretched out beside her. He connected his legs and arms to hers, her back to his chest, and rested his mouth to her ear. There wasn't an inch of her backside that didn't feel him. He clung to her, suffusing her with his strength. His heat was soothing, but the words he whispered were the balm to her shattered psyche.

"This is how you're going to get through this: your pain is mine. Sorrow, confusion, despair, anger, every tear—give it all to me. I will collect them all and pour them out on you in the sweetest joy you've ever known." He shushed her sobs with the slightest kiss to the sensitive space behind her ear. "Every time the baby moves, you say, *Richard's baby*. That's my baby growing inside you. She'll have my name and be as beautiful as her mother. We'll love her the moment we lay eyes on her. Why? How? Because she's a part of you." He rolled her onto her back and climbed on top of her, kneeling between her legs. Her skirt rolled up, but he didn't take notice. He lifted her shirt up over her expanding belly and placed his lips there.

"My baby." He kissed her there again and again, moving about her stomach kissing and declaring his claim on their little girl. "My baby."

The intimate contact with his lips on her skin normally would've sent her body into a frenzy, but his affection ramped up her wails. Her shoulders shook against the floor as the anguish consumed her. Richard kept at it, determined to make her understand. He knew the exact moment her mind grasped it and her heart accepted it. Agony left her sobs, and praise entered.

"Oh God." She shivered under the presence of God. All she managed to utter was, "Thank you, Jesus," but such praise in the time of such sorrow was more than enough.

She proclaimed her thanks over and again. Thanks for loving her. Thanks for healing her. Thanks for giving her strength. Thanks for giving her Richard.

Richard lifted her from the floor and helped her to the bed. "I'm sorry for being angry."

"You had a right to be. I can't imagine how my words must've hurt you."

"Yeah, but I should've talked to you first. I was just afraid to hear you actually come out and say you didn't want me anymore." He snuggled her under the covers pulling her as close as possible. "I hate that I hurt you."

"It's over now. The only thing that matters is you still love me and want to stay married to me. You're the best thing in my life. I don't want to lose you."

"Never." He smoothed her hair back out of her face and guided her head to his chest. He exhaled all the hurt, tension, and fear that had built over the week and relaxed into a peaceful sleep and vowed to communicate better. His marriage had literally been on the verge of being destroyed by a misunderstanding. He definitely had to do better.

30

"April Walker." She picked up her purse—trying to hide her smile at Richard's pissed off expression—and followed behind the nurse. She would have to remember to inform them of her name change. She sighed at the numbers glaring at her on the scale. *Just a couple more months*. She was in her last trimester and had just a few more weeks until her life and body would return to normal.

She smiled at Richard sitting in the chair next to her exam table. He had stayed true to his word and had attended every doctor's appointment. He finally noticed her staring and turned his attention to her. Her eyes roamed his face, taking in just how magnificent he was. He leaned forward resting his arms across his knees and raising a questioning brow.

"Come here," was her response to his unspoken question. He didn't hesitate to oblige. Her seat on the elevated table put her almost to his eye level. She took full advantage leaning in for his lips, locking on to them as if she was drowning and they were her life preserver. "I don't deserve you," she mumbled against his lips and snaked her hands under the hem of his shirt. "But since I have you, I'm going to enjoy every inch of you." Her hand tipped toward the waist of his pants and he caught her by the wrist.

"It'd be a shame for the doctor to come in here and find you tied to this table." He kissed the gasp off her lips and guided her hand back to safe territory. He chuckled at her shocked expression and reclaimed his seat.

"Richard?" A knock on the door interrupted her pouty whimper.

Richard watched her trying to compose herself as the doctor stepped in. She was the most beautiful woman he had ever encountered. It was he who didn't deserve her. Her strength was inspiring and he fell in love with her more each day.

"So Ms. Walker, how have you been?"

"Mrs. Hawkins." Richard didn't hesitate to flash the doctor with an annoyed look.

"I'm fine." April shook her head at Richard and the smile on her face softened his expression.

"A couple weeks ago I received a message that you fell down a couple of steps."

April didn't have to look in Richard's direction to know he was pissed. She felt his eye burning through her.

"It was more like stumbled down a few steps and I'm fine. I just called to see what I should be looking for just in case there was a problem. There wasn't any bleeding or cramping, and the baby was still moving. I'm fine." She chanced a glance at Richard, apologizing with her eyes.

"We'll talk." He grabbed her hand and stood to help her lay back, so the doctor could listen to the baby's heartbeat. Of all the things he had experienced through her pregnancy, hearing the rapid whirring of the baby's heartbeat was his favorite.

He squeezed her hand a little tighter and looked at her with the same enamored expression he had since the day they met. He spent the rest of the appointment kissing the back of her hand and rubbing her stomach, but as soon as the doctor left the room he started questioning her.

"When and where did you fall?"

"I didn't fall."

"Fall, stumble, or whatever you want to call it, if you were concerned enough to call the doctor, you should should've told me."

"I know, but I didn't want you to be upset."

"Why would I be upset?" She tried to turn from him, but he gripped her chin between his fingers searching her eyes for the answer. "What happened?"

The look in his eyes said it all. He wasn't going to let her go until she answered. She took a deep breath and prepared for his wrath. "I was pushed."

"What? Down the stairs?"

She nodded and the fury that spread across his face made her hesitant to say another word.

"Who in the…" He swallowed those words down his throat and took a deep breath to smother the heat raging through his veins. "Who pushed you?

"I don't know her name. I went to choir rehearsal and she was so adamant about me not joining that she followed behind me to reiterate that you closed the choir to new members and it would be better for me to go back where I came from."

Richard immediately saw red. It was the sheer power of God that kept him calm. "There is choir rehearsal tonight. You will show me who had the balls to put their hands on you."

"Please, just let it go. You're scaring me."

"I will not tolerate this jealous nonsense or you being threatened because of it."

"But, I'm fine."

"It's not up for discussion." He pecked her lips hopefully, conveying that he wasn't angry with her. "Now, if you don't mind, let's get out of here. I'd like to have lunch with my beautiful wife."

She opened her mouth to say something else but grabbed her purse instead. He had every right to stand up for her. If it was any other man, she would demand that he did. She followed him out of the room, not mad at all at the nurses checking him out as they walked down the hall. She was checking him out too and couldn't fault them for a weakness she had as well.

"What are your plans for the rest of the day?" She paused before getting in the car hoping he was free to spend the rest of the day with her.

"I'm going to take you to lunch, to a movie, and then we'll go back home." He helped her into the car, taking full advantage of how her skirt rolled up. The warmth of her thigh seeped into his palm and crept up his arm, temporarily making him lose his train of thought. "I'm going to make slow, sweet love to you until the sun sets, and then we'll go to choir rehearsal."

April let out an exasperated breath. He had stimulated her until she was almost squirming in her seat and then doused her with a bucket of cold water. She turned her head to keep from asking him to drop it and exposed the spot on her neck that he loved to nuzzle. He wasted no time attacking it.

He stayed true to his word and spent the entire day with her. When they finally arrived home, he had her panting, screaming, and trembling so hard she thought she was going into premature labor.

"Mmm...Richie." April rolled over and pulled the covers over her shoulder.

"Don't even think about going to sleep."

"Well, you shouldn't have done those things to me if you expected me to stay awake." She giggled and snuggled further under the blanket. "I don't see how you can do all that and still have energy."

"It's simple." He tapped her backside and stole one last kiss. "Being with you gives me an adrenaline rush. You have one hour to sleep and then we are going to church."

"Yes, Daddy."

"Go to sleep before I tame that little smart mouth." He walked out of the room softly shutting the door behind him. He let out a heavy breath and shook his head. Was it normal to be that obsessed with a woman? He had no idea. She didn't seem to mind, so he wasn't about to change.

He spent the hour on his knees asking the Lord to temper his anger and give him wisdom in dealing with the hatred toward April that seemed to be brewing amongst the congregation.

ॐ

April didn't try to hide her annoyance and for the first time, Richard didn't care that she was upset. He was going to let it be known that she was not to be messed with. They entered the church and he paused before entering the sanctuary to make sure she was okay.

"Richie, I just don't want people to think I'll run back whining to you every time someone does or says something I don't like."

"I hear you, but they will treat you with the same respect they give me."

"Honey, respect is earned; give them time."

"I've earned their respect and then some. Disrespecting you is disrespecting me."

She shook her head and conceded again, "Okay."

They walked into the sanctuary. When the musicians realized he was coming in to address the choir, the music stopped. All eyes were on him

"How's everyone doing tonight?" He waved the musicians over and they didn't hesitate to leave their instruments and join the group. "I understand that my marriage was sudden and some are having a hard time accepting it. Jealousy and hatred are strong spirits that can destroy this church if not properly addressed. You all are my partners in ministry. You're the backbone of every service, and I can't have such strong opposition standing behind me when I'm ministering to the congregation. Every harsh word, vindictive thought, evil eye, or act of violence directed toward my wife is an attack against me." His anger was rising, but April's soft touch to his back tamped it down. "A few weeks ago, my wife tried to join this choir and was denied. I appreciate you trying to follow my wishes, but she has the freedom to join anything regardless of my restrictions. Is that understood?"

April smiled at all the nodding heads hoping that Richard would end the conversation there. She wasn't that lucky.

"Now that we've come to an understanding, which one of you had the nerve to put your hands on her?"

Gasps echoed around the choir stand. April's eyes fluttered closed bracing for the fallout.

"Who is she?"

Her eyes popped open to his boring into her with an intensity she didn't dare defy. She pointed with her eyes and he zeroed in on her line of sight.

"Sister Jazmin, you are relieved of your membership in this choir and this church. You have about five minutes to get out of here before I call the police and have you arrested for assault." Fury rolled off of him and hovered around them.

"I'm sorry. I didn't mean to. I don't know what came over me."

"You pushed my pregnant wife down the stairs. Get out of here before I do more than have you arrested." She jumped at his harsh tone and fled without another word.

"I'm sorry, Pastor." Dedrick hopped up nearly in tears. "It's my fault. Jazmin said some pretty harsh words and I demanded she go apologize. I assumed everything went well. Lady April has always been welcome to join us."

"Good. I'd like for her to lead a song for the revival."

"Richie." He ignored her grumbling and kept looking at Dedrick for a response. "The revival is in a couple of weeks. I'm sure they have all their selections planned already."

"Actually, we do but maybe there is a song you already know that the choir knows as well. We won't need much practice."

"Sounds like a plan." Richard kissed her lips and ignored the look she was giving him. "I'll be waiting in my office until you're done."

She watched him walk away. No matter how mad or frustrated she was with him, she'd never get tired of watching him.

"Okay," Dedrick snapped her out of her trance. "What song do you have in mind?"

"Definitely something classic and upbeat, how about *Thank You Lord* by Walter Hawkins?"

"Yes. That's definitely a good one."

The musicians didn't hesitate to hop on their instruments, Dedrick passed her a mic, and the choir stood to back her. Right on cue, she came in singing:

Tragedies are common place
All kinds of diseases
People are slipping away
Economy's down
People can't get enough pay
As for me, all I can say is:
Thank you Lord for all you done for me

Her powerful melodic voice blared through the speakers and Dedrick missed the mark for the choir to join in, he was so caught up in it.

"Dang girl, sing that song!"

April laughed at the relief on his face and sang even harder, determined to shut up anyone who thought she didn't have the skill to lead a song. She sang the power of God down, shocking even herself. Before long, the choir had left her hanging and was praising the Lord like it was Sunday morning worship. April kept at it, letting the words minister to her as well as everyone else. When she finally calmed and opened her eyes, Richard was sitting on the front pew looking just as astonished as she felt. She seemingly floated toward him and kneeled before him. He cradled her to his chest and they both gave in to the presence of God enveloping them.

31

pril couldn't believe how fast time had flown by. She wished she had at least another month to prepare for the citywide revival, but the day was upon her and she was busy running around putting her stamp on things. She should've taken a more active role from the first meeting Richard had made her sit in on, but hindsight was definitely clearer when you had months to consider it. She decided on purple and silver as a color scheme and was anxious to see how many of the women who'd received the memo would join her.

She danced around the sanctuary humming one of the songs the choir would sing that night, oblivious to Richard watching her.

"Do you know how beautiful you are?"

April jumped and spun toward him. "When did you get here?"

"A few minutes ago." He watched her walk toward him not trying to hide the fact that he was checking her out. Her tights and tunic flowed over her curves. He loved it. Even her swollen belly excited him. He smoothed his hand over his face and shook his head. *I must be crazy.*

"What's wrong?" She sat on his lap and he welcomed her without hesitation.

"Nothing." He rubbed his hands up and down her thighs and "What are you doing here by yourself?"

"I just wanted to put up some decorations."

"It looks beautiful and I appreciate you doing this, but I wish you would call your deacon."

"Richard, that man has a life. I can't interrupt him every time I feel like coming down to the church."

"I hear you, but I'm going to catch a case the next time someone puts their hands on you. I'm trying to prevent that."

She tried to give him attitude and tell him he was overreacting, but his caress made that hard to do. The only thing she could do was place her lips on his.

"You know I've been looking for you for about an hour. Where is your cell?"

"Over there in my purse." She chased his fleeting pecks trying to deepen the kiss.

"I called Sheena, Candace, Meme, and Deacon Carl. No one knew where you were. You're trying to make me catch a case and drive me crazy."

April giggled and gripped the back of his head. "Don't tease me." His smile spread against her lips and she took advantage of his parted lips.

"Ugh, what are you doing to my little sister and in the house of God no less?" Sheena walked in front of them shaking her head. "You could've at least called and told me you found her before um…" She let her mischievous smirk finish the rest of her sentence. "Well, I'm here now. What can I do to help you finish decorating?"

"You blockin', Sis?"

Richard threw his head back laughing and Sheena's stunned expression did nothing to help him calm down. He was thinking the same thing and couldn't believe April actually spoke it. April laughed right along with him. Sheena gave her the evil eye and she nearly fell off Richard's lap laughing so hard.

"I'm sorry." April took a deep breath and threw her hands up in surrender. "It's getting late and I'd love some help."

"Okay, let's do this."

"You're helping, too?"

"Of course I am. This is important to you and I want to be a part of it."

She shyly grabbed his hand and led him to the floral arrangement she had been working on. His eyes and hands never even touched a flower. They were glued to her, massaging her shoulders, abdomen, and watching her gracefully move about the sanctuary. He was glad he wasn't preaching, because the word of God was the furthest thing from his mind.

They finished decorating. Sheena rushed home to get ready for service and Richard escorted April down to her office like he was dropping her off at home after a date. He didn't dare set foot in her office.

"You brought clothes and everything, right?"

"Yes. Did you?"

"I always keep clothes here. You go ahead and shower and get dressed. Take a few moments to relax and I'll come get you when we are ready." He unlocked her door and lightly kissed her lips He didn't trust himself not to do more, so he locked her inside.

Loud clapping and praying snapped April out of a sound sleep. The sound had crept under the door of Richard's office. She frantically jumped up looking around, trying to get her bearings and remember where she was. She was at church, in her office, and still in her robe. She wasted no time scrambling into the bathroom to get dressed and put on her makeup. She rushed to be ready before Richard knocked on her door. She ignored the ache in her lower abdomen signaling she had overdone it with decorating and running errands. There wasn't time to give into the pain or exhaustion.

The adjoining door clicked open and she took a second to examine herself in the full length mirror before joining Richard in his office.

"April, you remember Pastor Meriwether?"

April smiled brightly, shaking his hand as he kissed her cheek in greeting.

"And this is his lovely wife, Edith."

April embraced her hoping some of the woman's grace would rub off on her and maybe she'd mentor her in the ministry of being a first lady the way her husband had mentored Richard.

"And this is their son, Brent."

April turned her head toward the gentleman who had been lingering by the door. Her eyes focused on his face and her smile faded. She froze. Richard kept trying to hedge her forward to shake the man's hand, but April was rooted to her spot.

"Baby, you okay?"

Her eyes glassed over with that faraway look in them terrified Richard. Without hesitation, he radioed a deacon.

"Yes Pastor?" Jaleel stepped into the office followed by Deacon Carl. Jaleel's eyes instantly honed in on April. She was family and it didn't take him long to realize something was wrong. "I'll escort our guest to the fellowship hall and then get Sheena."

Richard was so focused on April he never acknowledged that Jaleel had entered and left or Carl standing guard at the door. "Baby, talk to me" He placed his hand on her forehead to check her body temp. It felt normal. He grabbed her wrist to check her pulse. It was hammering away faster than what he'd consider normal. "Baby, you're starting to scare me. Say something! Look at me and let me know you're okay.

Silent tears trickled down her cheeks. She didn't budge.

Richard stepped toward his desk to call an ambulance, but April's knees buckled and he jumped back to catch her. Deacon Carl was right there with him. Sheena barged through the door, saw her sister limp in Richard arms, and immediately assumed the worst. She rushed toward them, trying to wedge herself between them, but he wasn't having it. He carried her to the couch and sat with her in his lap.

"What happened to her?" Sheena sat so close she was practically in his lap, too. She felt April's body temperature and pulse, widened her eyelids to check her pupils, squeezed her cheeks to look at her throat, and checked the color of her fingertips.

Richard shook her and called her name several times, but got the same response. He looked to Sheena and her eyes were roaming his office. She turned her head back to him and asked the only logical question. "What were y'all doing before she got like this?"

Richard gave her a look that told her to not even go there. "I had just introduced her to our guest speaker and she just zoned out in the middle of our conversation."

Sheena opened her mouth to speak, but the office door clicked open

"Excuse me, Pastor, but the praise team has been up there stalling for like thirty minutes; should we proceed with offering?" At his hesitation, Jaleel continued, "And Pastor Meriwether wanted me to remind you that the guest speaker needs to be up preaching before eight, so he can make his flight."

"You go," Sheena said, more than likely sensing his struggle. "April is fine; she's just been under a bit of stress lately."

"What if it's something to do with the baby?" The concern in his voice was evident.

"It can't be. She just had a check-up. You take Pastor Meriwether on up to the sanctuary. I'll get her to snap out of it." She must have sensed his hesitation and touched his arm. "She'll be fine."

Richard set April aside and marched down the hallway toward the fellowship hall wishing he could kick every one out of his church and tend to his woman, but there were hundreds of people up stairs who'd been preparing for this revival for months. He couldn't let them down. "Sorry Pastor Meriwether, but you are going to have to run things without me. Jaleel will escort you up and the speaker for the night is on his way as we speak. The deacons know what to do when he gets here."

"It's no problem. With your wife is where you belong."

"Where's Brent?"

"Something came up, but he apologized for having to run off. He was so excited about finally being able to see you in action."

꧁꧂

"Lady April, we need you to snap out of this." Deacon Carl stepped forward and gave her a little shake. April slapped his hands away. Thinking he was getting through to her, he grasped both her shoulders and tried to turn her toward him. April snapped. Her hands slapped and pushed at his face. He struggled to hold her, but her flailing arms were hard to dodge.

"April, calm down. We are trying to help you." Sheena jumped out of the way to avoid being hit.

Carl succeeded in subduing her arms, but her legs joined in the fight. She stomped his foot and kneed him in the groin. He folded at the waist trying to contain the painful blow.

Sheena tried to help him, but he'd released April's arm and she swatted Sheena across the face. Sheena—stunned—stumbled back a little.

Richard stepped into his office and scanned the scene. April stood in the center of the room. Her once perfectly styled hair was fluffed about her head. Her beautiful face was distorted with red puffy eyes and wet cheeks. The pulse in the base of her neck thumped like a jack hammer, and her chest heaved with each breath as if she'd just run a marathon. He wasted no time gathering April in his arms, withstanding the slaps to his face, in order to get close enough to whisper in her ear.

"Remember…give me your pain, sorrow, heartache, and despair. Let me carry you through this."

She stopped struggling and he loosened his grip. His eyes shifted to Sheena. He noticed the speck of blood in the corner of her mouth and the blatant fear in her eyes.

"What happened?"

"I don't know. She lost it."

He turned his attention back to April. He touched her cheek and she swatted his hand away. He held her hand firm and snapped it down to her waist. She squirmed in the attempt to twist her hand out of his grip. Finding no freedom, April resorted to the tactics she used to subdue Deacon Carl. Richard was quick on his feet and rotated his hips. Her knee met the thick meat of his thigh.

"Baby, look at me. I'm not going to hurt you," Richard pleaded, praying she would snap out of it. He hated having to overpower her that way.

Sheena watched in horror as what seemed like a demonic presence had taken over her sister. She cried hard and when crying was no longer enough, she lunged toward April. She stretched her arm out, slapped April across the face, and yelled out, "The blood of Jesus!"

April stumbled back out of Richard's arms and the room went silent. Slowly she raised her hand to her throbbing face. Her eyes shifted to Richard, recognizing him again. Tears flooded her face and with the faintest of voices she whispered, "He raped me."

"Who raped you?" Richard tried to remain calm as he cautiously made his way toward her. Her statement had his heart racing a mile a minute. He reached her, but was afraid touching her would send her into fight mode so he resisted.

"He raped me," she cried more forcefully and collapsed against Richard's chest. He folded her into his arms and tried his best to soothe her. He wanted to press for an answer to his question, but feared she would snap again. He gently rocked her as he motioned for Deacon Carl to leave. Her wails tapered off and he dried her face with the sleeve of his suit. There was no way he was going to release her just to grab a Kleenex.

"He raped me," she mumbled against his chest

He slipped his finger beneath her chin and lifted her eyes to his. "Who raped you?"

"Brent." She would recognize him anywhere. Those round haunted eyes had invaded her dreams for the past six months.

Richard inhaled every expletive that was on its way out of his mouth. He prided himself on not being one of those foul-mouthed saints people spoke of, but the words swirling around his mouth were everything but Christ-like. April needed his peace to keep her calm. He'd give her just that, even if it killed him.

Richard looked at Sheena's questioning eyes and explained, "Pastor Meriwether's son, who conveniently left after I introduced him to April."

Richard didn't have to say another word. Sheena pulled out her phone and called Paul. One of the main things Richard liked about Paul was the brother knew how to handle business. He would definitely take care of Brent while he tended to April.

Sheena tried to peel April off of Richard, so he could talk to Paul, but she clung to him like they were surgically attached. Eventually, she got the hint and went to fetch a bottle of water. Her little sister didn't need her anymore. She had Richard, and from the looks of things, he was going to take good care of her.

"I think he rode with his parents. If he's on foot, he's probably nearby. Take all the deacons and start searching the area, but call the cops. I want him in jail alone, not sitting next to you." He read the look on Paul's face, and if he was the one to catch

Brent, he might not be able to control himself. He waited for Paul to speak up or nod his consent. He simply walked out and shut the door behind him.

April's wails ramped up and Sheena rushed over with the bottle of water. "April hun, think about the baby." Her shoulders trembled more fiercely, distress emanating from her. Sheena wanted to punch herself. She bit her lip and kept quiet.

"He raped me," she sobbed over and over again. Visions from that night came flooding back as pain, fear, and helplessness consumed her.

Her short hiccupping breaths were insufficient to provide oxygen for her unborn baby. The longer she continued, the more concerned Richard became. "Sheena, I'm taking her to the hospital. You stay here and wait for Paul to get back."

"That sounds good, but how are you going to drive with her attached to you?"

Richard looked down at April. He didn't know if she was attached to him or the other way around. He sure didn't want to let her go. "Call Cole and see if he'll come pick me up."

"He's here. I saw them when they came in." She was up and running out of the door before he could utter another word.

Not even five minutes later, Sheena burst through the door with Meme following behind her. "Cole is bringing the car around. Can you carry her out by yourself?"

"Yeah." He stood effortlessly. There was so much adrenaline rushing through his veins that she felt as light as a feather.

He had a hard time maneuvering into the back seat, but he managed to get there. Meme hopped into the passenger seat and Cole took off like his life was at stake. He drove with the same urgency his brother felt. In a sense, his life was on the line. If something happened to April, he didn't know if he could go on.

April tossed her arms over Richard's shoulders and rested her head against his chest. Her head was spinning, her lips and fingers tingled. She knew she needed to calm down, but she couldn't stop the images running through her head. The blood, the pain, her torn flesh, broken ribs, and her swollen face—Brent had done it and she had allowed his father to perform her wedding ceremony. How could Richard be friends with such a violent person?

Her thoughts trampled over her good sense and she gave into sorrow. Pain radiated from her side to her back. She cried out trying to control the pain, hoping it would subside. She took a deep breath to calm herself, but her sobs turned to panic and the throbbing intensified.

Oh God! No! Every negative thought she had about the baby charged to the forefront of her mind. How many times had she wished she wasn't pregnant? She even went as far as hoping for a miscarriage. In that moment—faced with the prospect of losing her child—it was the last thing she wanted.

"Richie, please," she panted, trying to force a calm she didn't feel. "Help me. Help my baby." She screamed as another wave of pain hit her abdomen.

"Cole, drive this car!" Richard's control slipped and he barked at Cole, feeling helpless to get April some relief. Liquid splashed into his lap and his eyes connected with April's.

"No! It's too soon." She shook her head, once again giving in to the anguish that seemed hell bent on destroying her.

"Listen to me." Richard silenced her with a look that she'd seen plenty of times, but he had never directed it toward her. "You have to calm down. Slow your breathing," He sucked in a slow deep breath and she mimicked his actions. He had no idea what he was doing, because April had outright refused to sign up for Lamaze or any birthing classes. He had seen it done on TV several times and just copied that.

Cole pulled into the ambulance entrance and Meme ran in to get a wheelchair. Cole opened the back door and lifted April from Richard's lap, so he could get out. He placed her into the wheelchair and gripped his brother's shoulders. "It's going to be all right. One thing I've learned in the past few months is that God can work miracles."

Richard took a deep breath and let those words sink in. Yes, he served a miracle-working God who was able to do exceedingly and abundantly above all he could ask or think. He would take care of April.

He wheeled her into the hospital—with Meme trailing behind him—and went straight to the labor and delivery department. It didn't take much of an examination to assess the situation. Fetal distress was imminent and she was rushed into an emergency cesarean section. Meme waited in the hall while Richard put on surgical scrubs and went to the operating room. By the time he reached April's side, she was calm. Whatever pain relieving medications they'd given her had taken affect. He kissed the tears streaming from the corner of her eyes and gripped her hand. "God's got you and our baby. We have to believe that."

April nodded and really tried to believe, but she was barely into her third trimester. How could the baby survive? She had wished her pregnancy gone so many times. Maybe God was finally giving her what she had asked for.

Out of the corner of his eye, Richard saw the doctor pass the baby to a nurse and he forced his face to remain expressionless. He didn't know much about childbirth, but the one thing he did know was that babies cried. The silence was suffocating. Everything seemed to be moving in slow motion. They laid the baby on a table and he saw fingers compressing her little chest just before a wall of nurses blocked her out of his sight.

Oh God, no! His eyes fluttered closed and April saw his distress before he could wipe it from his face.

"What's going on? Why is it so quiet?" She craned her neck to see what he'd seen, but it was pointless.

"Shhh, the doctors are working and God is in control." Her tears started again and he wiped them away. "No more crying, our little girl needs us to be strong."

"Okay." She sucked in a shaky deep breath, trying her best to remain calm.

Richard wanted to march over to where they were working on his baby and move the nurses out of the way. He needed to know what was going on. Why wasn't the baby crying? Was she alive? He needed to hold her and make sure she was okay as much as he required his next breath, but he held fast. Breathing freely would have to wait, April needed him. He rested his head against hers, softly calling on the name of Jesus. Moments later, the faintest little cry echoed through the room and it seemed as though everyone in the room sucked in a relieved breath.

Tears streamed down Richard's face. "See…she's going to be okay." He placed his lips on hers, more so for his own comfort than hers.

"Mr. and Mrs. Hawkins, we've stabilized your little girl, but she's not quite out of the woods yet. We are taking her over to the neonatal intensive care unit where we can monitor her progress. Once they've finished closing you up, I'll come to your room and explain where we go from here."

April was in her hospital bed replaying everything the doctor said: incubator to regulate the baby's body temperature, blue light to help with the jaundice, heart monitor, and a tube in her nose for feeding. They explained everything, so she wouldn't be shocked the first time she saw her little girl. She didn't care about any of it. She just wanted to see her baby, but she was stuck in the bed until the epidural wore off. The feeling in her legs was coming back, but that also meant she could feel the pain of her incision. They offered pain meds, but she refused them. She just needed to see her baby and then she'd take something for the pain.

"Hey, I hear you've made me an auntie."

April turned her head toward the doorway and—seeing Sheena—started crying all over again. "I haven't seen her yet. They keep telling me to wait."

"Can you walk?"

April didn't respond. She rolled her eyes and turned her head back toward Richard. He answered for her. "No, she can't. That's the only reason why they won't let her see the baby."

Sheena shook her head in understanding and sat on the edge of the bed. "Do you mind if I have a moment alone with my sister?"

"Of course not."

"Someone is waiting for you in the hall."

Richard knew exactly who she was talking about and hurried out of the room. "What's up, man?" He greeted Paul with a handshake and pulled him into a shoulder hug. "Did you find him?"

"I wouldn't be here if we didn't."

Richard exhaled his relief. Hopefully Brent behind bars would alleviate some of April's stress. "I take it, since you're here and not in jail that you controlled yourself."

"I didn't find him." The look on Paul's face said it all. Brent was lucky he was found by someone else. "Jaleel found that fool at the gas station down the street from the church, crouched behind the garbage can on his cell trying to call for a ride. He called me, but the police made it there before I did."

"Good, pretty boys like you don't do to well in jail." In spite of the situation, they managed a brief laugh.

Richard saw the nurse walking toward them and shook his head. He had stepped out of the room for not even five minutes and already April had gotten her hands on the call button. "Sorry."

"It's okay. Hopefully she's ready this time."

Richard followed the nurse into the room giving April a look letting her know he wasn't pleased.

"Okay Mrs. Hawkins, once again, I need you to be honest with me. Can you feel this?"

"No." She pouted trying her best to keep from crying like a baby.

Richard hid his smile. The nurse hadn't even touched her.

"What about this?" She scraped a pen along the bottom of April's foot and she nearly jumped off the bed with excitement.

"Yes, I felt that." She did the other leg with the same results. "Okay Richie, can I go now?"

He raised his brow, questioning the nurse.

"Let me go get a wheelchair."

"A wheelchair?" April bit her lip to keep from telling the nurse off. If they were going to put her in a wheelchair, she could've seen her baby a long time ago. She slid her legs to the side of the bed and Richard rushed to her side. He warned her to take it easy, but she didn't have a choice. She could barely move. He helped her to her feet and she was grateful for the chair being wheeled toward her.

The closer she got to her baby, the more her heart rate sped up. She had never experienced so many emotions all at once. Excitement, fear, anxiety, sadness, and regret roiled around in her. There were so many things she wished she could do over, but mostly she wished she'd loved her baby from the beginning. She would just have to spend the rest of her life making up for it.

Richard helped her to her feet and guided her hand into the slot in the incubator where she could touch the baby. He stood behind her for support and put his hand in the other hole. He heard her sniffles and kissed her temple. "It's all over. You delivered the baby and Brent is in jail. Now, it's time to heal."

April nodded her head and rested it back against his chest. Yes, it was time to heal. With Richard by her side, there was no doubt she'd make it.

Thank you for reading All I Ever Wanted. I hope you enjoyed. Visit my website or any of my social media pages and let me know your thoughts. I love hearing from my readers.

More books by

F. Y. Dawn

Surrender to Love Series

Book 1: Serenity of Passion

Book 2: What Love Feels Like

Book 3: What the Heart Wants

Book 4: All I Ever Wanted

www.fydawn.com

www.facebook.com/fydawn

Twitter and Instagram @fydawn

www.ingramcontent.com/pod-product-compliance
Lightning Source LLC
Chambersburg PA
CBHW020725210626
46807CB00016B/89

* 9 780615 965741 *